I0634770

Vital Sire, Cardinal Gibbons

Life of Father Charles Sire of the Society of Jesus

A Simple Biography

Vital Sire, Cardinal Gibbons

Life of Father Charles Sire of the Society of Jesus
A Simple Biography

ISBN/EAN: 9783744653725

Printed in Europe, USA, Canada, Australia, Japan

Cover: Foto ©Raphael Reischuk / pixelio.de

More available books at **www.hansebooks.com**

LIFE

OF

Father Charles Sire,

OF THE SOCIETY OF JESUS.

A SIMPLE BIOGRAPHY

COMPILED FROM HIS WRITINGS AND THE TESTIMONY OF THOSE
WHO HAVE KNOWN HIM BEST.

BY HIS BROTHER,

REV. VITAL SIRE,

Professor of Moral Theology at the Theological Seminary of Toulouse.

TRANSLATED FROM THE FRENCH.

With the approbation of His Eminence Cardinal Gibbons.

A. M. D. G.

NEW YORK, CINCINNATI, CHICAGO:

BENZIGER BROTHERS,

Printers to the Holy Apostolic See.

1890.

APPROBATIONS.

From His Eminence CARDINAL GIBBONS, Archbishop of Baltimore.

We cheerfully approve the Life of Rev. Charles Sire, a saintly priest of the Society of Jesus, whose even and gentle piety, zeal, and self-devotedness, may be well proposed to the imitation of our young clerics and of the Rev. clergy engaged in the work of the Sacred Ministry.

JAMES, CARDINAL GIBBONS,
Archbishop of Baltimore.

From Very Rev. THOS. J. CAMPBELL, S.J., Provincial, New York.

I have read with a great deal of interest and pleasure what its author calls "The Simple Biography of Father Charles Sire of the Society of Jesus." His boyhood reminds one forcibly of that of St. John Berchmans. His life in the Sulpitian Seminary is very attractive for the amiable but unyielding exactness with which every rule was observed, and the description of his work as a college prefect and teacher of the lower classes sketches a period which, as far as I know, has never been touched in other biographies of the Society. I trust that the book may do much good in many ways.

THOS. J. CAMPBELL, S.J.

COPYRIGHT, 1890 BY BENZIGER BROTHERS.

APPROBATIONS TO THE FRENCH EDITION.

From His Eminence Cardinal Desprez, Archbishop of Toulouse :

" REVEREND FATHER: We were pleased to receive your letter announc-ing your intention of soon publishing the second edition of the Life of your excellent brother. Father Charles Sire ; for we had already perceived. with great satisfaction, the favorable reception accorded the book on its first publication. It is not unlikely that the good it has effected will continue to increase with its re-publication ; hence, we cordially recom-mend it to every one.

" We especially desire to see it in the hands of our seminarians and priests, that the former may learn from its pages how to prepare them-selves worthily for the high functions of the priesthood—functions requir-ing angelic sanctity and the sublimest virtues ; and the latter be reminded anew that the only motive, guide, and stimulant of a priest in all his actions should be the salvation of souls, an end ever redounding to the greater glory of God.

" Whilst blessing you, Reverend Father, we also cordially give our blessing to the new edition on the eve of appearing ; and we express our sincere hope that the harvest of spiritual fruits this publication promises may be abundant.

" Receive, Rev. Father, the assurance of our devotion and affection.

" *Toulouse, April* 25, 1885."

From His Eminence Cardinal Donnet, Archbishop of Bordeaux.

" Thanks, Rev. Father, for your kind attention in sending me the biogra-phy of your brother, the Rev. Charles Sire. You could not have con-ferred upon me a greater favor, for I truly esteemed and loved him—good Father Charles, whom only to see was to love.

" His biography is not only a precious relic for your family, and especially for your own brotherly heart, but, moreover, it will serve as a model and guide in the ways of perfection to the priest and religious seeking to adorn their souls with the beautiful virtues of their vocation.

" The more one reads it, the more he is enamored of virtue, the practice of which seems easy and pleasant as one follows the pages descriptive of this holy Levite's life; and the reader finds himself unawares loving obedience, despite the constant self-renunciation it demands; the spirit of Faith holding unslackened rein over thought and feeling ; the spirit of sacrifice, even of all that is dearest to the human heart, required of those who devote their lives to the salvation of souls, and death itself, so precious in the sight of God when one has avoided evil and lived for duty.

" I therefore earnestly desire that so edifying a biography be in the hands of all the students of both our Preparatory and Theological Seminaries, feeling convinced that its careful perusal would accomplish among them, in a certain degree, that good which your worthy brother effected by word, deed, and example, when living.

" To be a saint—how beautiful both in life and in death! But can we say that the saints die? *Justi autem in perpetuum vivent.*[1] No, my dear Father, your brother is not dead, only gone to the Eternal Source of Life, towards which you, too, have been brought nearer through your deep and unalterable affection for him. The day will come when your now separate existences will be as one : *Cor unum et anima una !*

" *Feb.* 23, 1877."

From the Right Rev. Bishop Dellale.

The author of this biography, who, at the time of its compilation, was professor of Moral Theology in the Theological Seminary of Rodez, having submitted his work to his Bishop, Monseigneur Dellale, the latter requested his Vicar General, the Rev. Father Costes, now Bishop of Mende, to examine it himself or have it examined by some competent priest. After receiving the report of such examination, which was sent to him at Rome, Bishop Dellale gave his approbation as follows :

" Whereas, we have received a most favorable report concerning a manuscript entitled ' Life of Father Charles Sire, of the Society of Jesus,' examined by a thoroughly competent examiner, whom we ourselves appointed to do so ;

[1] The just live forever,

" And whereas, we have also been made acquainted with the approval passed upon said manuscript by several other learned and pious ecclesiastics, who have carefully studied it from a twofold point of view, that of the doctrines contained therein, and the incidents likewise ;

" We hereby declare that said manuscript merits our approbation ; and that, if published, the narration of the traits and incidents of this model of a holy life, and the description herein contained of such youthful perfection (all such knowledge being derived from the most reliable sources), will be as a sweet perfume of piety and virtue, offered alike to youth and to mature age, the clergy and the laity ; and that the perusal of the book will prove equally pleasant and profitable to mind and heart.

" Wherefore, we authorize and favor its publication.

" *Given at Rome, February* 14, 1870."

The foregoing approbation was sent to the author with a letter ending thus :

" In a conversation yesterday with Mgr. Maupoint, Bishop of St. Denis, Reunion Island, I mentioned your dear brother Charles ; and this prelate, who was well acquainted with him, paid the highest tribute of praise and admiration to his exalted character, which tribute may be summed up in these few words: ' *His was a holy life, crowned by a holy death.*' Such testimony, I am sure, will be a great consolation to you, and an additional guarantee of the fidelity of your narration."

† LOUIS, Bishop of Rodez.

From Monseigneur Bourret, Bishop of Rodez.

" My opinion of your work can be expressed in these few words: it is most edifying and well written.

" It must needs be edifying, the subject being one of that family of young holy religious of whom Aloysius Gonzaga, Stanislas Kostka, and John Berchmans are the types; the story of his life revealing the same piety, the same obedience, the same generous zeal, and the same consummation in the bloom of youth, as if God Himself were eager to clasp to His eternal embrace souls like these, who so ardently aspire after Him.

" As to the form, you have avoided a danger well-nigh inevitable in such works—that of introducing personalities and family affairs foreign to the subject. It is certainly a most difficult task for one to write his own brother's life without bringing in a little of his own. Yet you have proven the practicability of the contrary, by relating only what was intimately connected with your subject, and this in a manner at once clear, correct, and interesting. You make your young hero speak (and he speaks well) through his maxims, his thoughts, and the impressions derived from his letters, or preserved in the memory of his friends. And thus should the biographer ever do to render a work interesting and beneficial.

"*Dec.* 15, 1876."

___

From Monseigneur Leuilleux, Bishop of Carcassonne, present Archbishop of Chambéry.

"I have just finished reading your biography of Father Charles Sire. From beginning to end, it reveals a saint; hence, I am not surprised at the veneration with which every one speaks of him.

"From every point of view, your work appears to me worthy of eulogium. Allow me to thank you for it.

"*Feb.* 15, 1877."

___

From Monseigneur Foulquier, late Bishop of Mende, and Canon of St. Denis.

"How I congratulate you, my dear Father Sire, not only on having had such a brother, but even more on having him now as a protector in heaven! I also thank you most sincerely for having written the story of his life, and thus presented to us as a model that angel of youthful innocence and gentleness, whose holiness, daily increasing, filled up in a brief span of existence the measure of merits of a long life, and received the imperishable crown of the elect.

"Your narration reveals him to us as a model for children, students, seminarians, novices, religious, priests. We behold therein his heart filled with the most precious graces, ever faithful and generous, and animated solely by the ardent desire of loving and of immolating itself for the Beloved.

"I bless you for having given us this instructive and touching biography, which cannot fail to awaken in those who read it a zeal for perfection, love of God and souls, and, I may also add, confidence in the intercession of this predestined soul.

" In conclusion, I beg that you, his brother and biographer, who must needs have so much influence with him, will kindly place under his protection the old Bishop, who, whilst recommending himself to your prayers, hopes you will accept, etc.

" *March* 15, 1877."

From the Fathers of the Society of Jesus, former superiors of Father Charles Sire.

After two successive revisions, the Rev. Father Servières, at this time Provincial at Toulouse, sent the author the following approbation :

" Your biography of Father Charles has pleased me greatly, so much so, that I have been constrained to read it through, and carefully, which accounts for the length of time it has been in my hands. Doubtless, it will be appreciated and liked by all pious young students, its pages exhaling the sweet perfume of that rich harvest-field the Lord hath blessed."

After calling attention to some slight modifications he deemed advisable, the Reverend revisor ends his letter as follows :

" The Life thus abridged will be most useful. This living copy of Blessed John Berchmans [1] is worthy of its model, and will be its fitting companion picture, the more so, as Father Sire was, in so many ways, connected with students and college work. He will be the natural link between Saints Stanislas, Aloysius Gonzaga, and Blessed John Berchmans on the one hand, and the holy missionaries of the Society on the other. Here was a gap to be filled, here was needed an intermediate tint in the variegated crown of the Society of Jesus.

" *December* 21, 1869."

Several other prelates have expressed sentiments fully in accordance with those already given. These we will not quote at length, but content ourselves with adding that Monseigneur Maupoint, Bishop of St. Denis, after reading a short notice, which was published by his orders in the *Almanach religieux de Bourbon*, of the events which had just taken place, at the death of Father Charles, wrote as follows, June 22, 1863, to a correspondent at Versailles : " If the facts related in this notice are veritable, Father Charles will one day be canonized—truly, a great honor for

---

[1] Since canonized, and now St. John Berchmans.

the diocese. I visited this dear Father on his sick-bed, before he left St. Denis, and was much edified by him. I shall be happy to insert the notice in *Les Fleurs spirituelles de Bourbon.*"

We add in conclusion, that Monseigneur de Langalerie, Archbishop of Auch, after introducing at Rome, as Bishop of Belley, the cause of M. Vianney, the venerable Curé of Ars, did not hesitate to declare that the facts related in the biography of Father Charles Sire were sufficient to entitle him to the appellation of *venerable.*

The satisfaction, edification, and pleasure even, which their Lordships, the Right Reverend Bishops above cited, experienced in reading Father Charles's biography were shared by others ; and what these have thought of our hero's sanctity, amiability, attractions, and favor with God ; what they have believed concerning the author's fidelity as a historian, and his discretion in handling the subject ; what they have said eulogistic of the matter and style of the work itself, extolling its irresistible charms and the good it is everywhere destined to effect, especially in seminaries and religious houses ; what they have done to make the Life known—all this have many other priests, many lay persons of all classes of society, many members of various religious communities, also thought, believed, said, and done, as is evinced by the innumerable testimonies we have received from them.

We desire it to be understood that Father Charles's biography is not exclusively our own work, many of the witnesses of this good Father's saintly life having furnished us with much valuable and edifying information, expressed in fitting language and carrying with it the impress of authenticity, and numberless others having assisted us in a manner which, in our opinion, is not the least important—that of fervently and perseveringly praying Heaven to bless our efforts.

AUTHOR'S PREFACE.

THE publication of this Biography affords us much pleasure, as it is a compliance with many and oft-repeated requests. Innumerable favors having been granted through the intercession of the Rev. Father Charles, during the fourteen years[1] that have elapsed since he yielded up his soul to God, the recipients of them are naturally anxious to know more of him, to become acquainted with all the details of so saintly and edifying a life, that thus their affection for him be increased, their faith in invoking him, and their desire to imitate his virtues.

We ourselves have experienced, in a wonderful manner, the power of this generous intercessor's mediation; hence, in obeying the inspiration to write his Biography, we are likewise gratifying the promptings of our own heart, in thus laying at his feet our tribute of love and gratitude; happy, indeed, if these simple pages, the first fruits of our zeal for his glory, serve but to enkindle in other souls those sentiments of profound veneration for him and unbounded confidence in him with which we are animated; knowing that such will redound only to the glory of God, which this good Father so zealously sought to promote, the honor of Mary, who showered upon him her choicest blessings, and the consolation of the faithful themselves, for time and eternity.

[1] At the date of this translation, 1889, Father Charles has been dead twenty-seven years, having breathed his last August 4th, 1862.

Though doubtless lacking many requisites of a good biographer, we are nevertheless rich in that zeal inciting us to
a thorough knowledge of our hero, and the desire to present our readers with a scrupulously faithful portrait of his
character. Thanks to this zeal, we have been able to obtain from most reliable sources abundant information concerning him, on points wherein we were deficient.

His other relatives and friends, his fellow-students both
at the Preparatory and Theological Seminaries, his professors and teachers, even his superiors and the directors
of his conscience, have all vied with one another in ac-
quainting us with his virtues and defects, with the most
striking traits of his childhood, youth, and sacerdotal life.

His manuscripts, his correspondence, the journal he kept
so faithfully the last twelve years of his life, his notes written
under God's eye during the retreats, and intended especially for his director, were put in our hand ; and it is to
these we are indebted for the secrets of his religious life.
As to those incidents of his exterior life (the mere efflo-
rescence of the interior) herein related of his novitiate, of
the period during which he was employed in teaching, and
also of that in which he was pursuing his theological
studies, they, too, have nearly all been furnished us by his
brethren in religion.

To make the Biography as complete and as satisfactory
as possible, we have sought information from every possible
quarter—from his scholars, his other relatives, his fellow
travellers—even from those persons whose acquaintance
with him was limited to that of having been witnesses of
his death on ship-board. And we must say that to these
latter we are indebted for not the least interesting of our
details. So deep and lasting the impression his memory
made upon them, that the mere mention of his name,
which not one of them had forgotten, was the sole in-

troduction necessary to assure us a welcome and those many testimonies of kindness we shall ever remember most gratefully.

If among these persons, or, in fact, among any who read these pages, there be one acquainted with additional incidents or traits concerning the subject of this Biography, we beg him to consider these lines as an appeal to his generosity in forwarding us those precious souvenirs, which have everywhere been so cheerfully given.[1]

[1] Such information should be sent to one of the following Sulpician clergymen, brothers of Father Charles: the Rev. Vital Sire, at the Theological Seminary of Toulouse; the Rev. Dominique Sire, at the Seminary of St. Sulpice, Paris; the Rev. Césaire Sire, at the Theological Seminary of Puy-en-Velay (Haute Loire).

CONTENTS.

AUTHOR'S DECLARATION.

ERE beginning the narration of this beautiful life, which was crowned by so touching and glorious a death, we declare that, in applying the terms *Saint* or *Blessed* to Father Charles, and more especially in attributing to him anything of a miraculous nature, we do so only in the sense authorized by the decrees of Pope Urban VIII., dated March 13, 1625, and June 13, 1631; and that we are in no wise anticipating that final judgment of the infallible authority of Jesus Christ's Vicar, to which supreme tribunal we in all things tender a filial and entire submission.

SAINT-JORY, NEAR TOULOUSE, SEPT. 10, 1876.
Feast of the Holy Name of Mary.

LIFE OF

FATHER CHARLES SIRE,

Of the Society of Jesus.

CHAPTER I.

CHILDHOOD OF FATHER CHARLES.

BORN in France, in the village of Saint-Jory, near Toulouse, Father Charles Sire, the subject of this Biography, was descended, on his father's side, from two honorable families, the lives of several of whose members were most beautiful examples of virtue. We cite here but one of these, Margaret Sire, Father Charles's grand-aunt, whom the most venerable ecclesiastics of the neighborhood used invariably to call *The Saint*, and who, indeed, died in the odor of sanctity, at the age of eighty-three, only a few months before this good Father's birth. At the moment of her death, her face became beautiful and apparently transfigured; whilst after death from her body, which still remained flexible, exhaled a sweet and penetrating odor, like that of violets, perfuming the whole house. This wonderful fact was known to all the inhabitants of Saint-Jory.

On the maternal side, Father Charles was even more

17

highly privileged ; for Mme. Sire could count during her life fifteen priests in her family: six of her own sons, two uncles, one nephew, and six cousins. Several of these, since deceased, will receive especial mention in this book, as it was under their auspices and patronage that Father Charles became a priest. It suffices for us now to name but one, Monseigneur Savy, Bishop of Aire, whom all the priests in his diocese and the bishops in his province spoke of as a *true bishop,* and the two Matthieu brothers, who, on their return from exile in Spain, filled successively, for twenty-eight years, the important post of pastor of Saint Sernin at Toulouse. Illustrious as they were by reason of their talents, they were more so by their virtues ; and their memory is held in veneration in both the dioceses of Aire and Toulouse. '

Of the ten children who composed the Sire family, Father Charles was the seventh. A sister younger than himself and two brothers having died before they were old enough to make their First Communion, there survived seven brothers, only one of whom has remained a layman, the other six becoming priests, three of these belonging to the Congregation of St. Sulpice, which directs theological seminaries.

Father Charles was born on the 21st of December, 1828, and baptized on the 25th, God wishing, it would seem, that he should be born to grace on the day on which the Church celebrates the birth of the Author of grace. Throughout life, he ever regarded the day of his baptism as a blessed one, or, as he styled it, *a fortunate day,* the mere thought of which filled him with delight, and each recurring anniversary of the event was celebrated by him in a manner truly admirable, that could but reveal the trans-

---

' Monseigneur Savy was first cousin to Mme. Sire, and the two Matthieu brothers were her maternal uncles.

ports of love and gratitude with which the memory filled his heart. Hence was the name Noël, which he had received in baptism, especially dear to him.

Having been given as patrons the apostles Saints Peter and Paul, he had an especial devotion to these two pillars of the Church, always fervently invoking their intercession, and devoutly celebrating their feast; and it was a subject of great congratulation to him, after becoming a member of the Society of Jesus, that it was on this festival he made the annual renewal of vows. Even now, since he has left this land of exile for his true country, does it not seem as if he still wished to honor them, many of the remarkable favors believed to have been obtained through his intercession being received on some one of the days consecrated to them ?

But of all his Christian names the one he loved the best and honored the most was that of *Charles*, which the Church had also given him, and under which he was enrolled among her children. He loved to hear it, to pronounce it himself, to be called by it, to write it, and after the example of an illustrious saint, he often signed his less important letters with this single name. May we not see herein the reason why God has permitted him, since his death, to be called only *Father Charles*, this, in fact, being the name by which he is now chiefly known, loved, and venerated ?

It can be said of young Charles, as of so many of the canonized saints, that he imbibed piety with his mother's milk, Mme. Sire sparing no pains from his earliest years to make him a little angel. Gentleness and patience unalterable, caresses, promises, advice, and reproaches truly maternal—nothing was neglected that could form to virtue the heart of a child. Hence, he turned almost instinctively to God, and that amiable, child-like piety, ever one of his greatest charms, was not slow in manifesting itself.

The Blessed Virgin was its first and principal object. Mary had revealed herself to him from his tenderest infancy, as we learn from the following.

Margaret, a greataunt of Charles, had just died under his father's roof, and, as we have already said, in the odor of sanctity. Having been a witness of her holy life, Mme. Sire held her in great esteem and veneration, so much so, that when Charles was born she felt inspired to consecrate him to the Queen of angels through this pious relative, " believing," she said, " that in offering my newborn babe to Mary through her, I would thus draw down upon him countless benedictions." Nor were the mother's hopes deceived; for this consecration was doubtless the origin of his sanctity and happiness, the Blessed Virgin accepting the offering, and treating the child as a sacred deposit which she preserved through life from mortal sin, and upon whom she showered her choicest favors, not the least precious of which was his great devotion to herself. This she accomplished through the instrumentality of a pious peasant, named Catherine Beillard. As this person plays no unimportant part in our narrative, and especially that portion of it referring to Father Charles's death, we deem it advisable to mention here the origin of their subsequent relations.

In the year 1834, Charles being only six years old, Catherine, who had passed her twenty-eighth year, happened to call at Mme. Sire's house, at a time when this pious lady was reading a spiritual book to some devout neighbors. Impressed by what she heard, Catherine asked for especial instruction, and Mme. Sire, complying with her desires, acquitted herself of this office of charity so zealously and successfully, that Catherine soon became a fervent Christian, living only for God and duty.

The relations which henceforth existed between Mme.

Sire and herself brought her constantly in contact with the children, particularly Charles, who by reason of his tender age was nearly always with his mother.

Catherine could not fail to notice the child's good disposition; and struck by his candor, his innocence, and especially, what is unusual at that age, his pious inclinations, she soon became very fond of him, showing her affection by caresses, by trifling presents, and by talking to him, striving in all their little conversations to inspire him with still greater love for Our Lord and His Blessed Mother.

Charles, reciprocating her affection, was pleased to be with her, and his interest in these talks became more and more marked, Catherine's words, ever plain and simple, but full of faith and fervor, making the deepest and most salutary impression upon his tender soul. He was soon penetrated with such love for Jesus and Mary that within the space of two years his piety assumed the form of a zealous and privileged devotion. Excited by Catherine's exhortations, and interiorly directed by the spirit of God, his love for Mary was indeed great; and even at that early age he often repaired to the shrine of Our Lady of Good Gift, at the distance of more than a mile from his home, on his return expressing to his little sister the sentiments that animated his soul, hoping thus to make her participate in his devotions to Mary, and likewise in the graces he received from her.

Catherine was over-joyed at young Charles's rapid progress in piety. She could not understand how a child of so tender an age, who had scarcely begun to read, and whose heart had not yet known the visit of the Eucharistic God, could take such interest in conversations which turned altogether on subjects of piety. But above all did she admire the treasures of divine grace enriching him, and gave thanks to Mary for such especial favors. "Ah! how often," she has frequently said, "how often, as he was leaving the house, have not my husband and I, following him with looks of tenderness, exclaimed to each other, 'What a privileged child! what a beautiful soul! Some day he will be a great saint! He reminds one of the Child Jesus, at the age of twelve, teaching the doctors in the temple!'"

On his part, Charles loved Catherine with truly filial devotion, giving her his childish confidence and often recommending himself to her prayers. Later on, we shall speak of the salutary effects of this mutual affection, which, once established in their hearts by the Holy Spirit, never ceased to produce incomparable fruits of benediction, the chief of which to Charles, in boyhood, were the preservation of his innocence, a marked progress in virtue, and a faithful correspondence to the most precious of all graces—that of a vocation to the priesthood.

When but seven years old, he became one of the sanctuary boys at Saint-Jory. In this capacity, his modesty and good behavior excited the admiration of every one. Fervent and exemplary, he never gave way to levity. With his young companions he was kind, gentle, and even courteous, but never familiar; yet his was a warm, affectionate nature, as evinced by his gratitude to all who took the least interest in him.

At catechism, as at school, his application and study entitled him to a place in the foremost ranks. It is even related of him that when but ten years of age, in a protracted public examination, he answered so well all the questions put to him in catechism, that his astonished pastor said with a smile, "Sit down, my child, you know as much about it as I do."

This rapid progress at school delighted his family, and

filled them with the hope that he might, one day, make his mark in some of the professions. With this end in view (that of preparing him for a professional career), an elder brother, M. Marcel Sire, was charged with the duty of giving him Latin lessons during his (M. Marcel's) vacations. The child's gratitude for this act of kindness, as evinced by his perfect docility and great and successful application to study, was such that the astonished and delighted teacher devoted himself to his young pupil with reciprocal ardor, frequently stimulating his efforts by little presents. Nor was Charles's heart less capable of love than his mind of understanding, as the following anecdote will prove. One day, pricking a vein, he wrote with his blood a short note to this brother, simple indeed in style, but fraught with meaning. "I love you very much, my dear brother," it said, "and to prove it, I write this letter with my blood. Adieu."

M. Marcel was deeply touched at this act, which evinced great generosity and delicacy of sentiment, at an age when children are supposed to possess very little. Struck, moreover, at his intelligence, good sense, and piety, that daily became more apparent, he began to suspect that the child was called to the life of perfection. Nor was he long in doubt ; a few words that young Charles let fall, and his eager desire to enter the Preparatory Seminary, revealed the truth. M. Marcel now urged his father to send the boy to the seminary of Toulouse, but a serious obstacle, that the prudent parent deemed insurmountable, prevented the immediate accomplishment of this. Charles, now nearly eleven years of age, was distressed at the delay, but not discouraged. Making this trial the means of increasing his confidence in Mary, he resumed, with renewed vigor, his pious pilgrimages to Our Lady of Good Gift ; he also visited Catherine oftener, and deriving fresh strength from intercourse with her, he solicited, in union with her, more abundant graces, believing that redoubled zeal and his consequent advancement in virtue rendering him more pleasing to God, to whose greater glory it must needs contribute, would no doubt obtain, in time, a favorable answer to his petition.

His confidence was not misplaced. By a providential combination of circumstances, in which M. Sire could but recognize the hand of God, his son Marcel was made professor at the Preparatory Seminary of Polignan, and consequently Charles could be entered there as a pupil at the next session. [1]

On hearing this good news, Charles was almost wild with joy; and in contrast to his quiet, calm demeanor, he gave full vent to his feelings. Three things especially delighted him—the happiness of having his brother for his professor, thoughts of the progress he expected to make in study under his brother's direction, and the well-founded hope of being there admitted to his First Communion under the most favorable circumstances. His conduct now became more edifying, if possible, than ever, his countenance more cheerful, his diligence in his studies even greater than before. One thought absorbed him—that of repaying his parents for the sacrifices they were about to impose upon themselves for him.

One day, whilst walking alone in one of the public squares of the village, wholly absorbed in reflection, more like a man of mature years than a child, he was met by the parish priest of Saint-Jory. Astonished at his serious, thoughtful manner, the good Father said: "What are you doing here, my child? what is the matter? why are you so serious?"— "Father, I am thinking," was the answer. "Thinking?

[1] The Preparatory Seminary of Our Lady of Polignan is situated near the railroad station of Montréjeau (Haute-Garonne).

and of what ? " continued the priest. " Father, I am think-ing," said the earnest boy, " that if I go to Polignan this year, I ought to study very hard; as you know, we are a large family, and the education of so many boys costs our parents many sacrifices. I should feel very sorry to think that those they are about to make for me would be in vain. Yes, I must study very hard to compensate them for their trouble." " You are right, my boy," said the pastor, caressing him; " persevere in these sentiments, and you will one day be an honor to your family." Nor was this prophecy long unfulfilled.

CHAPTER II.

FATHER CHARLES AT THE PREPARATORY SEMINARY.

I.—His Conduct before and after his First Communion.

YOUNG Charles was too well disposed not to conduct himself from his very entrance into the seminary at Polignan as a most conscientious pupil, who to fulfil his duty had but to know it. As to this, there is not one dissenting voice, either among his superiors or fellow-students, all of whom unite in declaring that his life there was from the very start uniformly regular; that he became in a short time a model of virtue and piety; and that, during the last four years especially, he was foremost even among the most fervent. Always respectful and devoted to his teachers, full of gentleness, courtesy, charity, and thoughtfulness towards his companions, he soon became a favorite with all.

"His first care," said Father Lacomme, then his friend and fellow-student, later, his brother Jesuit, "on entering Polignan was to associate himself especially with those pupils whose virtue was well known, and who, by reason of their influence, their experience, and more particularly their piety, could hold the place of mentors to us younger boys, and keep us in the right path. Charles always joyfully sought their pious rendezvous, was docile in receiving their advice, and faithful in following it to the letter. Among these young friends was one for whose society he had a great predilection, but who, alas! died

soon after Charles made his acquaintance, leaving in the
seminary a memory embalmed in the odor of sanctity.
Charles was frequently in his company, and, indeed, made
it a practice to pass certain recreations with him and
another student, for the express purpose of conferring together on spiritual things. It was from these salutary conversations, always so full of charms for Charles, that the
sweet and amiable piety already implanted in his heart
assumed a new and more vigorous development, from the
first months of his entrance into the seminary.

"It became especially manifest a little later, when the
superior made known the names of the twelve boys who
were to be admitted that year to the Holy Table. Both
Charles and myself had the happiness of being among the
number. As soon as Charles knew who they were he hastened to them in recreation, spoke to them of the great
event with an overflowing heart, and associated himself with
them in an especial manner. It was easy to perceive that
his soul was deeply penetrated with the importance of the
solemn act we were about to perform, all his conversations
turning naturally upon this one subject. But when the
preparatory exercises began, ah! then it was his piety and
zeal knew no bounds. Not content with preparing himself for this eventful day, he was likewise desirous of seeing
his companions do the same; and to excite their fervor, he
would frequently say to them: 'How happy we are in being twelve in number, like the apostles with Our Lord!
but, alas! there was a Judas among them, and let us take
care!' The happy day came; it would be impossible to
describe the joy that inundated his soul; so great were his
transports that he could not restrain them. Ever to bear
in mind the blessed remembrances of this day, he wrote
the date in a little blank-book that he carried constantly
about him, and each recurring anniversary was celebrated

with that gratitude and love that revealed the unfading impression made upon his heart. It was, as he styled it, one of his *most fortunate days,* which he must give entirely to God.

"The eleven other boys who were admitted to the Holy Table with himself became, for this reason, especially dear to him. Not only did he preserve their names and ever recommend them to God in his prayers, but annually he made himself their substitute before this good Master, offering to Him for each one of them in particular that testimony of gratitude and love due from each. Later, when wishing to give any of his fellow-students an especial mark of his affection, he would add his name to this list of First Communicants, saying with great feeling, 'Although you did not make your First Communion with me, we are such good friends that I am going to write your name among those who did.'

"This remembrance of his First Communion," adds Father Lacomme, "was ever fresh and unfading in his heart, and undoubtedly the inexhaustible fountain of his fervor. Eight months before his death, meeting me in the Isle of Bourbon, after several years of separation, he spoke of that great day, and with unaffected delight. 'Oh! don't you remember our First Communion?' he said; 'what has become of the other ten?' Our inquiries gave us reason to bless God for His especial favors to ourselves; for of the twelve we were the only two called to the holy ministry and the religious life."

This vocation to the priesthood of which Father Lacomme here makes mention, and unequivocal evidences of which had already manifested themselves in Charles, was, on the beautiful day of his First Communion, so clearly made known to him, or rather so deeply impressed upon him, that he could not refrain from running to his director and opening his heart to him on the subject.

Very few of the boys of the lower classes of study in the Preparatory Seminary of Polignan were permitted to wear the cassock; a more than ordinary share of virtue must needs be his who would obtain this honor; yet Charles was thus clothed very shortly after making his First Communion. He was indeed very young, but his heart was pure and given unreservedly to God, and his conduct most exemplary. Moreover, he had great good sense, application, and a fair share of success in his studies. Hence, as his vocation seemed solid, and his desire to wear the cassock was very strong, his director deemed it advisable to grant him this privilege. The time for so doing could not have been better chosen. The Archbishop of Toulouse, then making a pastoral visitation in the Pyrenees, had promised to be at Polignan on the feast of the Holy Trinity, to administer Confirmation to all those students who had not yet received this sacrament, but especially to those who had just made their First Communion, eight days previously.

And it was on this day, so memorable for Charles, that he had the happiness of receiving the holy habit—that habit he had so often envied his brothers, and which, we must say, he always strove to honor. His joy was such that he wrote immediately to his pious mother, that she might share it. " He could not," said this devout lady, " behold himself clothed in the cassock without experiencing genuine delight. Two months later, having come home for the vacation, he hastened to the shrine of Our Lady of Good Gift, to offer there his tribute of thanksgiving. Impelled by gratitude, he also visited Catherine, and he took advantage of his stay at home to do his little sister's soul all the good he could, exhorting her to piety, obedience especially, with this end in view relating to her numberless edifying stories."

Indeed, piety and obedience were at this time his two most

brilliant virtues. "From the day of his First Communion," says Father Lacomme, "his piety ever went on increasing. He frequented the Holy Table regularly, and soon became a weekly communicant. His piety was tender and full of unction; he knew how to converse with Our Lord, heart to heart, as one friend with another. This could be seen even in his exterior, and I know that it was so. Noisy, boisterous sports were distasteful to him, his preference being for those quiet relaxations which did not interrupt his union with God. With this good Master he could remain all day, like a loving child with its father. He went to Him in all things with a simplicity that was astonishing, and he asked for graces with such confidence as knew not the shadow of doubt. His lively faith and his charity made him see and love God everywhere, especially in his superiors. Hence his respect, esteem, and devotedness for them were marked; and no one remembers ever to have heard him express the least unfavorable word of any one of them."

He obeyed them in all things, with a simplicity truly remarkable. Obedience, in fact, was already so deeply rooted in his heart, that it had become one of his most salient characteristics; and he himself states, in some of the notes taken during one of his retreats, that this was the virtue for which, since his twelfth year, God had given him the greatest predilection. So habitual and precious, from that time, did it become to him, that he practised it at home, during vacation, as perfectly as at college.

Not satisfied with obeying, even in the slightest details, both his mother and the elder brother who kept him busy with his books five hours every day, he observed, with unflagging exactness, the vacation rule laid down at Polignan for those who wore the cassock; and this boy, scarcely thirteen years of age, cheerfully performed, during those days of freedom and repose, all those pious exercises, fidelity to which even fervent seminarians sometimes find very difficult.

Every morning he devoted a half hour to mental prayer, and assisted at the adorable sacrifice of the Mass. During the day he said his beads and recited the Little Office of the Blessed Virgin; then, towards nightfall, he made a visit of at least a quarter of an hour to the Blessed Sacrament, and gave a half hour to spiritual reading. And these acts of devotion, usually so wearisome to children, he performed with loving fervor, for his obedience was not that of fear or mere routine—it was the fruit of love. He obeyed his superiors and parents because he loved them, and beheld in them the representatives of God Himself.

This same motive it was that impelled him to study with diligence, and gave a supernatural character to all his actions. "Charles," says one of his most intimate friends, now a pastor in the diocese of Toulouse, "studied hard, and always with the sole view of pleasing God, by thus doing His will, and qualifying himself the better to save souls—an end ever redounding to His greater glory. This was his dominant thought, and he appeared comparatively indifferent to everything else. Hence, after the distribution of prizes on exhibition days, he never failed to make an offering of his to Our Lord, through His Blessed Mother."

In the lower classes, his efforts were crowned with success annually, notable rewards in every branch of instruction being conferred upon him. For various reasons, however, these triumphs were but little noticed in the family circle. God doubtless permitting this that young Charles's heart should be directed solely to Him, and all the faculties of his soul employed in making Him known and loved. Indeed, it was at this very time that the child's zeal, taking

fresh expansion, became more active and generous ; and
the principal means God used to work this happy trans-
formation were the associations or sodalities into which
he was admitted as member.

II.—Charles's Zeal as a Sodalist.

There were now three distinct sodalities at Polignan:
that of St. Aloysius Gonzaga, for all the lay-students and
such members of the lower classes as wore the cassock; that
of the Holy Angels, for the ecclesiastics [1] of the fifth, fourth,
and third classes; lastly, that of the Blessed Virgin, the
most honorable of all, into which only the most pious ecclesiastics of the second and the rhetoric classes were admitted.

Charles was successively admitted into each, " and it was
then," says one of his fellow-students, " was born that
zeal for the salvation of souls and God's glory which,
during the rest of his life, was to be his distinguishing
characteristic. Its first manifestations were the fraternal
admonitions which, upon occasion, he gave to his young
friends—charitable admonitions, given with such tact,
delicacy, and gentleness, that they never offended—and yet
Charles, at this time, was not more than twelve or thirteen
years of age."

To these passing remarks he soon added the apostleship
of the word, and the edifying stories and anecdotes he
used to relate are still remembered. Full of faith and
fervor, his words always impressed upon those who heard
them some good thought or holy resolution.

Says a pious lady of Saint-Jory, " He often called at
my house, and at every visit he had something charming to
relate, some incidents of Our Lord's life, or of His miracles ;
and his usual topic of conversation was the Blessed Virgin.
Of this he never grew weary. Oh! how truly pious he

---

[1] Those were called *ecclesiastics* who wore the cassock.

was. His was a heart of gold. His soul was all for God, and he had no desire save that of making others love God and the Blessed Virgin. I could not help thinking and saying that this child, so young and yet so zealous, was surely one of the predestined."

Another inhabitant of the same village, whom Charles used to visit, never heard his name mentioned without exclaiming, " What a beautiful soul was his! he was an angel!" and then, with tears in his eyes, he would repeat some of the many edifying things he had listened to from Charles; and on seeing his picture latterly, he cried out in delight, wiping away the big tears that filled his eyes, " Oh! yes, that is he, he who was goodness itself! He was a lamb, a true lamb of the good God."

Not less vivid and lasting was the impression Charles made at Polignan. His fellow-students, long since mature men, even now never think or speak of him without feeling impelled, almost in spite of themselves, to render testimony to his praise. " I should be a veritable ingrate," said one of them,[1] " were I to forget his kindness to me. The first time I saw him was the day of my entrance into the seminary. I was just crossing the threshold, and though a perfect stranger to him, he came forward with a word of welcome. From that moment we were friends. I have always believed there was something providential in this meeting, for his friendship has ever since exercised over me a most salutary influence. I never think of him without recalling that good angel whom God sent to the young Tobias, and who guided him and bestowed so many favors upon him during his long and perilous journey.

" A few days after my entrance at Polignan, Father Contamin came to preach the retreat for us. Yielding to

---

[1] M. Sénac, now a priest in the diocese of Toulouse.

the attractions of grace, Charles, from this time, entered upon an entirely new path in life, in which he ever after continued, making great progress. It was now, at the suggestion of this Father, and after the example of some of the older inmates of the house, he established with two of his fellow-students the Association of the Holy Family. This association, whose end is to honor the Hearts of Jesus, Mary, and Joseph, to promote God's glory and the salvation of souls, drawing down upon those who constitute it the graces needed to maintain themselves in fervor, is composed of only three members, each of whom must honor these holy Hearts in general, and in particular that which has fallen to his lot to represent in the society.

"Charles was always the soul of this reunion. It was he who ever directed and stimulated the associates' zeal. One of the members having fallen sick, shortly after its establishment, I was chosen to fill his place, and God alone knows the inestimable blessing this proved to me ! I feel confident that whatever of that spirit of piety and fervor so essential to a true Christian, and especially a priest, I still possess, is altogether due to this association, which I can never recall without the most lively emotions of gratitude, and a renewal of my faith and charity.

"It would be difficult indeed to recount all the little devices of piety and zeal by which he sought to preserve our fervor. He was a true apostle, animated with celestial fire, and never lacking words of good counsel or pious reflection. Among other practices calculated to promote God's glory in procuring the salvation of souls which he induced us to follow, was that of always, no matter where, when, or with whom, giving our conversations a pious turn, he himself setting us an admirable example in this respect, of prudence, delicacy, and tact. Often, when in company

with him and other young men, I was constrained to admire
the manner in which he quietly and gently led our conversation upon pious subjects, and that without annoying or
wearying any one.

"He frequently recommended to our prayers some of
our less edifying comrades. Nor did his zeal for souls stop
here ; it went beyond the enclosure of the seminary, and
from time to time he would beg us to pray and do penance
for sinners in the world.

"These exhortations were strengthened by example ;
God's glory and his neighbor's salvation he sought to advance not by prayer alone, but by exercising vigorous penances upon his body and soul, adding to those sacrifices
inherent to his position other mortifications and practices
of perfection most painful to nature. After the example
of St. Berchmans and several other holy youths, besides
following scrupulously the ordinary rule of the house, he
imposed upon himself an especial rule of prayers and penitential exercises. Among other means of chastising his
body, he used a whip of knotted cords tied together. This
whip I myself have seen.

"The winter's cold, which is very severe in the Pyrenees, was for him another source of bodily mortification,
particularly to his hands. Yet this he bore cheerfully and
in a spirit of penance, taking, however, like every one else,
the proper means for warming them, thus practising three
beautiful virtues : mortification, charity, and obedience.
Sometimes, seeing his fellow-students shivering with cold
and lacking courage to warm themselves by exercise, he
would take hold of them and force them into a lively tus-
sle that soon set their blood into brisk circulation and imparted warmth to their members. This was so much the
more meritorious for him, as he really had no fancy for
such games (preferring rather relaxations of a sedentary

nature), and herein did violence to his own inclinations in order to follow the spirit of the rule and render a service to others.

"He practised mortification in many other ways, but always so quietly as scarcely to be noticed, even by his fellow-students, habituating himself to those numberless voluntary privations, apparently trifling, but which Our Lord deems of great value as the offerings of a fervent, loving heart. I have frequently seen him in the morning or evening, when one's appetite is sharpened by the mountain air, whilst pretending to eat the piece of bread given him (deeming himself unobserved), quietly slip a portion or even the whole of it in a safe place, where he knew a friendly hand would be sure to get it for the poor.

"His love for Jesus, Mary, and Joseph suggested to him a penitential practice that to me appeared most austere. He engraved the three initials of these names upon his arm, and every day renewed the incisions, even so deeply as to draw blood. This voluntary crucifixion of the flesh, which we would have considered barbarous in any one else, in him seemed admirable and truly edifying.

"After what I have already said it is useless to speak of Charles's conduct in the house, and the influence of his example. His regularity, piety, and modesty were really wonderful. All admired and praised him, all loved and even venerated him. They whom grace attracted most strongly to God sought him out, delighted to be in his company and inhale that atmosphere of faith and piety in which he lived. Ah! how many children, how many of his fellow-students, are indebted to him not only for their peace and happiness, but for their regularity of conduct and piety."[1]

---

[1] The identical testimonies of Fathers Lacomme, Sénac, and several others of Charles's fellow-students.

III.—Charles's Zeal whilst in the Second Latin and the Rhetoric Classes.

Thus passed the first five years of young Charles's life at Polignan; and from the account we have just given of these, the reader may be prepared to judge of the last two he spent there; for, according to the testimony of his friends and teachers, it was especially whilst in the second Latin and the Rhetoric classes that he revealed himself what he ever after remained—a pious, fervent Levite, a zealous, indefatigable apostle.

He had completed his sixteenth year when he began his humanities. At this time the Sodality of the Blessed Virgin at Polignan was very flourishing, and counted among its members, even according to the testimony of those who did not belong to it, only the most exemplary young men. Charles was in every respect worthy of being received into it; but as his natural timidity and humility made him shrink from asking admission, it was deemed advisable for some of the sodalists to invite him to join them. He was deeply touched at this, and in expression of gratitude to those members who had thus taken the initiative in the matter he wrote their names on the list of those for whom he prayed especially.

He was received on the 28th of June, 1846, the vigil of the feast of SS. Peter and Paul, his two patrons. Says M. Sénac, already quoted:

"So great was his happiness, and so inundated with grace his soul, that he actually wept some time for joy; and he wrote to his mother that his reception into the sodality was one of the greatest blessings that could have befallen him. In testimony of his gratitude to God, he recorded this day as one of those the anniversary of which he must ever keep a holy-day, consecrated entirely to Him."

His title of sodalist imposed new duties upon him; and these, for love of Jesus and through gratitude, he resolved to perform generously.

The first was indeed easy to him—to love the Blessed Virgin with a filial love and boundless confidence; zealously to propagate devotion to her, and both by word and example induce others to do the same. In this duty he never failed. " Having become her child by a new title," says Father Lacomme, " he not only endeavored to love and honor her more than ever himself, but he also assumed the obligation of striving by all means in his power to make her known and loved by others. He really became her advocate, using all his influence (which was very great) to inspire devotion to her. I see him now, radiant with joy at the opportunity of speaking of her, which was frequent, for, as all knew, he was ever on the alert to seize the occasion. He made a resolution, after his admission to the sodality, of never refusing any favor asked him in her name. This he told me himself. He always called her the " Good Mother," and only God knows the depth of his tenderness and love for her."

" My especial remembrance of Charles," adds another of his brother sodalists,[1] " is, that he spoke of the Blessed Virgin and St. Joseph with the same simplicity as he did of his father, his mother, his brother, or any of his own family; indeed, just as one would speak of writing a letter to a relative or friend would he of addressing himself to the Blessed Virgin or St. Joseph. One might really have supposed from his reverential familiarity that he was accustomed to seeing St. Joseph and conversing with him. One day he said to me, ' I am going to ask a certain favor of St. Joseph, and I think he will grant it. When you are very anxious to obtain anything, go to St. Joseph, and you

---

[1] Rev. Father Maubé, Dean of Saint-Bertrand d'Alan, in the diocese of Toulouse.

will not be disappointed.' Poor Charles! I see him now,
everywhere, as of yore—in recreation, in the evenings of the
month of May, when he would speak so joyfully and tenderly of the Blessed Virgin; in Mary's chapel, after the reception of some new sodalist, at which times his piety and
fervor were truly contagious; and on the eves of her principal feasts. The day after one, of these he said to me, ' I
was so happy last night, that I could not sleep; I was at
the foot of Mary's throne all night long: the' joy that
filled my soul surpasses understanding.'

" During his hours of study and work, as during prayer,
his face was ever radiant with that happiness which springs
from keeping one's self in the presence of the Blessed
Virgin. If there be a time when enthusiasm must needs
prove contagious, it is certainly on Distribution Day, when,
crowned and bearing their prizes, the scholars are surrounded by their relatives and friends. Yet, just amidst
such excitement and joy, did I see Charles, the year of
his second Latin and Rhetoric, calmly join some friends
he had been seeking amid the tumult, and say to them with
a mysterious air, easily understood by the initiated, ' Let
us go to the chapel for the last time, and lay on the Blessed
Virgin's altar the ribbons around our prizes; we must separate in her presence.' None. of us have ever forgotten
the silent tears of that adieu, nor the poesy of that first love
at the feet of the ' Good Mother.' As for me, my heart
reverts continually to those early friendships, that sanctuary, the tenderness of those impressions, and the enthusiasm that filled us youths of eighteen; and I know that
the memory abides with me as a never-failing fountain of
benediction, strengthening and encouraging me when
weary, and urging my faltering steps in the paths of perfection. Charles appeared less moved than any of us; and
what struck me especially was his perfectly calm and nat-

ural manner, as if this were a familiar and ordinary scene. This quiet, gentle self-possession was, in my opinion, one of his most salient characteristics."

To give a better idea of his zeal in Mary's service, we add to the above testimonies a brief mention of some devotions he practised himself and incited his fellow-students to practise during vacation.

Not content with uniting himself to them every day in the holy Hearts of Jesus, Mary, and Joseph, at the usual hour of their three daily meals, he engaged himself to pronounce these blessed names whenever he heard the clock strike, and to consecrate himself to the Heart of Jesus, through Mary, by uttering those sweet words, which were the last to fall from his dying lips: "All for Jesus through Mary!" or, "I am all Thine, and all that I have is Thine." *Tuus totus ego sum, et omnia mea tua sunt.*

To inspire others with devotion to the Blessed Virgin, he would say to them, "Let us go to the Heart of Jesus through that of Mary; let us lose ourselves and be immersed in the love of that divine Heart, so that we act but from the impulse of grace. There let us make our meditation, there hear Mass, there say our Office, take our spiritual reading, hold our conversations, but always united to Mary.

"Let us also offer our prayers and actions in union with the prayers, actions, and dispositions of the Blessed Virgin. At the beginning of each, let us always, if possible, recall our general intention, to which we will join the especial one of asking great love for Jesus in the Blessed Sacrament, great love for Mary, the knowledge of our vocation, and the grace of corresponding to it.

"Yet more; one day we shall be priests, and as such, after the example of Jesus, we are bound to labor zealously for the salvation of souls. Hence, let us now, during the vacation, begin to exercise this zeal, regarding ourselves as

instruments in Mary's hands to promote the glory of her Divine Son; and inflamed with an ardent desire for the salvation of souls, let us ever preach our appointed mission by good example, by words of piety and gentleness, but especially by prayer."

Every Monday he recited the Little Office of the Blessed Virgin, to place himself under her protection, and draw down the more abundant benedictions from Heaven; Tuesday he consecrated to the Heart of Jesus, and, as was his custom, through that of Mary; and there, far from tumult and distraction, he meditated upon his motives for embracing a true and solid devotion to the Mother of God; on Thursday night, during the holy hour, that is, from eleven o'clock until midnight, he placed his heart in Mary's hands, thus to adore with her and the holy angels the Sacred Heart of Jesus. During the month of August he said the "Memorare" daily, and in addition to fervently celebrating all the feasts of the Blessed Virgin which occurred during vacation, he made several Communions with the intention of obtaining great devotion to her, and the favor of being preserved through her intercession from all sin, mortal at least, during this time of freedom and repose.

Next to his devotion to Mary, no obligation of a sodalist was dearer to him than that of loving his brethren in the sodality and of having but one heart and soul with them. "He loved us," says M. Sénac, "from the depths of his heart, and I remember his often accosting us in these words: 'How good it is for brethren to dwell together,' *Ecce quam bonum!* In maintenance of this fraternal cordiality among us, he loved to give and receive those material tokens (objects of piety, for instance) by which holy souls are impelled to communicate their sentiments to one another. I received from him many, many such evidences of friendship, especially during vacation, when, more exposed to worldly influence, one felt the great need of protection in his isolation from the sodality.

" He loved also to cultivate these friendships through correspondence, and what did he not accomplish with each of us in this way? As for me, I received numberless letters from him, all redolent with the perfume of piety, and which I read and re-read. Oh! why did I lose them, for they were the picture of his pure and beautiful soul."

To the above-mentioned evidences of affection, Charles never failed to add many ingenious devices of a heaven-born zeal. Daily, at vocal prayer, he remembered these friends; likewise did he make visits for them to the Blessed Sacrament, spiritual Communions, and practise voluntary mortifications, even offering Our Lord all his good works for the preservation of regularity, good example, and fervor in the sodality. Oh! you should have seen him as a sodalist, especially when filling the offices he so appreciated, of *promoter* and *apostle*. Then, indeed, nothing escaped his vigilance. He exhorted some, and encouraged others, inspiring all with renewed animation, cordiality, and joy.

This truly apostolic fervor was not confined to members of the sodality; the whole community felt its effects. When quite young, he had always taken great pleasure in the society of those students who, by reason of their age and piety, could serve him as mentors, faithfully listening to their advice and following their counsels. On becoming a sodalist he sought to express his gratitude for such favors by rendering these same good offices to others in turn; and it was truly his delight. I may say he deemed it a duty, to collect around him, at certain recreations, the younger boys, especially those who had not yet made their First Communion. Happy in the opportunity and hope of inspiring their young hearts with love of Jesus, Mary, and Joseph, he showed them great tenderness, and strove to prepare them far in advance for the visit of the Euchar-istic God, by conversations fragrant with piety, relating to them many edifying little stories and charming practices, in nearly all of which the Blessed Virgin was prominent.

Moreover, he never let pass an occasion of speaking to them of God and the things of God, even setting apart a portion of the hours of relaxation for Christian conver-sation. Divine love had already inflamed his soul with apostolic zeal, and the manner in which he insinuated himself into the hearts he wished to gain for Jesus Christ, gaining first for himself their esteem and confidence, was really wonderful.

"He was in the second Latin class," says Father Dupuy, of the Society of Jesus, "when I entered Polignan. The impression produced upon me by his appearance is still quite fresh in my mind. There was a mingling of sweet-ness, goodness, and affability which served as a veil to some-thing I could not see, but the influence of which I felt. I was not constrained with him, as new scholars generally are with older ones. Very soon his characteristic gayety almost effaced the difference of age and class existing between us; and in a few days I became one of the fruits of his propa-gandism for the Sodality of the Holy Angels.

"From that moment I felt that I had in him a true friend. I was not always very good, and in one way or another I, no doubt, caused such pure and disinterested affection as his great anxiety; but my assurance of the depth and sincerity of his charity was to me a wonderful and irresistible power, most beneficial in its effects. Know-ing that I would ever find in him not caresses or demon-strations, but what is far more precious in holy Christian friendship, it was impossible for me to refuse him any re-quest. This same apostolic zeal he exercised among others, sparing no means to induce them to join the sodality, and persevere therein with edifying fervor. One rule of this association was that the members assemble once a week, during recreation, in groups of three or four, for conversation on spiritual subjects. For these conversations Charles seemed to have an especial gift; and so natural his manner, so bright and unaffected all he said, that his words never failed to leave us impressed with a sense of satisfaction, even when they did not produce more important effects."

" I also had the happiness," adds the Rev. Father de Guilhempey,[1] " of belonging to one of these groups in which he every week exercised the ardor of his zeal; and I can say that it was truly his soul's delight to speak of the good God, and the happiness of loving Him and living for Him. Even at that early period his motto was the well-known one of St. Ignatius : *Ad majorem Dei gloriam*, To the greater glory of God ; and his principal occupation, or, at least, the motive of all his actions, to gain souls for Him.

IV.—The Memory Charles Left at Polignan.

Ah! what good did not Charles accomplish at Polignan, and how precious the memory he left there! Those who knew him best, never speak of him but with love, gratitude, and veneration, all congratulating themselves on having been his friends, and some, especially, on being the conquests of his zeal. Several of them, on hearing the news of his death, were unable to restrain their admiration for his virtues, but exclaimed in a tone of the deepest conviction, " Ah! Father Charles is a saint. He was an angel at Polignan, living but for God, and seeking only His glory. Yes, for God he would do and sacrifice all, even himself,

---

[1] A priest in the diocese of Toulouse.

and that without effort or hesitation, and with child-like simplicity; so familiar had this disposition of soul become to him, that it was almost second nature. Hence, none of those who knew him there are astonished, either at the odor of sanctity embalming his memory, or the irresistible attraction which has already moved souls to invoke his intercession before God. Had I heard of his working miracles on leaving Polignan, it would not have surprised me." [1]

" As for myself," writes one of them, [2] April 26, 1872, " I owe everything to him, and if some day I am so happy as to bless God in heaven, it is to him, as the human agent, I will be indebted for it. At Polignan I loved him; since his death I invoke him; and God grant that through his powerful influence I may, some day, resemble him."

Such was the impression made upon the pupils. Let us now listen to the testimony of his teachers.

Writing to one of Father Sire's brothers, a short time after his death, the Rev. Father Dencausse, then superior of the Seminary at Polignan, and now Vicar General of Toulouse, expressed himself as follows: " I congratulate you much more than I condole with you, at the death of your fervent religious. *Beati qui in Domino moriuntur.* [3] He has left our midst, young indeed, but with his work finished, having, in that brief time, wrought out his sanctification and accomplished his appointed mission here. His life was given to God entire; his heart had never known division. The moment seemed to have come when his charity and zeal, hitherto concentrated in his own soul, or rather confined within a narrow circle, were to extend

---

[1] The above is the testimony of various pupils at Polignan with Charles, who are now priests, religious, professors, etc.

[2] The Rev. Father Debernat, now a priest in the diocese of Toulouse.

[3] " Blessed are the dead who die in the Lord."—Apoc. xiv. 13.

their bounds and embrace a far wider horizon, but the hand of Heaven intervened.

" This soul had the ardor of an apostle, yes, of a martyr, and God, Who is sometimes pleased to reward holy desires, even ere their execution, prematurely crowned his generous offering. I must confess to you that we at Polignan are, like yourself, a little proud of this young saint; we claim him as ours in great measure, for we are convinced that in our midst was awakened and developed, up to a certain point, the germ of that sanctity which was to be matured later. On leaving us, he was nearly prepared to enter into that narrow way where one is occupied solely in following the Divine Master, after renouncing all things for His sake. Of this his edifying life among us is incontestable proof.

" We can say of him what the sacred writers deem allsufficient testimony of the Model of children: · He . . . . was subject to them. . . . And Jesus advanced in wisdom, and age, and grace with God and men.' Ask for nothing more; this embraces all: his ever regular, edifying life, his implicit obedience, his renunciation of his own will—unequivocal marks of holiness.

·· I remember perfectly his unvarying sweetness of manner, his blind submission, his eagerness to execute my wishes. I do not know that I ever heard a complaint about his conduct or work, and I never had to correct him for any bad tendency; on the contrary, his behavior was such that I used frequently to place him near some of the more giddy and thoughtless pupils, in hopes that his good example might happily influence them.

" He was at Polignan during that blessed period when was formed in our house that legion of young religious, nearly all of whom, like himself, sought the Society of Jesus. Charles lived with them, was their friend, and also, like them, was a member of the Sodality of the Blessed Virgin, in which, I assure you, they practised virtue in an eminent degree, and from which sodality sprang nearly all these vocations. Ah! what a comfort and joy the spirit of holy generosity which reigned in that pious association was to me. Charles's subsequent life ever bore the fresh, unfading stamp of the sodality.

"I am confident he is in heaven, and that he will watch over a house which must needs have had some share in forming his heart to piety; and over *me*, who as director of the association so often spoke to him of heaven, of souls and their priceless value. He derived far more profit than I from my own lessons; and it is now my turn to study those he taught me, lessons truly rich in their eloquent piety. Yes, I hope and believe they will not be lost; and this remembrance, so dear to me, shall likewise be beneficial to my soul; nor am I the only one here who will cherish it."

The Rev. Father spoke truly; he was not the only one, for all at Polignan, the teachers especially, have preserved the most precious recollections of Charles. Rev. Father Bize, his confessor, spoke of him, even to the day of his death, only with veneration, and frequently with tears. "Oh! what a beautiful soul!" he would exclaim, "what a beautiful soul! His life was so pure, his imperfections so slight, his faults so few, that it was with difficulty I could find in his confessions matter for absolution." Speaking of Charles's conduct as a pupil, he said: "Of the many who passed through my class during the thirty-three years I was professor of Rhetoric, I knew but two who during an entire year never once violated the rule of silence in class, and Charles was one of these two."

V.—Charles's Dispositions on Leaving Our Lady of Polignan.

Nor did Charles, on his part, forget Polignan. Whilst pursuing his studies there, his love for his fellow-students and veneration for his directors had been such, that the ineffaceable memory of those days abided with him ever after. "My soul is really oppressed, and my heart filled with the keenest regrets," he writes towards the close of his Rhetoric course, "at thoughts of the separation from these zealous teachers, who have lavished so much care upon me, these pious seminarians, these fervent sodalists, who called me by the dear names of friend and brother."

On returning to his home, a month later, he expressed the same regret in terms so unmistakable and earnest that his pious mother was really surprised; and fifteen years afterwards she thus spoke of it in one of her letters: "Charles left the Preparatory Seminary after a sojourn there of seven years, but sad and tearful at his departure. He had found it, he said, such a blessing to be in a house where reigned innocence, recollection, and fervor, and where the Blessed Virgin had granted him so many favors."

This feeling of gratitude towards Polignan never grew cold in his heart; and during his annual retreats he would always revert to the happiness of having been a pupil there under his two brothers, and of having had a good, zealous director, and warm friends in the sodalities of St. Aloysius Gonzaga, of the Holy Angels, and of the Blessed Virgin. Two years before his death, having heard that one of his nephews had been entered at Polignan, he sent his congratulations to his brother and sister-in-law. "May the good God bless and reward you," he wrote, "for having made such a judicious selection for your son."

On leaving this cherished spot, Charles made a pilgrimage to Our Lady of Garaison,[1] about twenty five kilometres [2] from Polignan, the object of which pilgrimage is thus explained by Father Lacomme, who accompanied him.

" When about to enter the Theological Seminary, Charles determined to begin this new life under the auspices of the Blessed Virgin. He moreover wished not only to obtain enlightenment and guidance concerning his future, but also to thank this heavenly Mother for all the favors she had heaped upon him the last seven years. Having already made preparations for the journey, on the first day of vacation, after bidding adieu to Our Lady of Polignan, we started on our way."

" At the moment of departure," adds Mme. Sire, " the weather was so threatening that a brother of one of Charles's companions tried to dissuade them from setting out. Alarmed by the flashes of lightning, which succeeded one another with frightful rapidity, and the peals of thunder, making all the neighboring hills reverberate, several of the party would not venture on their journey; but Charles, who was not to be deterred by such obstacles, remained firm, declaring that he had confidence in Mary, and would accomplish his promises. He had been the recipient of too many of her favors at Polignan, not to feel assured of that succor which seemed indispensable to him now, and he set out with the two companions he had succeeded in reassuring. Mary responded to his confidence ; the storm burst, but on either side of them, and the rain, which fell in torrents, accompanied them in such a manner that they reached their destination with dry clothing!

" During the journey, Charles commented with the fervor of an angel upon the magnificent canticle of the

---

[1] Before the apparition of the Blessed Virgin at Lourdes, the pilgrim-shrine of Our Lady of Garaison was the most celebrated and most frequented in the diocese of Tarbe.

[2] A kilometre is 1093.6389 yards.

Three Children in the Furnace, and his heart was so inflamed with divine love that his companions frequently heard him exclaim, 'Oh! let us be devoured by that love which burns without being consumed!'

"As soon as they came in sight of the miraculous chapel, they prostrated themselves to thank Mary for the providential assistance she had just rendered them, and kissed the sacred ground. On drawing near the fountain where the apparition had appeared, they approached it on bended knee."

"Charles was greatly fatigued," continues Father Lacomme, "but his love for Mary would not suffer him to rest ere saluting her. Reverently entering the sanctuary, he prayed a few moments in that holy place, which so truly reveals the piety of our ancestors, and the aspect of which alone is sufficient to inspire devotion to Mary, fully justifying what is said of the shrine, 'No one can go to Garaison without being touched.'

"Early next morning, Charles hastened to satisfy his piety by a worthy Communion; and great indeed was his spiritual consolation in receiving Our Lord on this occasion. The whole day was passed in visiting the various spots connected with the remembrance of the shepherds so honored by the Blessed Virgin; and when we resumed our journey, it was with souls full of regret, and a desire of returning hither some day, to renew that fervor with which Mary had here inspired us."

"On his return from this pilgrimage," adds Mme. Lacomme, "Charles spent several days with my son, at Anan.[1] We were so edified by his lively faith and charity, that I have never forgotten him, and the memory of his visit is truly a precious one. I had just experienced one of the most terrible misfortunes that could befall the mother

[1] District of the Haute-Garonne.

of a family; and my grief was so much the greater, as my overburdened heart refused to give vent to it. Charles's sensitive, sympathetic nature understood this, and among the words of consolation which fell from his lips none touched me so deeply as these, which I shall ever remember: ' Great sorrows, like Mary's at the foot of the cross, may not be expressed in words and tears; and it is this good Mother alone who can console us when Divine Providence is pleased to send us such trials.'

" He suggested to me the idea of my joining the Arch-confraternity of Our Lady of Victory, and kindly offered to take charge of the matter himself. Soon after leaving, he sent me the ticket of admission, accompanied by a medal of the Blessed Virgin and a relic of the true cross, doubtless intimating to me, by these two presents, that if I would be consoled with and by Mary, I must, like her, bear my portion of her Son's cross."

After the pilgrimage to Garaison, Charles returned home to spend his vacation. It was now he began to make special preparation for his entrance into the Theological Seminary, by increasing and perfecting his acts of virtue, making his own bed, for instance, under the pretext of wishing to know how when in the novitiate, as if such a trifling thing demanded long apprenticeship. This habit he ever after adhered to, from a spirit of charity, desiring to give others as little trouble as possible, of humility, delicacy, and more especially mortification, as he could thus un-perceived remove the mattress at pleasure, and lie immedi-ately next the straw bed.

It was about this time, also, he commenced to rise early in the morning, to repair to the banks of the Garonne and pray amid those magnificent forests of poplars and wil-lows—there, where the beautiful scene spread out before him, the song of the birds, and the murmur of the waters, were all so many eloquent tongues inviting him to praise God. " I remember," says one of his friends, " he wrote me, during this vacation, a long letter, the pages of which clearly revealed the ardent love of God which consumed his soul. In it he spoke in all freedom and simplicity of the joy, the fervor with which, on the banks of the river, he made his morning's meditation;—' one step,' he said, ' in preparation for the Theological Seminary!' This letter, the memory of which has always remained in my heart as a powerful incentive to good, touched me deeply, and inspired me with the highest esteem for him."

It was at this period, too, he began the custom which he never relinquished, of visiting, from time to time, the sanctuary of Our Lady of Grace, in the village of Bruguières, five kilometres from Saint-Jory; likewise, of inclining his head in salutation to Mary, whenever, in any church, he passed her statue or chapel.

Meanwhile the day was approaching when he must cross the threshold of that blessed sanctuary, where, far from the world and its pleasures, he hoped to give himself wholly to God, in an irrevocable consecration of his life to the service of the altar. To render himself as worthy as possible of this celestial favor, he made a fervent novena to the Blessed Virgin, with charming simplicity and humility begging his friends to compensate for the coldness and feebleness of his prayers by adding their own petitions thereto, that God would deign to grant him through His powerful Mother's intercession the grace of remaining to the end a faithful, pious seminarian.

CHAPTER III.

THE THEOLOGICAL SEMINARY AT TOULOUSE.

I. Virtues most conspicuous in Charles during the First and Second Years.

1. *His regularity and obedience.*—On entering the Theological Seminary, Charles had but one desire, that of becoming a good priest, which, of course, included the necessary preparation for this high estate, by being a perfect seminarian.

Hence, in imitation of one of the dearest and most amiable patrons of youth, he practised that maxim which has become so celebrated by reason of the number of saints it has formed : " For me, the best of all penances shall be the ordinary life." [1]

" It was by the aid of this maxim," says one of his fellow-students,[2] " that Charles made rapid progress in the path of perfection. Long before, when pursuing his literary studies, penetrated with its spirit, he had followed it scrupulously ; and now, at the Theological Seminary, his fidelity to it was perfect, and he often dwelt upon it in his conversations with unaffected delight. 'It seems to me,' he would say, 'very easy for us to become saints—merely to observe our rule (which is the infallible expression of God's will in our regard), both as God wishes and because He wishes it, performing all our duties as if in God's presence and directed by Him; is there anything difficult in this ? Oh, how little does the good God require of us ! '

[1] Maxim of St. John Berchmans.
[2] M. Birot, treasurer of the Theological Seminary at Lyons.

"Truly, it was not difficult for him, and he kept the rule perfectly, with all simplicity, without constraint, without apparent effort. His obedience was admirable, and his name at the Theological Seminary was synonymous with regularity itself. He seemed born to live according to the rule, and the rule seemed made for him. He observed it in every detail ; I do not believe he was ever found remiss on any point whatever, being always where the rule wanted him and as it prescribed, without either delay or unseemly haste. So well did he manage his time, that he could always preserve that amiable and pious gravity our masters taught us whilst practising it themselves. Being regulator for one year, which office obliged him to ring the bell for all the exercises, and at the precise time, I can truthfully say that I do not think he was ever one moment late, but that the first stroke of the clock found him with his hand on the bell-rope.

"His piety was never intermittent ; just as I saw him on the first day, so was he on the last. Under no pretext whatever did he allow himself the least departure from the rule. One day I saw him at his chamber door, confronted by a fellow-student, who asked some information of him. This new Aloysius Gonzaga made his friend a sign to wait until he could obtain the necessary permission to speak, which granted, he complied with the request, with his accustomed suavity.

"This regularity embraced not only the common rule of the house, but, as I can attest from observation, even the minutest details of his *private rule.*" By this term in seminaries are meant those regulations one imposes upon himself with the approval of his director, and which include everything one proposes to do or to avoid during the whole day, for the purpose of honoring God, sanctifying one's actions, correcting one's defects, acquiring virtues, and employing one's time most profitably. "Like all good semi-narians, Charles had his private rule, wherein everything was mapped out with such precision that not a moment was left at the disposition of caprice." "A similar rule," says one of his brothers, "determined, during vacation, the actions of each day, week, and month. This plan of life, approved by his director, became for him an inflexible line of conduct. Alone or in company, travelling or at home, he was so faithful to it that one could truly say he lived under strict obedience, both when in the world and in the seminary."

One point of his rule to which he attached the greatest importance was silence, and herein his fidelity was perfect. Whether the exercise at which he assisted were presided over by his superiors or one of his fellow-students mattered little to him; if silence were prescribed, he kept it inviolably, and never spoke without permission.

In his cell it was the same; his room-mates, who are still living, say that he invariably asked only in writing for what he needed; and fear of displeasing a fellow-student had no weight in inducing him to the slightest deviation from the fundamental rule of silence. "On taking up the study of philosophy," says one of them, "I was put with Charles in a chamber where there were four beds, two of them occupied by two students who, though good and well-behaved in the main, were by no means scrupulous in observing the rule—one especially, who gave up his cassock at the end of the year. Hoping to gain him by gentleness, Charles would smile at his confrère's innocent nonsense, but never once did he break silence to please him."

In every way imaginable Charles's companions tried his fidelity, especially at the beginning, but he always remained firm. "One day," says Rev. Father Birot, "as

he was returning to his cell from evening class, modest
and recollected as usual, he was confronted by a fellow-
student, who, otherwise good and amiable, but a little more
frolicsome sometimes than the rule allowed, had resolved,
it seems, to try the measure of our dear brother's patience
and charity.   First, he mimicked Charles's pious gravity,
then pushed him to the right and left of the corridor, and
lastly barred his way.   To be sure, it was all done good-
humoredly, yet few could have preserved their composure
as did Charles, who, without smiling, though without any
sign of irritation, not even taking his hands out of his cassock sleeves, in which they were concealed, contented
himself with trying to avoid the blockader and pursue his
way.   Finding all his resources fail, the young scamp at
last cried out, ' It's no go !'   And he was right; for vain,
indeed, was any attempt to turn Charles from the rule and
the even tenor of his way.   Meeting him afterwards in
recreation, his mischievous friend said to him, ' I fear you
have a grudge against me.   I meant only a little fun.'   ' I
have no cause to bear you a grudge,' answered Charles,
' but I really think you ought to observe the rule better ;
you would be happier, and God would be more pleased
with you !'"

In pursuing his studies, Charles was likewise generously
obedient, allowing himself no hour of rest, nor of negligence.   Day after day, at the exact time, one beheld him
change, through obedience, from one prescribed exercise
to another, whether alone or in company mattering little
to him: God's eye was upon him, and that was enough.   To
form an idea of his perfect obedience, it suffices to read his
private rule or glance over his class notes.   It were impossible to find anything more complete, precise, or carefully
executed than these.   All the branches, not excepting the
less important, are there analyzed and noted down, day by

day, class by class, without the least interruption or gap, in a manner truly admirable.

His teachers and fellow-students, in perfect accord with the foregoing, likewise declare that Charles's success in his studies was due not so much to talent as to his application, docility, and obedience.

2. *His mortification and modesty.*—Next to regularity and obedience, the virtues most to be remarked in him at this period of his life, especially during the first year at the Theological Seminary, were mortification and obedience. " I lived with him a long time," says one of his brothers, " and our intimacy was such as ordinarily exists in Christian families between brothers. I can positively declare that after most carefully searching my memory I am unable to recall anything in his conduct contrary to the spirit of Our Lord, and especially as regards mortification and recollection.

" Never was he known to seek himself in anything, but frequently to sacrifice his own ease and convenience, after the example of our divine Master. At home we generally passed through the garden on our way to church, or when going out for a walk ; and whilst the rest of us would sometimes indulge ourselves by partaking of the fruit or plucking a flower as we went along, Charles never did. Nor do we ever remember to have seen him eat or drink between meals, not even during the hottest days of summer, when, especially towards noon, one's thirst is usually so great. As for those comfortable positions the debilitating influences of the heat tempt one to assume at this season of the year, I do not believe, in fact, I am sure, he never allowed himself to indulge in them, these words of the holy Council of Trent being continually before him : ' Since nothing is better calculated to lead the faithful to piety and the service of God than the example of those who are consecrated to the divine ministry, it is especially desirable that these, called by their vocation to be Our Lord's chosen ones, so regulate their exterior that their deportment, clothing, gait, conversation,—indeed, everything about them, be grave, modest, religious, in a word, commanding the veneration of all.' Docile to these instructions, Charles, whilst at the seminary, labored so zealously and effectually to conform to them, that all who saw him at this period, either during vacation or during the scholastic year, are unanimous in declaring that his conduct was ever in perfect accord with ecclesiastical modesty and mortification."

"I had occasion to see him very often about this time," says Sister Mary of Providence, a religious of Anglet, near Bayonne, "and never did I approach him without being edified. What struck me especially, after the great respect he showed his parents, his gentleness and frankness, were his modesty and reserve in all conversations, even the least serious, his amiability and gayety being always governed by circumspection. He looked at a woman's face only when obliged to do so, and then with great reserve, and merely for the instant. But the virtue which shone brightest in him was mortification, of which I had one day a manifest proof. Being indisposed at his home, where I had been spending several days, I was lying down in a chamber near his own. I had been asleep some time, when the door of the next room suddenly opened and shut ; and listening, I soon perceived that it was Charles, who, happy to find himself alone on the first floor, as he believed, came hither to pour out his soul before the good God and satisfy his love of penance, the sighs and pious aspirations which, after the use of the discipline, exhaled from his heart, all aglow with love, betraying his secret. I also ascertained, unknown to him, that he would remove the mattress from his bed and sleep upon the bare boards, next morning carefully replacing everything as before, so as not to be discovered. These marked and undeniable proofs of his spirit of mortification pleased me greatly, and gave me a very exalted idea of his virtue."

Of all the exterior mortifications which young Charles practised that of the eyes cost him the most ; hence, it was on this point he made the strongest and most precise resolutions, examining himself carefully three times a day as to the fidelity with which he had kept them. Under circumstances likely to cause a violation of these resolutions, as, for instance, the general movements of the community, he would, from time to time, take up his rosary, or fix his eyes upon his cassock, which by its color and length reminded him of that universal mortification the pious Levite should ever practise.

Thanks to these precautions, the control of his eyes became so natural to him that in all the ordinary exercises, even in class or in the refectory, he seldom looked one in the face. His eyes, habitually lowered, were lifted only occasionally to regard the reader, the professor, or whoever presided over the exercise. Those unforeseen events which in large gatherings of people usually excite a general and simultaneous movement of curiosity never took him by surprise—he seemed unconscious of them. When passing one of his superiors or brethren in the hall, he would gently incline his head in token of salutation, but without fixing his looks upon him or otherwise withdrawing his attention from that recollection that seemed his natural element.

This holy modesty was so perfected, by degrees, that even in his room or during study hours he never amused himself looking at his brethren; neither did he go near the window unless it was necessary, and in recreation he carefully avoided glancing up at the door when strangers entered. Likewise, when we went into town on the appointed days for walking out, he ever guarded his eyes in the most mortified manner; and during vacation, when carriages were constantly passing under his window, he would not even so much as cast a glance at them.

To all these exterior mortifications, which Charles practised with the greatest simplicity, and so naturally that the most observant could scarcely detect them, he added similar interior ones, required less by the necessity of doing penance than of acquiring or of cultivating in his heart the sublime virtues of the priesthood : virtues which, being opposed to nature, demand sustained efforts, and sacrifices renewed every day, every moment.

What privations, for example, did he not impose upon himself to preserve unsullied, in the depths of his heart, the beautiful flower of purity: keeping at a distance from the fire in winter, refraining from rest and sleep in the sultry summer days, holding himself aloof from persons of the other sex, by having intercourse with them only when and as necessity required it.   He spared himself nothing to protect the life and vigor of this inestimable virtue. And then, how he labored to detach his heart from creatures, that thus it might be the more strongly united to God, by resisting not only all such affections as were bad or dangerous, but even those which were too free or ardent, avoiding in his intercourse with the most pious of his brethren all excessive familiarity, every word or action savoring of too much natural tenderness, or not in accordance with true ecclesiastical detachment.

Later on he began, by degrees, to diminish, with his director's approval, the pious correspondence he had heretofore kept up with his friends outside the seminary, that thus he might give himself unreservedly to his chosen work; and as to his sensitive, shrinking nature, so timid in the face of pain or struggle, and continually placing obstacles before his zeal, he resolved to combat and mortify it to the utmost, thus realizing in his conduct that maxim of the pious author of the " Imitation: " "There a man makes greater progress, and merits greater grace, where he overcomes himself more, and mortifies himself in spirit."

By the aid of this universal mortification, in a little while he became altogether master of himself. " From about the second year of his course at the Theological Seminary, he had so completely subdued his nature," says one of his fellow-students, "that it really seemed dead in him, and his affections were under such control that he appeared less a man than an angel. Of course, like every one else in the seminary, he doubtless found many occasions that cost him a struggle, but I must say, I never saw the least trace of it in his countenance. With an ever tranquil heart and serene face, his voice was never raised above its usual pitch, not even in those discussions in which he was assigned a part. His reasons once clearly stated, but without any exhibition of temper, obstinacy, or undue animation—that was all; he insisted no more, and his last argument was the example he gave us of that unalterable gentleness of disposition we all admired without being able to imitate. Astonished at such virtue, I would sometimes congratulate him thereupon. 'Of what use is it to get excited and lose one's peace of soul?' he would say; 'Our Lord never lost that which he also requires of us, and it is so sweet to walk in His footsteps.' "

This self-control, the fruit of so many efforts, and that perfect recollection, its necessary consequence, permitted him to devote his energies, sole and undivided, to the workof the seminary; for, master of his passions, he could make them subservient to his task of self-detachment, of the eradication of his defects and those vicious inclinations inherent in our nature, thus establishing in his soul, on the ruins of the old man, the new man in Jesus Christ, whom the priest must represent to the faithful, and with whom every pious Levite should, in consequence, strive to be clothed whilst at the seminary.

Ever laboring, then, to die to self that he might live only in Jesus Christ, Charles made the acquisition of charity—beautiful virtue, which is the summary of that life, or at least its perfection—the continual object of his efforts.

3. *His charity.*—A thousand charming practices, chief among which was the holy exercise of God's presence, daily fostered the growth of his tender charity.

" I believe firmly," says one of his fellow-students, " that he practised to the letter this maxim of Scripture, ' Walk before Me and be perfect.' [1] Yes, he seldom lost sight of God, but lived in, with, and for Him; all his thoughts, words, actions, even the serenity of his countenance and the expression of his eyes, being so many unmistakable evidences of his walking ever in the continual presence of God.

" Even in class and during recreation it was the same. When interrogated by a professor, his answers were always given with such modesty and respect, that one could not help perceiving that this man to him was the representative of his Master, Jesus Christ. And in conversing with us, we felt how truly his heart was united indissolubly to God. Moreover, he often spoke to us of the Divine Presence, profiting by every occasion to remind us of it, even in recreation, but always so unaffectedly and sweetly that every one was charmed and edified. ' Oh! how happy we are,' he would say, ' to be here in the seminary, where we can love God to our heart's content! Yes, everything around us is calculated to lead us to Him. Oh! how cul-

[1] Gen. xvii. 1.

pable were our conduct, did we fail to fill our hands with those treasures of God's graces so necessary to the welfare of our own souls and of those our holy vocation will hereafter entrust to us!'"

Impossible, indeed, would it be to recount all the holy transports of love that filled so tender and beautiful a soul as this in the course of the day. The morning prayer, the holy sacrifice of the Mass which followed, his Communions especially, and his visits to the Blessed Sacrament, were all but so many pious colloquies in which Charles spoke to his Beloved as to a dear friend, or a child to its father. Always united to the Source and Centre of Love by prayer, he was ever inflamed therewith, and if one may judge correctly of the interior by what appears exteriorly, rapturous, indeed, must have been the intercourse between God and his soul.

Says one of his friends: "Every time I saw this holy fellow-student at the foot of the altar, I could not but remark his angelic piety. The mere sight of him after he had received holy Communion did me good. Nor was I the only one impressed by his demeanor at such times; every one noticed and admired it, even children."

"I was very young," says a person who lived at Saint-Jory, "when Father Charles used to spend his vacation at home; yet never can I forget the impression he made upon me, especially at church, nor how much more pleasing to me it was than that made by other young ecclesiastics, all good and edifying. He looked so recollected and holy at the altar in his surplice, that I could scarcely turn my eyes from him, and at the moment of his receiving holy Communion my own sensations were delightful, as, closely questioning his exterior, I sought to comprehend the sentiments with which his ardent soul seemed animated. His demeanor at church, in every particular, was always such as to edify every one, as I have frequently heard remarked."

His devotion in all exercises of piety was noticeable. Were the prayers long or short, his modesty and fervor whilst assisting thereat convinced every one that his heart accompanied the words—a heart inflamed by divine love. "Yet there was nothing strained or exaggerated about his virtue," says one of his fellow-students. "He loved much his good Master, as he called Him, and did nothing except for His glory, but his love was that of great simplicity. Immeasurable, too, was his love for Mary, and faithful his service, yet of a nature that did not attach itself exclusively to this or that practice, and which sought to be unnoticed."

The prevailing sentiment of his prayers was that of love, gratitude, admiration, praise. He thanked God for all his gifts, even those apparently the most common—his not being deformed, his having been born in the bosom of the Catholic Church, in a country so profoundly Christian as France, and of a family making open profession of God's holy service. He also thanked Him especially for the many supernatural gifts lavished upon him in his baptism and infancy, as well as whilst both at the Preparatory and Theological Seminaries. And touched at thoughts of these benefits, he was frequently unable to restrain the transports of his heart, but, like the Prophet, would invite all creatures in heaven and on earth to supply his deficiencies, by uniting with him in praising, blessing, and exalting the Lord. "Oh! magnify the Lord with me, and let us extol His name together,"[1] he would exclaim. "All ye works of the Lord, bless the Lord: praise and exalt Him above all forever."[2]

[1] Ps. xxxiii. 4.
[2] Dan. iii. 57.

Says Catherine: " That admirable canticle of the three children in the fiery furnace was frequently upon his lips. He loved it, and such were his transports in commenting upon it that he seemed a seraph, all burning with love."

As to other sensible evidences of divine love that Charles must have given vent to whilst in the seminary we know very little. All that we can learn from a perusal of his writings whilst there is, that he ever aspired to the most perfect. A pious individual who observed him closely, especially during his vacation in the bosom of his family, assures us that in all his conversations there was some reference to God. "And when he spoke of this good Master," she says, " particularly of His love for man and the return of love we should make Him, his countenance became so radiant that one easily read therein the ardor of his heart and the zeal for souls with which he was consumed; he then, indeed, appeared rather a seraph than a mortal! Oh! how I esteemed him for his wonderful love of God!"

" Regarding all his superiors as the representatives of God," says M. Birot, " his respect, docility, love, and gratitude towards them amounted to veneration. When circumstances favored it, he would speak of them in recreation, expressing such esteem and admiration for their exceedingly meritorious yet often misunderstood life that we could not help sharing it with him. It was especially on occasions like these that Charles's heart was revealed to us. Never can I forget these happy hours of youthful confidence, which did me so much good."

This filial affection which he testified for his teachers during his stay at the seminary, by unequivocal marks of esteem, love and veneration, never grew cold; and all through life he was pleased frequently to give expression to it. The year of his death, passing through Toulouse, ere setting sail for Bourbon, Charles made them several visits, and one of his old teachers being absent, the following grateful message was left with his confrères: 'I beg of you to remember me to M. N., and tell him how pleased I should have been to see him, and thank him for all his kindness to me, for I feel that I owe him much.'"

Charles's filial piety towards his superiors was equaled only by that fraternal charity with which his heart was filled for his fellow-students.

"I shall never forget," says one of them, "the angelic expression of his face when he spoke to me of unity and love among brethren. He would say: 'Oh! the beautiful life of the seminary! It is here we realize that admirable motto of Scripture: Behold how good and how pleasant it is for brethren to dwell together in unity." [1] To see Jesus Christ in each of them, to love and respect them for His sake, patiently bearing little contradictions, closing our eyes to their faults, and seeing only their good qualities, believing good of them, never evil—is not this truly heaven upon earth? Oh! if the world but knew the infinite sweetness of charity! But to taste this charity the spirit of God is necessary, and this the world has not.'.

"This spirit of God Charles himself possessed abundantly. How happy he was to render a service, compassionate a trouble, console a grief, or restore peace and joy to a suffering soul! Ah! then, indeed, was he rich in those blessed words the secret of which is known only to the saints; and they whom he thus solaced were convinced that they had found in him a veritable friend, a true father.

"His charity, moreover, was not exclusive; it embraced all his fellow-pupils, for which reason he was a slave to that point of the rule ordering one to take recreation with those companions Providence first brings to us. Also, in repair-

[1] Ps. cxxxii. 1.

ing to the chapel after dinner, walking with his eyes
modestly cast down, as he always did, he quietly took the
place naturally assigned him by Providence. Some one
praising his fidelity one day in this regard, he answered:
' The rule forbids our making a choice, but even if it did
not, why should we wish to choose? Are we not all
brethren? And should we prefer to associate with others
rather than those God gives us ? '

" Such charitable sentiments soon obtained for him among
his fellow-pupils a flattering epithet, which must have
touched his heart—that of *good*. When I entered the Theological Seminary in 1848, it was the distinctive appellation he then bore, and which he has borne ever since. In
speaking of him, they always said, *the good M. Sire*. Goodness was so identified with him that, take what pains he
would to conceal it, one must needs have perceived it in all
his acts and words, even in his very appearance, and have felt
instinctively, in approaching him, that here was the goodness of God, here was a soul actuated purely by charity.

" This virtue, however, did not blind him to the faults
of his brethren requiring fraternal correction. How often
have I not heard him gently reprove such of them as, more
giddy or thoughtless than malicous or ill-disposed, would, in
his presence, discuss those little disagreeables of community-
life that, frequently forming the subject of conversation,
have a tendency to diminish charity, cool one's fervor,
and even create a disgust for duty. And these reproofs
were always given with characteristic tact, a prudence far
superior to his years, and so mildly ! He had veritable talent for placing things before one in the true light, and
bringing back to a sense of right and justice those who had
allowed their better judgment to be misled.

" On such occasions, there was in his person and words
an air of confidence, in strong contrast with his ordinary ti-

midity, an authority which, however, wounded none, an out-
pouring of justice and love which penetrated the hearts of
all who heard him.   We all felt that Charles was far better
and more pious than ourselves, and it sufficed for one to
be with him but a short while to realize the ennobling influences he shed around him.

"I do not believe these fraternal corrections ever made
him an enemy ; he was loved and respected even to veneration by all his fellow-students, which veneration must
surely have been inspired by his sanctity."

4. *His less striking virtues.*—And this sanctity was great
indeed ; for to the practice of those eminent virtues which
we have just mentioned, and which constitute the foundation of the Christian life, he added those thousand little virtues, interior and concealed, which, having humility for
their origin and perfection for their end, lend to their pos-
sessor something charming and celestial—virtues commonly
designated condescension, Christian urbanity, simplicity,
gentleness, forbearance, etc.   All these were so inseparably
his whilst he was at the Theological Seminary that they really seemed a part of his nature.   He was habitually goodness, sweetness, and affability itself, with never a trace of
temper or impatience in his conduct, much less affectation,
inquisitiveness, or a desire to encroach upon the rights of
others.   So pleased did he always seem with everything and
everybody, that one might readily have supposed his tastes
and wishes identical with those of all around him.   With
that truly Christian kindness and politeness so strongly
recommended by St. Paul, he overlooked the defects of
others, and gave none cause to suffer from him.   His words
were ever mild, his manner simple and affable.   He was
bright and lively in recreation, yet without undue frivolity
or familiarity, carefully avoiding the least word or action
not in accordance with humility, modesty, Christian suavity.

He kept equally aloof from whatever savored of worldliness, luxury, and self-ease on the one hand, and slovenliness and disorder on the other. "Scrupulously clean and neat in his appearance," says one of his room-mates, " his cell, his clothing, all his effects were ever in perfect order. His note-books were admirable specimens of neatness ; and upon his table there was not the least trace of carelessness. And the time devoted to these material cares was not that set apart for study (this he deemed too precious to be employed in any other manner than as prescribed), but the half-hour given us of the philosophy class, every Wednesday and Saturday, after midday recreation."

" This spirit of order," adds one of his brothers, " Charles carried everywhere. His appearance was faultlessly neat ; as to his hands, they always looked as if just out of the water. Scarcely was he under the home roof for his vacation, ere every one felt the presence of this friend of order. After a most careful arrangement of all his effects, he quietly settled down to his studies. We still remember in the family how, in order to leave his brothers more room, and, at the same time, be himself more alone with God, he contrived a study at the end of the corridor, partitioning it off by curtains."

This evident regard for the comfort and pleasure of others was manifested on so many occasions, under such a variety of circumstances, and was withal so frank and sincere, that it could but win our admiration, gratitude, and love ; and it is no wonder that every one at his home and at the seminary. fellow-students as well as teachers, praised his virtue and exalted his character only so much the more as he sought to be unnoticed.

"The life at our seminaries, says Rev. Father Houbart, superior of the Theological Seminary in Angers, " is not that calculated to produce brilliant virtues. The best seminarians are those who make little display in spiritual matters, quietly working out their sanctification, whilst practising the beautiful maxim inculcated by the author of the 'Imitation,' 'Love to be unknown and to be accounted as nothing.' And such was Charles—ever striving to conquer self, at the same time shunning the notice of men, he became in a very short time one of the most remarkable models of the house."

"I see him now," adds another of his professors, the Rev. Father Maréchal, former superior of the seminary of Issy, near Paris, "with his angelic face, the expression of which I can never forget. I see him come and go, in observance of the rule, answering in class, ever the same, the manner his own, yet somewhat like the others, striving always to lose himself, as it were, and to be unknown. He appeared very pious ; I trusted him fully, and ranked him in my esteem with our best seminarians."

"He was so skilful in concealing everything under the veil of humility," says one of his fellow-students, "that, at first one observed in him nothing more than simply an edifying life. His great virtue was precisely this concealment of merit, exposing only to the eye of God the rich treasures of his interior."

Realizing that the sacerdotal novitiate is a tomb in which the young Levite, dead to the world, must be buried, by striving to escape the notice even of those with whom he lives, Charles made it his chief endeavor to attract no attention. "I will labor," says he, in his resolutions of 1848, "to remain unknown and forgotten."

"And it was precisely this," adds one of his brethren, the Rev. Father Dore, diocesan missionary of Toulouse, "that increased our esteem for him. Like the humble violet, vainly did he seek to hide himself from our notice ; the sweet perfume of his soul betrayed him everywhere. One felt in his presence as if virtue escaped from his person and revealed his sanctity ; hence, all venerated him, especially those who were the most inclined to piety. Our teachers themselves had something more than respect and esteem for him ; indeed, they considered him a saint and cited him as a model, several even recommending their penitents to cultivate his acquaintance, and none ever speaking of him except as a type of goodness, an angel of good counsel. The eldest of these, the Rev. Father Vieusse, who directed his conscience, and consequently knew all the beauty of his soul, loved to contemplate him during the exercises, feeling for him that veneration holy mothers have for their pious children."

On hearing of his death, twelve years later, the teacher [1] who had for two years taught him natural philosophy and the sciences exclaimed, "Oh ! how I loved that good Charles ! He was an angel ! He had no remarkable talent, but what piety! what candor ! what innocence! His modesty, regularity, and charity edified every one. What a model seminarian he was! Never did I hear the least thing to his disadvantage. From the first year of his entrance into the seminary he was what the hour of his death saw him—a saint, wholly devoted to God. How happy I am to have had a saint under my tuition ! Ah ! may he from the heights of heaven deign to look favorably upon our scholars and upon me, poor servant, whom the good Master was pleased to make use of in teaching him something of human sciences during his stay on earth."

[1] The Rev. Father Chambon, then superior of the Seminary of Philosophy at Autun. He was the first priest outside of the Sire family who invoked Father Charles. As soon as he learned the circumstances of Father Charles's death, he began to beg his intercession, and continued to do so until his own death, which occurred August 14, 1873.

II.—Charles's Promotion to the Tonsure.—The Vacation Which Followed.

After reading the above testimonies, one readily understands with what confidence and security the Rev. Fathers, directors of the Theological Seminary, invited this pious Levite to take the first step towards the sanctuary. "It was in the middle of his second year at the Theological Seminary," says his professor of philosophy,[1] "that we all invited him to receive the tonsure; we, as well as his fellow-students who were brought in closer contact with him, fully persuaded that he would one day be a good, holy priest, according to the heart of God and of the Church; not that he possessed brilliant talent, or marked aptitude for the studies assigned us (although on this point, his studies, I can truly praise his docility, application, judgment, and success, to a certain degree), but because of his most edifying conduct. Without revealing yet that ardor of zeal he manifested later among the Jesuits, he exercised in the house an influence none the less real because hidden, a most precious influence, which every pious, modest, regular scholar sheds around him, and which in communities is so powerful in maintaining the spirit of order, discipline, and fervor."

Charles was promoted to the tonsure[2] July 1, 1849, the feast of his two patrons, Saints Peter and Paul. How fervent his remote preparation was, one may judge from what we have just read, and the immediate one was even more so. We learn from his writings that at this time he entered seriously into himself, reproaching himself severely for his slightest faults and negligences ; and feeling the need of

[1] The Rev. Father Gassot (now deceased), director of the Theological Seminary of Orléans.

[2] Mgr. d'Astros, archbishop of Toulouse, being too indisposed at that time to officiate, the ceremony, which had been deferred, was performed by Mgr. Doney, Archbishop of Montauban.

giving himself irrevocably to God, he endeavored to empty his heart of all its human attachments, that the void might be filled by God alone. Then, resuming all his most pious practices, and renewing all his most generous resolutions, he promised Our Lord to be more fervent and generous than heretofore, never recoiling before any sacrifice whatever, and devoting himself, even in the seminary, to the advancement of His glory in the salvation of souls.

" Yes," he writes in his notes of the retreat, " yes, I desire to belong to God entirely and forever. *Jam non dicam vos servos,* He says to me, *vos autem dixi amicos,* ' I will not now call you *servants,* but I have called you *friends.*'[1] Dost thou understand this, Charles? Thou hast had friends; thou hast been no stranger to the blessings of friendship, and it is this that has rendered thee so happy in the past. And hadst thou known no love save that of Jesus for thee, would not this alone have sufficed to make thee appreciate the title of friend and all it implies?

" Behold, it is this Jesus, this good Jesus, Who wishes to be thy Friend: *vos autem dixi amicos.* Art thou disposed to be His? Art thou ready to immolate thyself for Him, renouncing for His sake thy goods, friends, parents, country, even life itself ? Yes, I am ready to do all things for Jesus —to renounce pleasures, honors, and riches, that I may live of His life; to strive to tear every passion from my heart and acquire every virtue, immolating myself, if needs be, to advance His glory in gaining souls for Him.

" Gaining souls....*Sitio!* I thirst! Oh! who can comprehend that burning thirst of the Heart of Jesus upon the cross! Who will find in this simple word those earnest exhortations He addresses his priests to gain souls for Him! More than once has Jesus from on high addressed these exhortations to me, and I have been deaf to them.

[1] St. John xv. 15.

He has reproached me for my indifference to the salvation of souls, and the abatement of my piety. Wherefore is my heart now inflamed with love, and my understanding enlightened to see that I was created to gain souls for God? Woe to thee now, Charles, if thou prepare not thyself for the life of sacrifice God demands of His priests! Woe to thee, if, whilst in the seminary, thou labor not incessantly for the acquisition of learning and piety! Woe to thee, if thou give not thy companions there good example, both in word and conduct!

" Is not thy courage strengthened, thy fervor enkindled at the contemplation of a St. Francis de Sales, a St. Francis Xavier, a St. Vincent de Paul? Knowest thou not that the priest is that advance-guard charged with defending the flock of Jesus Christ, and snatching it from the hands of the impious? Consider their zeal, their energy of character, the rude labors these faithful servants impose upon themselves, the wearisome privations they undergo, the cruel sufferings, not only being spent and worn out in the service, but oftentimes even massacred, whilst we, knowing the price of souls, are so slothful in the Lord's vineyard! Was it not to us the good Master said, *Ecce ego elegi vos, et posui vos ut eatis et fructum afferatis, et fructus vester maneat?* [1]

" O my soul! let the remembrance of the past gloriously re-animate thy future. Mindful that Jesus has so often urged thee to gain souls for Him, even in the seminary, take now the firm resolution of bringing many to Him, by thy words, example, prayers. Set thyself manfully to the work. Mary will aid thee."

To ensure success in this mission of saving souls, Charles, after giving himself wholly to Jesus in his ordination, gave

---

[1] I have chosen you and have appointed you, that you should go and should bring forth fruit: and your fruit should remain.—St. John xv. 16.

himself in like manner to Mary, constituting himself her devoted servant by a solemn vow, written and signed by his own hand, wherein he assigned her his body and soul, all that belonged to him, exteriorly and interiorly, the fruits even of his good actions, past, present, and future, to dispose of solely according to her good pleasure, and as she saw most conducive to God's greater glory, in time and eternity. After which offering, followed by an attestation of loyalty, he conjured her to present him to her dear Son, that, received thus by the good Master, he might, through her intercession, become a most faithful disciple and perfect imitator of His virtues.

In consequence of these promises, Charles, after receiving the tonsure, made greater efforts than ever to regulate his exterior, but more especially his interior (thoughts and motives), as became a worthy and fervent ecclesiastic. Hence the vacation which followed close upon this event was spent in practising those two grand virtues of the priesthood: religion and zeal.

On arriving at Saint-Jory, his first care was to offer his services to the pastor, to perform under his direction whatever offices of the holy ministry the latter might assign him. Knowing his modesty, piety, and zeal, the worthy pastor not only accepted his offer of co-operation, but gave him entire charge of the material cares of the holy place —the sacristy, ornaments, the sacred vessels, and the sanctuary. In a short time Charles had everything there the picture of neatness, and order was the reigning spirit. The altar boys, duly trained and instructed upon the importance of their duty, gave evidences of it by their silence, the gravity of their behavior, their uniformity of action— in a word, they were subjects of edification to the whole parish.

Charles himself set them the example. It would be impossible to describe the modesty, piety, and lively faith, with which he served the altar, chanting the offices, standing or kneeling before the Blessed Sacrament, or assisting the pastor at the baptismal font, the Holy Table, the bedside of the dying. Everything directly or remotely connected with the sacred liturgy went to his heart. The Church chants filled him with delight, and his raptures were beyond expression, as his soul drank in those magnificent harmonies which resounded so often in our parish church and the chapel of the Theological Seminary on Sundays and feasts.

"It was during this vacation," says his pious mother, "that Charles abandoned himself to all the holy impulses of his heart, and glowing with the ardors of zeal, he made us live in an atmosphere wholly spiritual, by means of his conversations, supported by incessant acts of virtue and admirable practices of piety, which could but fill our souls with greater love for God."

Continues one of his brothers, "Several times I accompanied him on his visits in the parish, and I remember the delight with which he was ever received, so charming his manners and conversation. Pious subjects were usually the sole topic on these occasions, and the impression of his words was such that many of his sayings are still remembered, and quoted to re-animate one's fervor."

"I cannot forget," adds Catherine, "how entranced we were when he spoke to us of the Blessed Virgin, which was very often. 'When one addresses himself to Mary,' he used to say, 'he should speak to her as to a good, sweet, gracious mother, who is happy to see us approach her like children. It is then she smiles upon us, caresses us, and covers us with her graces, for everything comes through her; she is mistress of the Heart of Jesus, the source of grace. As for me,' he added smiling, 'when I invoke the Blessed

Virgin, and she seems not to hear, I pull her gently by
the robe, and she grants my petitions !'

" Instructing us, one day, as to what we must do to
touch the Blessed Virgin and make sure of her powerful
mediation, he said, ' We must give ourselves entirely into
her hands, reserving nothing—give her our thoughts, desires, affections ; all our goods, our happiness, joy, consolation ; all our actions, our good works, epccially our
confessions and Communions; even our last sigh, our first
sight of God's face after death, our first raptures on beholding her in glory when we enter heaven !'

" All these instructions frequently recur to me," adds
Catherine, "and I make them my spiritual nourishment.
After Charles's example, I endeavor to unite myself to the
Blessed Virgin and live ever in her presence, thinking of
her during the day, and placing her statue near me at
night, for I desire with all my heart to belong wholly to
Jesus and Mary."

The fruitful zeal this young Levite exercised in his
parish by word and example likewise extended its sphere,
with the same blessed results, by means of his letters. His
correspondence, which was considerable, gladdened the heart
of many of his friends, and had a wonderful power of inclining them to piety.

" He wrote to me regularly," says one of them, " and
his letters always did me much good. They were all really
little discourses wherein he described, in all simplicity, the
pious practices with which zeal inspired him for the correction of what he called his faults, and the sanctification
of each of his actions."

These spiritual relations, which Charles always initiated,
and to which his good heart, his frank gayety, and amiable
candor gave a double charm, made such salutary impressions upon his friends that they always spoke of them in

terms of unaffected delight, and as if they scarcely knew
how to express their gratitude to him.

III.—Charles's Notable Progress in Virtue During His Third Year at the Theological Seminary.

After spending his vacation in the pious manner above
described, Charles returned to the seminary, determined
to become a saint and to prepare himself for the priesthood by striving to the utmost to procure God's glory and
the salvation of souls.   Fully convinced that sanctity consists not only in merely avoiding evil by perfect detachment
from creatures, but also in doing good, that is, sanctifying
all our actions by giving them a divine character, he endeavored to purify his intentions, and act henceforth only
from supernatural motives.   And as in the order of grace
one can do nothing without God's assistance, which assistance is so much the more abundant in proportion to our
desires and prayers, he every morning, with renewed fervor, earnestly besought Our Lord Jesus Christ to guide
and direct his conduct, both interior and exterior, throughout the day.   Those multiplied invocations, which in all
truly Christian communities are addressed to the Holy
Spirit and to Mary at the beginning and end of every exercise, he made with great attention and piety ; and if the
exercise were prolonged, from time to time he would continue these invocations by reciting at least the first words
of the *Veni, Sancte Spiritus* or the *Ave Maria.*

Thus completely renouncing self and relying only upon
grace, he blindly followed its guidance.   Under this all-
powerful stimulant, his soul made wonderful progress in the
paths of perfection, leaving far behind him those less generous souls who serve God by halves or only at intervals.

To this interior sanctity Charles made it a duty to join
that of the exterior, which, manifesting our good disposi-

tions to others, is most efficacious in leading souls to God
and urging them to become holy.

In addition to the powerful motives which had heretofore prompted him to edify his brethren, there was another
this year, giving a new impulse to his zeal. Being made
regulator,[1] he believed, and justly, that this dignity, evinc-
ing the esteem and confidence of his teachers, thereby imposed upon him so much greater reason for setting good
example, which he labored most effectually to do.

" I saw much of him at this time," says one of his fellow-students, [2] "and, to his praise be it said, I never knew
him to infringe the least part of the rule ; nor did I ever
hear him criticise the conduct or judgment of his superiors;
never did he offend against mortification ; never complain
of our fare, of the heat, the cold, the length of study-hours,
the shortness of recreation; in a word, I never knew him to
be guilty of the least fault, but, on the contrary, everything I saw and heard of him then confirms my belief of
his extraordinary sanctity, proclaimed by voices innumerable since his death."

Even at the period to which I refer, his conduct was so
exemplary, his piety so manifest, that other seminarians,
led by his example, became likewise veritable models.
Several of them even attribute to him the success of their
ministry, and continue to thank God for having given
them in the seminary this exemplar of every virtue. Nor
was mere good example (though a powerful agent in itself)
all ; Charles's zeal displayed its activity in word and deed.

Says Father Maupomé :[3] " Yielding to the ardor of his
zeal, Charles profited by his influence to exercise in the

---

[1] This is the first dignity of the house. It imposes upon the person invested with
it the duty of announcing all the daily exercises by ringing the bells.

[2] Rev. Father Cazal, a pastor in the diocese of Toulouse.

[3] A member of the Society of Jesus. He died a missionary on the coast of Madagascar.

house a veritable apostolate, linking together by the bonds of piety numbers of his fellow-students, and forming them into little associations, governed by rules voluntarily accepted and easily kept, such as meeting on appointed days and hours to recite some prayers selected in advance, or practise some virtue, or exciting one another by pious conversations to love of God and zeal for His glory. Later, these associations became centres of zeal and virtue. Several of them were formed in honor of the Holy Family, for which Charles had an especial devotion. Twelve years afterwards these associations were still flourishing and bearing admirable fruits of virtue."

Before undertaking this work, Charles consulted his director, who answered him thus: " The more of these reunions there are, the greater your advancement in virtue ; frequent intercourse with the most pious seminarians will teach you yourself to become pious and to do good." Encouraged by this advice, Charles abandoned himself to the natural inclinations of his heart, and set about commencing at the Theological Seminary what he had already so successfully accomplished at the Preparatory. "Though less ostensible," says one of his confrères, " his apostolate at Toulouse was not inferior to that at Polignan. Seeking the society of his younger fellow-disciples, he did them much good by his conversations, as he profited by every occasion of speaking to them of God ; and this he did in such a manner that no one was wearied, but all delighted with his simplicity, his frank gayety, his fervor. It was thus recreations passed with him were spiritual reflections, which he provided for us through some of those pious remarks ever falling from his lips, those reflections ever abiding in the hearts of the saints."

" Never can I forget those moments," adds one of his friends, " when, finding ourselves in circumstances where we could not speak of God, he would give me one of those glances worth a conversation, and which seemed to say: ' Oh! how restrained we are! But let us take our revenge by conversing with Jesus in the depths of our hearts ! "

In all these reunions and pious associations, as in all his talks with his confrères, Charles had but one end in view— to procure God's glory and the salvation of souls, by inciting his brethren to continued progress in the paths of sanctity, and inflaming them with the sacred fire of divine love which devoured himself. It was this that induced him to accept so willingly *the* rôle of *monitor* whenever offered him ; and it is needless to say with what charity, devotion, and success he performed its duties. Such of his fellow-pupils (and there were many) as had asked this service of him, declare unhesitatingly that they are indebted to his zeal and tact for the correction of those faults they overcame in the seminary. Moreover, all his friends say he had an especial talent for insinuating himself into souls, particularly the most beautiful, first winning their affections unalterably, and then establishing them firmly in God's service, by the bonds of love and fervor.

" When he was with us," says one of his fellow-students, " we could but feel how tenderly and devotedly he loved us, and that he had only one desire: to do good to our souls and make us better by inspiring us with those holy sentiments animating himself. The more effectually to lead us to God, and to stimulate us especially to a keen sense of gratitude, he would often remind us of all the favors this good Father had showered upon us. He even marked in a note-book *the fortunate days* (as he styled them) of his most intimate friends, and when these anniversaries came around he would say with a smile and a voice truly angelic : ' Remember that to-morrow will be such or such an anniversary; I, too, will bear it in mind, and help you to thank God.'

Often, to excite us to zeal, he would deplore, in our presence, the sad lot of those innumerable sinners who offend God without knowing Him. To pray for such himself, and get others to pray for them, was one of his favorite devotions.

" He also prayed much for infidels, even shedding tears over their unhappy condition ; and when he spoke to us of them our hearts were filled with like sentiments of love and compassion. He was greatly rejoiced whenever, at the end of the month, he found himself in possession of an abundant collection for the Propagation of the Faith. His eloquence in favor of this work was proverbial, and it was impossible to refuse when he solicited a contribution towards it."

The two friends who had formed with him at Polignan the Association of the Holy Family being this year also at the Theological Seminary, he was happy to renew with them the spiritual tie which had proved mutually so beneficial. It was in this holy relationship especially that the riches of his heart overflowed, inundating other hearts with its divine treasures. He was the head, the director, and the soul of this association, ever stimulating all its members to increased fervor, by his word as well as his example.

Though absent from the seminary in the body, after leaving Toulouse, he was nevertheless present in spirit, of which he gave frequent evidence by his letters. The only one of his confrères we know has often told us how much he owed to Father Charles of his fervor, his love of study, his devotion to St. Joseph, the fruits of his ministry, and of all his virtues and merits generally.

" Twelve years later," adds one of the heads of this association, " Father Charles, about to take passage for Bourbon, came twice to see us at the Theological Seminary. He spoke to us with much affection and simplicity of the association, earnestly entreating us ever to keep it alive and vigorous in the house, and giving us some holy counsel thereon, which will never be effaced from my memory. These two visits wrought great good in this respect, and I can say to his praise that the associates of the Holy Family since then have been more fervent and united in the Hearts of Jesus, Mary, and Joseph. Oh ! may he from the heights of that heavenly abode, wherein his intercession is so powerful, obtain for its members continued and increasing fervor and union !"

CHAPTER IV.

THE RELIGIOUS VOCATION.

I.—The Divine Call. Charles Responds to It.

THE first link of that mysterious chain drawing our pious hero. to the port of religion was his love of community life, his natural fondness for association with others in charity and piety, which first showed itself in his earliest years, and was gradually developed in the Preparatory Seminary by his admission into the Sodality of St. Aloysius Gonzaga whilst in the seventh Latin class, and that of the Holy Angels, whilst in the fifth. It was here he began really to taste the happiness of dwelling together in unity with brethren, having but one heart and soul, and each striving to aid and encourage the other in the paths of perfection. Likewise, when Charles, at the end of his year in the fourth Latin class, saw one of his elder brothers joyfully embrace the austere life prescribed by St. Sulpice, he was filled with holy envy, and promised himself to imitate his example, were it the will of God.

This was the Lord's first call to Charles, and his first step towards the religious life. A more definite call urging him towards the Society of Jesus soon followed. Completely transformed whilst in the fourth Latin class by the influence of Father Contamin, also impelled towards holiness by Father Nègre, Charles began to realize the grandeur, nobility, and usefulness of a society that aims at naught but God's glory in the highest degree and the salvation of souls. It was, nevertheless, not until about the time of his

84

second class in Latin that this esteem for the Society of Jesus began to produce in his heart a marked attraction for the life of a Jesuit. The sight of so many of the Jesuit Fathers, and the pious conversations he had, from time to time, on the subject with his brother sodalists, were the gentle allurements Mary used to turn his heart towards the society which bears her Son's name. I use the expression *turn his heart ;* for, to determine his will, always bent upon good, yet ever uncertain and wavering in its choice, stronger lights and a more energetic action of Providence were necessary. Nor did these fail ; but it was only whilst at the Theological Seminary that these graces were bestowed upon him, the occasion being as follows.

In consequence of some measures Charles had believed it his duty to adopt in the education of one of his brothers, and which were severely condemned by the family, he found himself during the vacation of 1849 the object of their stern and (in our opinion) unmerited reproaches, especially as he had acted thus only from deference to an elder brother, whose skill and wisdom in the management of children he knew from experience. Though smarting under the pain and humiliation of such misunderstanding, Charles, conscious of the purity of his motives, offered no word of excuse or explanation ; filial piety, the fear of thus turning upon his brother these reproaches, and especially that spirit of humility and penance which was his in an eminent degree—all combined to make him preserve a silence so much the more meritorious before God as it was painful to nature.

It is easy to understand that so tender and loving a heart must needs have been steeped in sorrow on perceiving that even his mother blamed him and mingled her reproaches with those of others of the family.

The absence of letters and visits from them, during the

first three months after his return to the Theological Seminary, was likewise one great means God used to draw him to Himself. In thus detaching him from those whom it was his inalienable right and duty to love, but whom, perhaps, he cherished too tenderly, this-good Father gently, yet strongly, inclined his heart towards such of his companions as had entered the Society of Jesus. It was during the course of this third year at the Theological Seminary that Charles felt urged to visit them at their novitiate, and never did he leave them, he said, but most reluctantly, and as if oppressed by sorrow. One day, when these emotions were stronger than usual, he believed it his duty to make known the fact to his director, and tell him that his former inclination towards the Society of Jesus had been aroused, and was keener than ever; but his director, who doubtless wished to test his vocation, appeared to attach very little importance to this disclosure. Astonished at his apparent indifference, the probably true reason of which he did not suspect, Charles thought his spiritual guide not favorable to the religious life, and fearing this might prove a great obstacle to the realization of his hopes, he fell, in spite of himself, into a state of dejection which gradually undermined his strength. Shortly after returning home to spend his vacation, it was noticed by the family that he seemed to have lost his spirit of frank cheerfulness. Then he grew silent and pensive, his appetite was impaired, and sleep forsook his pillow at night.

Alarmed at these symptoms and his perceptible loss of flesh, his elder brothers earnestly inquired the cause, on learning which they advised him to go to Toulouse, and make a retreat of several days with the Jesuit Fathers there, with the intention of being enlightened as to his vocation, and of consulting them as to whether or not he should enter their novitiate; the brothers promising, if he did this, they themselves would obtain their parents' consent to his carrying out this his most cherished wish.   To aid in the accomplishment of this plan, without its being suspected by members of the family other than those already in the secret, one of them, under the pretext of spending a few days of rest and quiet with a friend in Toulouse, offered to accompany him thither, and, introducing him to the Reverend Novice Master, obtain a prompt and decided answer to the momentous question.

Charles agreed to the plan, and greatly encouraged by the kindness and proffered assistance, now looked forward to the realization of his dearest hopes.   But ere taking any step towards it he must consult Jesus and Mary in prayer. Accordingly he made known his desires to Catherine Beillard, begging her daily and continued prayers, but more especially that she would now unite with him in two novenas in honor of Jesus, Mary, and Joseph, thereby to obtain the grace of knowing and faithfully following his vocation, and of becoming a Jesuit, if such were God's will. These novenas, which he sanctified by fervent Communion and holy pilgrimages to Our Lady of Good Gift and Our Lady of the Heath, brought their own reward in renewed consolation and an ardent desire of going at once to Toulouse for his retreat, and to make application to the Jesuit Fathers for reception into the novitiate, if deemed advisable.

Prepared, meanwhile, for their son's journey, his pious parents gave their consent, and followed him with fervent prayers for the re-establishment of his health.

It was about the middle of September that he went to Toulouse.   The Reverend Father de Foresta being Novice Master [1] at this time, naturally it was to him our young

---

[1] This Father died at Avignon in the odor of sanctity. His Life, which has been written, is most edifying.

student was presented, and by him also, upon exceptionally favorable reports from Charles's brother,[1] permitted to make there a three days' retreat, during which his religious vocation would be carefully examined, and his entrance into the Order as a postulant positively determined.

At the end of the retreat, in writing down the motives which induced him to join the Society of Jesus, Charles speaks at length of the great happiness he experienced, the brilliant lights that illumined his way, and especially of the marks of divine grace shown him in the attraction he felt for holy things. Even at the risk of considerable repetition, we cannot refrain from giving the literal text of these notes, just as they came from his pen and heart. Whilst confirming our narration, they will edify the reader, and serve, some day, perhaps, as a model for those numerous timid, hesitating souls, who, longing to know the divine call, are ignorant of the means of recognizing it.

Charles's first choice, made at the novitiate of Toulouse, about the middle of September, 1850.

" *Ad majorem Dei gloriam !* To the greater glory of God !

" Having consulted God in prayer, and meditated upon the end of my creation, the following I set down as my impressions, past and present. From the time I have known what a community is, I have felt a strong desire to enter one (without, however, an inclination for any especial community), there to be directed by wise and enlightened superiors, and living in obedience, thus do God's will.

---

[1] In speaking of young Charles to Father de Foresta, M. Vital Sire, then director of the Theological Seminary of Rodez, told him simply and frankly that his beloved brother had been very pious all his life; it was more than probable he had never lost his baptismal innocence : his docility and obedience were such that he would attempt to walk on water, if commanded by his lawful superior; his only defect was in having too scrupulous a conscience ; and that skilful guidance on this latter point was all that was necessary to make him a perfect Jesuit.

" Whilst in the second Latin class and in Rhetoric, I felt a decided attraction for the religious community known as Jesuits, this attraction proceeding as much from the voice of the Holy Spirit in the depths of my soul, as from impressions made upon me by conversations with Jesuits on the subject, and the deportment of the various members of the society that came under my observation.

" On entering the Theological Seminary, more serious occupations, an increased application to study, a diminution of fervor in God's service, [1] the cultivation of ideas of another tendency—all combined to dim these impressions that had been made upon mind and heart during the last two years at the Preparatory Seminary,—years, I must say, which were passed in the society of some most fervent and edifying companions of the Sodality of the Blessed Virgin.

" This indifference towards the Society of Jesus lasted about two years, during which time I became by degrees imbued with prejudices against it. or rather against some of its members.

" In the course of the last year, having gone to see the Brothers (novices) of the society. my heart felt a renewal of its old attraction for this community, and I was conscious of leaving the house most reluctantly and sorrowfully. During the same year I had quite a long conversation with a young Brother (novice), with whom I was yet unacquainted, which made such an impression upon me that I spoke of it to my spiritual director, who treated the matter with indifference.

" During this vacation I also had two conversations with a Brother (novice), my friend and confrère, which affected me deeply. Some days afterwards, another talk,

---

[1] What we said in the preceding chapter proves that he here refers to a diminution of sensible fervor, which his humility made him believe was a diminution of real fervor.

familiar and unconstrained, with one of my own brothers, a priest, removed all doubts from my mind; and from this moment (it was about three weeks ago) I have never for an instant ceased to think of the Society of Jesus, to love it, to long for admission therein. Immediately after this talk, I made two novenas in honor of the Sacred Hearts of Jesus, Mary, and Joseph, with the intention of obtaining the grace to know and to faithfully follow my vocation, and enter the Society of Jesus if it were God's will. The result of these two novenas has been to me great consolation of heart, and an ardent desire of making a spiritual retreat and applying at once for admission to this society. During the three days passed here, the desire has increased to such a degree as to make me fear it may be an obstacle to a vocation of this kind.

" Everything in the society pleases me and attracts me to it—the conduct of the priests in the house, the sanctity of the superior, the edifying behavior of the Brothers (novices) and Brothers coadjutors, the spirit which reigns here, a spirit St. Ignatius demands of each and every member—zeal for God's glory and the salvation of souls (this has for a long time been my motto), and lastly, devotion to the Sacred Hearts of Jesus, Mary, and Joseph.

" During these three days I have been impelled interiorly and supernaturally towards the Society of Jesus, the thought being ever before me, coming to me whilst at meditation, during my visits to the Blessed Sacrament, the recital of the Litanies, at meals, in recreation—in fine, always and everywhere, the whole day. Moreover, since entering this house I have breathed and tasted devotion to St. Ignatius, St. Aloysius Gonzaga, St. Stanislas Kostka. Finally, I feel that God calls me to live in the Society of Jesus, there to expiate my past faults by a life of mortification, or at least of obedience and retirement ; there to prepare myself to become a priest according to the heart of God, by long trials of my vocation ; there to find a remedy for those waverings of spirit that ever beset me, ever striving after the most perfect, and knowing not which to choose ; there, also, to obtain an antidote for my sloth and indolence of disposition ; there to spend my time in preparation for the priesthood ; there to avoid the many dangers hovering around the secular ministry. I believe that God calls me to the Society of Jesus, for the divers motives just exposed—motives which, in my opinion, proceed not from reason alone but from the voice of the Holy Spirit.

"Hence, in yielding to these influences I am but acting as a reasonable being. I obey the inspiration of Heaven, the divine voice that calls me, the impressions of grace upon my soul, and ask admission into the Society of Jesus.

"May the Holy Trinity, Father, Son, and Holy Ghost, bless, accept, approve, and ratify this election made in Its presence and to please It alone !

"*Laudetur Jesus Christus! Amen.* Praised be Jesus Christ ! Amen."

II.—Charles Requests Admission into the Society of Jesus, and is Received as a Novice.

The events following close upon this first choice are so well related in a letter written by Charles's mother about this time to one of her other sons, that we are prompted to quote her own words :

"My very dear son :—

"After three years at the Theological Seminary, my beloved Charles quietly determined to make a short retreat with the Jesuits, to be the more surely enlightened regarding his vocation. The will of God being manifested to him most clearly, he thought only of entering the novitiate of the Jesuit Fathers at Toulouse. My consent and your father's being necessary for this, he endeavored to obtain it, and you know the means he took to succeed. It was not an easy task. Having first laid before us all those natural motives calculated to influence us, he made an appeal to our consciences, in the name of faith—a strong and touching appeal. When at last, vanquished by his entreaties, we yielded to his wishes, oh! how great was his joy! He was really unable to restrain his transports!

"He soon set about disposing of everything not absolutely necessary to him, distributing among his friends his books, images—all those innumerable little objects one generally values so highly. At last there remained in his possession but a little chaplet enclosed in a case, and this he gave me. Having thus reduced himself to a state of religious poverty, he now sighed for the moment of his departure.

"The poor child! but one thing troubled him—to see me so sad. I was indeed overwhelmed; the sacrifice seemed beyond my strength. I was truly grieved when you left us for St. Sulpice, you and Dominique; but that sacrifice was nothing to this, for I could at least see you occasionally. But a Jesuit! he is lost, as it were, to his family; he returns to them no more; oh! the thought is crushing! Charles did his best to console me, seeking my presence and saying all manner of kind and gentle words. Then he would sing with an air of joyful tenderness: 'Oh! how happy one is when he lives in solitude!' I would smile, but with a heavy heart.

"The day of his departure having come, I could not tear myself from him. In spite of everything, I would accompany him to the boat. The poor child! It was on the water's edge I left him ; it was upon the water he died. Doubtless, he was very sad, too, but he concealed his grief, and appeared not to feel the sacrifices he was making. He seemed delighted when, as we were awaiting the boat, I related to him that I had consecrated him to Mary on the day of his baptism, and in what manner. It was the first time I had ever mentioned it to him."

"He left us towards evening," adds his youngest brother. That room which is the usual witness of the joys and sorrows of the family was the theatre of the separation— there where twelve years later, after a pious ceremony, full of joy, our dear parents were to be informed of the death of their son on the bosom of the ocean.

"Every one was affected, even myself, at seeing this great grief, which I could not yet altogether comprehend. The men were silent : the women wept. In spite of all remonstrances, my mother would accompany her son, and I followed her to the canal. The boat arrived, and our mother saw gradually disappearing from her sight our beloved Charles, who henceforth belonged to the family only by the ties of affection."

Arriving at Toulouse about three o'clock in the afternoon, Charles immediately entered the novitiate, and that same evening began his retreat of probation, which lasted eight days. This was on the 15th of October, the feast of St. Teresa. This date and the 24th of the same month, that of the close of his retreat, when he was admitted as a novice into the Society of Jesus, are inscribed in his notebook as among *the fortunate days* which he must consecrate especially to the Lord.

On the morning of the fourth day he was admitted to the novitiate ; and great, indeed, was his joy on hearing the Reverend Father de Foresta say with a smile to his new brethren : " Turn down the brim of his hat, take off his band, and receive him into your midst; one day he will imitate you." "'O happy moment," writes Charles, in the notes of this retreat, "happy moment!" And he continues to pour out thus his holy transports of gratitude and love.

It is Jesus, Mary, and Joseph, his friends, his protectors, who share his affections. It is from their hearts he wishes to imbibe strength, love, courage. He will enter the novitiate only by and with them. He even desires that his name be inscribed on the list of those already in the silver heart around the Blessed Virgin's neck in the chapel, and at the name of *Jesus*, reminding him of the new title he expects soon to bear, his joy is beyond expression.

"*Jesus*!" he exclaims, "*Jesus*! I desire no other name than this. It is the one sweetest on the lips, the most charming to the ear, the most grateful to the heart. It drives away the demon, dispels temptations, and attracts heavenly benedictions. I would write it everywhere, I would murmur it ever—in trials, temptations, in the hour of desolation, in all penitential actions, accompanied always by the names of Mary and Joseph, but that of Jesus being ever the fairest and the most beautiful! And only think, I shall be a Jesuit, a member of the Society of Jesus!"

All his notes of this retreat are redolent with the same freshness of fervor and love. At the thought of Jesus, Mary, and Joseph, and all their favors to him, his soul is overpowered with gratitude, and the greatest sacrifices appear insignificant to him. These words of the Beloved in the "Imitation" became his rule of life: "Esteem the whole world as nothing; prefer the attendance on God before all external things. For thou canst not both attend to Me and at the same time delight thyself in transitory things. Thou must withdraw from thy acquaintance and those dear to thee, and keep thy mind disengaged from all temporal comfort." (Imitation of Christ, book iii., chap. liii., v. i.)

"In these words," says he, "is comprehended the sacrifice of all—parents, friends, confrères. I must no longer occupy myself with family affairs, nor with health, nor with anything that passes away with time; my life must be devoted to the interests of the soul—the souls of my brethren and friends as well as my own. Yes, Charles, this is henceforth thy only care; otherwise, thou wilt never be a true religious, thou wilt be but a demi-Jesuit. Read these words frequently and put them in practice: 'At the age of thirty, Jesus quit the society of His Mother'—and such a mother! Wherefore did He leave her? Out of charity for men, to go to preach to them, to catechise and save them —behold my model. I am not yet twenty-two years old; and, like Jesus and John the Baptist, I shall not preach until I am thirty. Yes, I resolve not to become a priest ere attaining that age."

The last sentiment Brother Charles expresses in his notes of the retreat is that of confidence, unbounded, unwavering confidence in Jesus. The example of the apostles, especially St. Peter, his patron, re-animates his courage. "Peter," he writes, "asks permission of Jesus to come to Him, and at His word casts himself into the sea. Oh! the power of faith! Peter walks upon the water! But scarcely does he hesitate, losing confidence, than he begins to sink. Jesus approaches and enters into the bark, and immediately the wind and the storm are lulled. Ah! every week at least shall Jesus enter into my soul, and with His presence I shall have a calm, untroubled conscience.— Who were the apostles? Men of the people, and of the common people; and who am I?—What did Jesus make of these rough, untutored men? Priests, preachers, apostles! And will He not transform me in like manner?—

Through chastity one becomes an angel; by obedience and poverty, another Jesus Christ ; by contemplation and retreat one imitates Mary.—Oh! what motives for love! *Non fecit taliter omni nationi.* ' He hath not done in like manner to every nation ' (Ps. cxlvii. 20). God does not act thus towards all; He selects, taking one and leaving another. What motives for confidence !

" Every day and every hour let me recall these words of Jesus, *Ego sum, nolite timere.* ' It is I, fear not ' (St. Luke xxiv. 36) ; and let this be my principal resolution—to fear not, ever beholding Jesus in the persons of my superiors and directors. May He be praised forever ! *Laudetur Jesus Christus! Amen.*"

In the course of this retreat, Charles made a second election, more serious and more clearly defined than the first ; and it was after this second election he was received as a novice into the Society of Jesus.

The present chapter could have no more natural conclusion, nor all the preceding portion of Charles's life, as portrayed in our pages, a more perfect crown, than the exact reproduction of this interesting paper, which we give below.

Second Election of the Society of Jesus, made by Charles Sire, in his retreat of probation, October 24, 1850.

" For the greater glory of God, the salvation of souls, and the benefit of my own soul especially.

" Having contemplated the end of my creation, and examined my interior as that of a stranger whose perfection I desired, the following is my decision at the tribunal of reason.

" I establish as a principle in the beginning, that in the choice I am about to make of my own free will everything should tend towards the end imposed upon me by the Creator—His glory and my salvation. I am not now considering whether my vocation is for the world or for the ecclesiastical state, that point having been already decided upon before God and my director, with the help of reason and faith. But the question is: Am I called to the Society of Jesus, or to some other community, or to the secular priesthood? Now, here is the answer reason enlightened by faith gives me, after a careful examination of my interior—that is, of the dispositions of my soul: I should enter neither the secular ministry, nor any other community save that of the Society of Jesus, and these are my reasons:

"1. In the secular ministry I am in great danger of being lost, either because of the perils to which I should sometimes be exposed by the hearing of confessions in the sacred tribunal, those especially of women, without my having a director at hand to whom I could have immediate recourse; or, because routine, to which I am inclined, might easily glide into my actions ; or, because I would find myself continually in the presence of persons of the other sex, to the detriment of chastity (and I am impressionable) ; or, because I might be praised and never reproved; or, led by the example of some of my confrères, I might become attached to the goods of this world; or, because from lack of fixed plans and a systematic course of life I might yield to the ever-changing caprices of one's mind and thus lose my time, neglect my duties, etc.

"2. On the other hand, I have no especial taste for preaching, which would lead me to the Missionaries of Calvary,[1] nor for the apostolic life, attracting me to foreign missions ; nor for the training of candidates to the priesthood, the object of the Sulpicians ; nor for the instruction of youth, as in the Preparatory Seminaries (although I

[1] The diocesan missionaries of Toulouse.

must say the latter has some attractions for me),—in a word, I am not drawn towards any religious community where from the very beginning one's mind and faculties are bent towards some particular duty; hence there remains for me to select but the Society of Jesus, which alone can satisfy my tastes.

" Moreover, in the Society of Jesus are many advantages which I find in no other religious community, much less in the secular priesthood. They are as follows :

" 1. I make a vow of obedience, and all my duties are specified—a certain remedy for those perplexities and waverings of the soul ever urging me to seek the most perfect.

" 2. Slothful by nature and dilatory in action (the opinion of all wise and enlightened persons with whom I have lived concerning me, an opinion fully endorsed by myself), it is in the Society of Jesus I shall be urged onward, the example of my brethren, the voice of my superiors, the necessity of daily advancing in perfection, and the numberless graces I hope to receive, all being so many stimulants to my courage.

" 3. I have made no progress towards the virtues and perfection of the priest, and remaining at the Theological Seminary I should be ordained in three years. What a future ! Here, I shall have abundant time to prepare myself for the priesthood, and I shall learn well what a priest according to God's own heart should be.

" 4. In the Society of Jesus I discover no danger, but, on the contrary, everything leading me to virtue and towards the end of my creation.

" 5. I have no decided taste for any particular function either of the secular or religious priest ; here, wise and enlightened superiors will mould me to whatever duty they deem me best fitted for.

" 6. I wish to expiate my faults by a life of mortification ; here, I will be inspired with courage to do so, whilst in the holy ministry of the secular priesthood I would not have the strength. Finally, as I have always felt the desire of living in a religious community, and that called the Society of Jesus is the one which suits me best before God and reason enlightened by Faith, it is this I should select.

"Now, having examined thoroughly my inclinations and tastes, descending into the depths of my soul, I feel impelled towards the Society of Jesus ; and as this impulse comes not from the senses but the interior, it must needs be my vocation to correspond to it. The present moment is propitious, there being no obstacles to overcome, either as regards the authorities of the society or from my parents (which obstacles might present themselves later), neither have I formed any bad habits. I am young, and, with the grace of God, I can easily be turned towards perfection. However, as I may make a mistake were I to decide so important a matter for myself, I leave it entirely in the hands of my superiors, and hold myself in readiness to accept and do whatever they deem best.

" Yet, whilst thus awaiting guidance, I ask, in the presence of God, admittance into the Society of Jesus, and this election, which I believe good and excellent, I make with a perfectly unbiassed, tranquil mind, and I would confirm it, were I to die this moment. It is for you, my superiors, to decide."

CHAPTER V

THE NOVITIATE OF THE JESUIT FATHERS AT TOULOUSE.

IN entering the novitiate, Charles made the firm resolution of being, if not the most perfect, at least the most fervent of novices, which, consequently, included the determination of observing all the rules of the house scrupulously; of recoiling before no sacrifice whatever; of placing himself at once in his director's hands, as a piece of wax which he could mould at will; of making known to him with simplicity all that passed in his soul, even temptations and interior movements most painful to acknowledge, such as aversions, suspicions, exaggerated affections, the necessities of health, his slothfulness, and lukewarmness.

To realize this resolution, he selected from among the virtues exacted by the Society of Jesus of its members those which seemed to cost nature the most, and swore to practise them until death—obedience the most entire, the blindest and most perfect; angelic purity, absolute poverty, universal charity; complete detachment from friends, family, self; humility and perfect mortification, embracing, after the example of Jesus Christ, all that nature abhors most, and flying from what the world seeks eagerly.

1.—Brother Charles's Conduct during the First Months of His Novitiate—His Fervor and Joy.

These resolutions, once made, became immediately the constant rule of his actions. All who were brought in contact with him, at this time, attest that from the very beginning his fervor and generosity were such that he seemed to have a thirst for justice, that is, for sanctity in general and religious perfection in particular; that he sighed for these ornaments of the soul as worldlings do for pleasures; and happy to find within his reach the means of obtaining them, he embraced them joyfully and with an ardor truly admirable in practice.

"He had been in the novitiate but a little while," says his youngest brother, "when I was placed in a boarding-school in Toulouse. I used to accompany my mother in the many visits she made to him, and I can say that never had I seen Charles appear so tranquilly inflamed with divine love, so gentle, yet so zealous. His whole exterior bespoke a heart that felt itself born to a new life. One might have said he was a captive who had just broken his chains. This soul, so profoundly pious, already tasted the exquisite happiness of seeing itself drawn nearer to God, and that by the strongest bonds of religion. Nothing seemed an effort to him. Happy in his new life as a fish restored to the water, he wondered how he could ever have breathed and lived out of this, his present element, the religious life. He sought, on several occasions, to convince us of his happiness, but it was unnecessary, his radiant face speaking more plainly than words. He took great delight in extolling before us the tenderness of the society, his new mother, whom he loved with an ever-increasing fondness. Oh! what a true religious he had already become!

"Nearly all his conversations during these visits turned upon the happiness of belonging no longer to himself, but instead to a religious community. 'Oh! how happy I am,' he would say; 'when obliged myself to obey, I think of Jesus obeying!'"

"Speaking to me one day," says another person, "of

detachment from temporal goods, even as regards necessary things, he said that it was a great pleasure in using
these articles to be able to say, ' Nothing is mine, not even
the cassock I wear, and I am pleased to know that in asking for it I make an act of submission.'   Oh! how he
loved poverty, calling it his good mother, his faithful
companion, his beloved; and what pious devices did he not
make use of to practise it to the utmost ! " -

This love of the religious life, this fervor and zeal,
Brother Charles manifested everywhere—in his visits, his
conversations, his letters.   He felt it impossible to restrain
the enthusiasm that filled his soul; it must be communicated to every one, especially his parents and friends.   About
a month after his entrance into the novitiate, he wrote
thus to one of his brothers:

" I cannot resist any longer the great desire I have of
expressing to you my happiness.   You have doubtless
heard, though without the details, that I have entered the
Society of Jesus, a merciful God having deigned to call
me to the life of perfection in this holy community.   Oh!
the mercy of my Jesus! I have been in the novitiate since
the 24th of last October, and far from any abatement of
my eagerness to become a Jesuit, since my acquaintance
with the usages of the novitiate I feel that the longing increases daily.

" What a happiness it is, O my dear brother, to relin-
quish our liberty, that we may be guided by wise and
skilful directors, and pushed forward in the path of perfection by so many saints !   What a happiness to have as
models not only our Fathers and Brothers in heaven, a
St. Ignatius, a St. Francis Xavier, a St. Francis Regis, a
St. Aloysius Gonzaga, but numberless Fathers and Brothers
living under our own eyes, and who give us the example of
every virtue !   Blessed are they who comprehend this hap-

piness ! Blessed, a thousand times blessed, they who enjoy
it ! May Heaven accord me this grace ! Let us bless the
Lord ! "

11.—Brother Charles's Conduct before, during, and after His Grand Retreat of Thirty Days.

1. *His preparation for the retreat ; his vow to the Hearts
of Jesus and Mary.*—A few months only after his reception
into the Society of Jesus, Brother Sire was admitted, with
all the other novices, to participate in the exercises of the
grand retreat of thirty days.

This is the work *par excellence* of the novitiate, the most
decisive of all, and the powerful lever St. Ignatius used
and established in his Order to transform the novices. The
proposed end is not to decide one's vocation and choose, if
advisable, the Society of Jesus, this choice being made in
the retreat of *probation,* but to reform one's self, by a thorough examination and study of one's defects, his natural
inclinations, his vicious tendencies, and especially his predominant passion, so as to attack and extirpate them as far
as possible, replacing them by those Christian virtues, religious and sacerdotal, of which Jesus Christ sets us the example. With this intent, the novices are engaged for thirty
days in a number of spiritual exercises, all properly arranged and dependent upon one another, which must needs
bring about in a well-disposed soul an entire transforma-
tion.

This retreat is considered of such vital importance, that
no means are neglected to insure its success, the precious
results being confirmed by an experience of three hundred
years. The novices are prepared for it long in advance ;
and towards the approach of this blessed period, the superiors redouble their zeal to inspire the novices with a great
appreciation of and ardent desire for these exercises.

Wishing to increase the efficacy of this retreat, already so powerful, the Reverend Father de Foresta, director of the Novitiate of Toulouse in 1851, pledged himself to have made by all the novices an especial Communion, to fast with them on the eve of this day of the Communion, and to burn two tapers on Mary's altar all day long, if the thirty novices about to go into retreat succeeded in making it without hindrance and successfully. This grace having been obtained, the vow was fulfilled the following July, on the feast of the Visitation.

Nor did Brother Charles, on his part, remain inactive at the approach of the retreat; he sighed too ardently for these happy days to rest content with ordinary preparation. Mortifications, abstinences, laborious employment twice a week, the Way of the Cross on Fridays and Saturdays, even disciplines and iron cinctures—nothing was spared that might touch God's heart and incline Him to hearken; but the most powerful and the most efficacious of all these means to which he had recourse was prayer. Not content with his own increased supplications to the Lord, two months in advance he begged prayers on all sides— from his friends at Polignan and Toulouse, his fellow-students at the Theological Seminary, his parents at Saint-Jory —all were invited to unite their prayers to his, their efforts to his; but his most pressing solicitations were addressed to his brothers who were priests.

"My dear Marcel," he wrote to one of them, "it is with great pleasure I inform you of the approach of my grand retreat of thirty days, which we are going to make during the month of May, that month consecrated to our good Mother Mary. Oh! since your love for her is so great, strive to obtain from her the favor of having her fix her eyes of mercy and sweetness upon me and my brethren; beg her not to lose sight of me for an instant, but to be to me a radiant Star, the Morning Star, harbinger of the Sun of justice.

"I almost long for the retreat to be finished, that I may tell you of the marvels this tender Mother will have wrought in me, during her grand feast of thirty-one days. In this beautiful month, let us both ask of her the knowledge and love of the Sacred Heart of Jesus, of her own holy heart, and of St. Joseph's ; let us pray to her in unison, that, taking our own hearts from our dangerous keeping, she place them in security, I mean in the divine, the amiable Heart of Jesus, close by her own and St. Joseph's, and forever !

"Let us love Mary, my dear brother, let us converse of Mary in our letters, let us speak of her everywhere and on all occasions, striving to make her known and loved by all; let us be ever her most faithful servants, her slaves through love. It is in her heart I bid you adieu."

The letter to his brother Dominique was not less importunate. We give below a few extracts from it:

"Jesus, Mary, Joseph. For the greater glory of God ! "After excusing myself for my long silence towards my charitable brother, I must thank him, the pious brother who consecrated me to Mary in the chapel of Loretto at Issy. Oh ! consecrate me anew to that tender Mother, particularly during my novitiate. Tell her that I ratify the first consecration, and offer myself to her anew in all sincerity and earnestness. Pray especially for me, and with increased fervor, during the beautiful month consecrated to her, for it is then I am to make the grand retreat.

"Praying daily for you, and the more assiduously as you advance towards the priesthood, I ask you to render me a like service, and to remember me, a poor novice, who, although thanking God for having led him into a house of spiritual abundance, yet knows not how to open his heart to grace, and lend an ear to the voice of the Holy Spirit...

"Oh ! I beg of you your first free Mass ; I have a right to it because of the many and close ties uniting us, and likewise because of the love I bear you, which is ever increasing in proportion as the object of it draws nearer God, Who is charity.

" Excuse me for having so little interesting news to tell you ; far better than entertaining you thus is it to apply one's self to the love of the Sacred Hearts of Jesus, Mary, and Joseph, in which I embrace you most tenderly."

Who can fail to perceive, after the perusal of these two letters, that the most powerful means Brother Charles used to draw down the benediction of Heaven upon his grand retreat was devotion to the Sacred Hearts of Jesus, Mary, and Joseph, a devotion which, even before his entrance into the Society of Jesus, had become very dear to him, and which during the novitiate increased perceptibly, or, rather, was more manifest exteriorly.

At the first interview with his director, in which his whole life as a novice was to be regulated, Charles acquainted him with his favorite devotions to Jesus, Mary, and Joseph, and to his guardian angel. The Reverend Master of Novices, approving them, congratulated his pious penitent upon so privileged an attraction, and encouraged him to practise them unreservedly. Henceforth, they were the most powerful, I might say, the only means Brother Charles made use of to obtain those especial graces of which he felt so keenly the need in his ardent desire to be transformed. " Every new action, work, exercise, practice, plan, note-book," thus he writes in his first notes of his novitiate, "everything, do I put under the especial protection of Jesus, Mary, Joseph. Yes, all that I desire for becoming a perfect religious, and all that is necessary thereto—lights, guidance, will, strength, courage, I will ask of the Sacred Hearts of Jesus, Mary, Joseph ; and to win these amiable Hearts, I will be very

exact in saying the prayers in their honor ; I will consecrate
to them each of my actions, by a little sign of the cross upon my mouth or heart, and I will receive, as from their
hands, whatever may happen to me.   At study, in recreation, everywhere, will I regard Jesus, Mary, Joseph ; and a
thousand times a day will I exclaim : Jesus, meek and
humble of heart, make my heart like unto Thine ! Mary,
meek and humble of heart, make my heart like that of
Jesus !   Joseph, meek and humble of heart, make my
heart like those of Jesus and Mary ! "

Three months later he asked and obtained his director's
permission to take every Sunday, after holy Communion,
a half-hour's reading upon devotion to the Blessed Virgin.
Finally, hoping thereby to draw down the most abundant
benedictions from Heaven, he at the time of the grand
retreat conceived the idea of devoting himself by a formal vow to the Sacred Hearts of Jesus and Mary, with
the especial promise of propagating, all his life, the *cultus*
to them, according to his power to do so, and the spirit of
the Church.   On Holy Thursday, April 17th, he made, with
his director's permission, this touching vow, couched in
the following terms :

" Omnipotent and Eternal God, Holy and Undivided
Trinity, I, Charles Sire, in thanksgiving for Jesus Christ's
innumerable benefits to me, a miserable sinner, and others
of the human race, especially for the institution of the
Holy Eucharist, and in reparation for all the injuries this
most loving Heart daily receives in this ineffable Mystery
of Love, devote myself entirely, with all the faculties and
affections of my soul, in the presence of the Blessed Virgin
Mary and the whole celestial court, to the Sacred Heart of
Our Lord Jesus Christ, to Whom I deliver up all my
merits, past and future, whether before or after my death
(suffrages of Masses, and prayers), and Whose perpetual

servant I constitute myself, promising to do all that lies in my power, that of a feeble creature, to propagate, for love of Him, devotion to His loving Heart.

"Moreover, I choose, in an especial manner, the Blessed Virgin Mary for my mother, and I likewise devote myself similarly to her holy Heart, with the promise of extending devotion to her, according to the spirit of the Church, particularly devotion to her Immaculate Conception, as occasion may require.

"For the exact and faithful accomplishment of this vow, relying upon the merits of Our Lord Jesus Christ and the assistance of the Blessed Virgin Mary, I humbly pray Thee to deign receive this holocaust as a sweet odor, and also that, as Thou hast given me the desire and grace to offer it, Thou wouldst likewise bestow upon me abundant grace to accomplish it. Amen."

One might suppose that after this vow Brother Charles had done all he could to ensure for his retreat Heaven's choicest blessings; yet, to touch more deeply the Sacred Hearts of Jesus, Mary, and Joseph, he promised to make during this time three especial fasts in honor of each of them; and a week's fast, after the retreat, to thank them for his success: to maintain during all the exercises a most profound recollection, a continual vigilance, in order to ward off or combat all those temptations of weakness, discouragement, or human respect, which the demon might suggest to him; finally, to live during these thirty days in great purity of heart, in a love most courageous, and, above all, in a state of sweet serenity under the eyes of Jesus, Mary, and Joseph. [1]

[1] This devotion to the Sacred Hearts of Jesus and Mary, being approved by the Church, may be publicly practised and in the public Offices. Devotion to the Heart of St. Joseph, however, not yet being approved, may not be introduced into public worship, although nothing interdicts the usage in private

2. *Brother Charles's conduct during the grand retreat.*—
Beginning May 5, 1851, the exercises of the grand retreat
ended on the feast of Pentecost, June 8th. Among the
thirty novices who made it, Brother Charles, according to
the testimony of the Novice Master himself, was one of
the most docile, generous, and fervent.

Starting from this fundamental truth, that man is upon
earth only to serve God, consequently, to know Him and
love Him with all his mind, heart, and strength, Charles
occupied himself, during the first week, in striving to
eradicate from his heart every fibre not in unison with
God; combating every affection purely natural, all attach-
ment to sin however slight, all voluntary imperfections.
To give Jesus, Mary, and Joseph proof of his sincerity
herein, he promised them not only to purify his intentions
every time he met his friends, his parents, or confrères,
but likewise never to begin himself a correspondence with
them, to be briefer and less tender in writing to them ;
never to remain in the parlor more than a quarter of an
hour, not even with his mother ; and, if possible, not to go
to Saint-Jory during vacation, at the time his brother
Dominique would there sing his first High Mass.

The day of rest, following this first week of retreat, was
employed by the good Brother in thanking the Sacred
Hearts of Jesus, Mary, and Joseph for the precious graces
he had received, and in considering what he could do
whilst in the novitiate, during his whole life, and especially during this retreat, to express his gratitude for them.
The Holy Spirit having enlightened him thereupon in the
second and third weeks, behold how this generous heart,
ever docile to grace, obeyed its inspirations :

Thoroughly convinced that Jesus Christ is the true way,
the narrow and sure way to eternal life, he determined to
walk in His footsteps, and follow Him, cost what it might,

in the painful paths of poverty, abnegation, self-contempt, and zeal. To strengthen himself in this resolution, he meditated for eight days, a quarter of an hour daily, upon the claims Jesus had to this imitation, the inestimable advantages to be derived from it, and the manner of practising it.

Once decided thereon, he turned his gaze inward, examining before God his interior; and striving to discover whatever in his nature, intentions, habits, might offer serious obstacles to his imitation, he conjured the Lord, in incessant prayer, to give him strength and courage to triumph. Collecting then, as in one picture, his predominant fault, his motives for combating it, the means of destroying it, and the stimulating thoughts that all his life should impel him to pursue the opposite virtue, he made, in the profound silence of midnight, a decisive meditation, which, aided by the numberless penances and most fervent prayers which had preceded it, produced upon his heart incomparably salutary effects. It is in this meditation, facing the most painful sacrifices, he overcomes, through grace, all obstacles of nature, and makes Our Lord, in the following words, this donation of himself, than which none more entire and perfect could have issued from heart or lip. [1]

"It is done, O God, my Saviour, it is done; to Thee alone do I give my heart, senses, faculties—all that I have, all that I am; yes, all, and willingly do I sacrifice upon the altar of my heart all within me that displeases Thee.

"Hence, sacrificed be my aversion for and desire to escape anything that fatigues, pains, annoys, or wearies me, such as discipline, study, essays, visits to the hospitals,—

---

[1] This meditation was followed, next day, by a very important one upon *fear* as one of the most serious obstacles to the entire donation of one's self to God. One feels in reading his notes of this retreat that Brother Charles was marvellously wrought upon by grace, and, moreover, that he had rude assaults of nature to sustain.

and this, in spite of nature, the senses, parents, and friends. Angels, record it !

" Again, sacrificed be pride and self-love, listlessness and self-ease ! To extremes ! to extremes, for Jesus, Who has given for me His goods, His honor, His life, thus saving me and restoring to me my goods, my honor, my life !

" Thirdly, for love of Him, I will urge myself forward, I will constrain myself to a scrupulous observance of the rules that press hardest on me ; I will do violence to myself to advance in virtue, to converse about God in recreation with the confrères least congenial to me. Angels, record it !

" Finally, forgetting the past, I will have no solicitude for the future, and be indifferent to all things. To Thee, O Jesus, do I commit the past, present, and future ! Without Thee, I am nothing, but with Thee I am all-powerful.[1] Jesus, Mary, Joseph, come to my aid!

" Mortification, exterior and interior, be my sole remedy. Yes, Lord, such is my desire, and I feel that I offer too little in return for so much love Thou givest me. Yes, I wish to be a saint, I desire it ardently, and with all my heart : *Volo fieri sanctus, et coram oculis Jesu acceptus ; hoc volo, hoc desidero, hoc toto corde concupisco.*"

Brother Charles did not stop at generalities, but descending into the depths of his soul, and searching out even his least faults, his slightest imperfections, he took most vigorous means for their extirpation. Nothing escaped him, and all that was defective in his nature he resolved to cut off, or, if possible, eradicate. Let us take a glance at that interior work, which, whilst revealing a character unusually slothful, and a temperament naturally indolent, likewise shows us a strength, fervor, and generosity unexceptional.

" I will labor seriously and efficaciously at my santifica-

---

[1] *Nihil possum sine te, omnia tecum.*

tion, wherefore I must be careful to regulate my actions well. To this end are the Rules and Constitutions of the Society given me ; but to keep these Rules, and sanctify all my conduct, I must combat and destroy, if possible, the principle, the foundation of all my faults and imperfections—in other words, my predominant passion ; this it is I must combat without truce. And now, what is this predominant passion ?

" If I examine all that is bad within me or reprehensible, that for which I have been most reproached, even in childhood and boyhood, by my parents, superiors, friends, brethren ; if I consider my actions, past or present, my inclinations, the true motives influencing me, I clearly perceive that my predominant fault is a natural aversion for everything that wearies, inconveniences, or fatigues me, and a tardiness of execution. I am naturally slothful, without energy or activity; my spirit timorous, my will cowardly and sluggish, I am not truly a man, *vir*. Ah ! it is this defect, then, I must strive to eradicate by unceasing efforts.

" To succeed therein, I must habitually practise the opposite virtue, which is an active, joyous generosity in God's service—*alacritas ;* let this be my predominant virtue. And as it may not be seriously practised without the aid of universal mortification and the profoundest humility, I resolve to make these two virtues the principal object of my efforts.

" To excite myself thereto, I will frequently read the lives of those saints who have been most generous in God's service, that of St. Francis Xavier, for instance. Then, storing my memory with various incidents related of their courage, I will, at my meditations, often recur to the numberless motives that should influence me to cultivate these virtues and combat my predominant passion. In moments of trial and difficulty, I will stimulate myself to the most painful sacrifices by such thoughts as these : " God wills it. Jesus desires it. *Ego sum, noli timere.* [1] For love of Jesus ! For the greater glory of God ! What would Jesus do, were He in my place, and how would He do it ? *Quid timidi estis, modicæ fidei ?* [2] *Tantum proficies quantum tibi ipsi vim intuleris.* [3] What are not worldlings willing to endure for temporal interests? Courage, then, courage ; heaven awaits us, heaven and the society of Jesus, Mary, Joseph, of the holy angels, the apostles, the saints, those of our community and all the others ; *comfortare, et esto robustus.* [4]

" I will ever bear in mind this last maxim, remembering that man's life upon earth is a continual warfare, in which I must never grow discouraged. If I fall, let me arise immediately, prepared to resume the struggle with renewed ardor. " [5]

To these general resolutions, which constitute the principle and foundation of the *reform of life*, Brother Charles added others, descending into particulars, and classed under the head of *Defects to be corrected in my relations towards God, my neighbor, and myself.* We regret that our circumscribed limits prevent the reproduction of this important paper, as its perusal would edify and produce most salutary effects upon all who read it. Brother Charles finished it in the fourth week by a resolution some glimpse of the difficulty of which we catch from his notes, and the merit of which only those who have been intimately acquainted with him can comprehend.

[1] " It is I fear not."—St. Luke xxiv. 36.

[2] " Why are you fearful, O ye of little faith ? "—St. Matt. viii. 26.

[3] " For there a man makes greater progress, and merits greater grace, where he overcomes himself more and mortifies himself in spirit."—Imitation of Christ, book i., chap. xxv., v. 3.

[4] " Take courage, and be strong."— Dan. x. 19.

[5] Election of his grand retreat.

In meditating upon the glorious mysteries of Our Lord's life, and seeing this divine Master deprive Himself after the Resurrection of all the joys and pleasures of earth, separating Himself from His relatives and disciples, and snatching Himself from even the embraces of His Mother, that in heaven He might be more perfectly united to God, Brother Charles promised the Lord to detach Himself from friends and relatives, to pluck all purely natural affection from his heart, no longer loving anything on earth except for God and in God, realizing thus, in all their perfection, the end of the novitiate and the grand object of the retreat.   This was also the last and most perfect of his resolutions—no, I am mistaken; his loving, generous heart suggested another, outweighing this ; for on the feast of Pentecost, which was the day whereon the retreat closed and also the anniversary of his First Communion, having pondered the thought before God, and with his director's hearty consent, in the presence of his good angel and holy patrons and the whole celestial court, he immolated himself entire upon the altar of the Lord, by the vow of perpetual chastity.   And that this vow might not prove a rash one, he assured its accomplishment by efficacious resolutions, to which he was ever faithful.

3. *Brother Charles's conduct after the grand retreat. His means for ensuring perseverance.*—Before the retreat Brother Charles was, beyond doubt, a fervent novice, a true religious ; for, as we learn from his notes,[1] he ever sought the most perfect ; nevertheless, there yet remained to him a goodly number of defects, especially of character and temperament, his natural sensitiveness, timidity, and indolence being such as to lead him into faults that must be corrected : a sluggish bearing, slowness of speech, and undignified gait, an embarrassed manner, especially with certain confrères, lack of energy in action, etc.

[1] We shall produce them later on.

After the retreat, all these and several other less important faults which had been pointed out to him became immediately the continual object of his attacks, and so vigorous were these attacks, so persevering, that in a very short time the defects were supplanted by the opposite virtues. A radical change was wrought in Charles; to be sure, his nature and temperament remained the same, for these cannot be uprooted, but his constant efforts at correction made such an impression upon his character that he seemed completely transformed.

Instead of that timid, embarrassed, even pusillanimous manner heretofore remarked in him, one beheld him frank, cordial, obliging, lacking neither firmness nor energy, detached from everything, and forgetful of self. Although obedience had ever been his favorite virtue, yet, even on this point, there were some imperfections to correct. After the retreat, all these disappeared. Nature no doubt asserted herself, and murmured loudly, but he heeded her not, and his only answer to all such obstacles was: "God has spoken, and that suffices; to do His holy will, and procure His glory, I will not recoil before any sacrifice." The following anecdotes will illustrate this generosity and obedience.

Says a pious lady of Toulouse: " Brother Charles used occasionally to visit my house, for his youngest brother was boarding with me at one time, and I can positively declare that he never came without the *socius*.' Frequently the *socius* would offer to allow Brother Charles the privilege of being alone with us, saying he would wait for him at St. Sernin's, a church about two steps from my dwelling, but never was his offer accepted.

"One day he came to see us with one of his old friends, a fellow-student in the seminary. They were

---

' The companion who ordinarily accompanies a novice when visiting.

both very thirsty, and I offered them some refreshment. His companion, who was not a Jesuit, accepted ; and when he rallied his friend on refusing, the good religious merely replied : ' You have not tasted, my dear, the rule of the Society of Jesus.' Nor did he appease his thirst, preferring rather to find his happiness in this occasion of practising obedience and mortification.

"Oh ! how dead to self he was already ; nature being so subjugated in him that even his least, his involuntary actions and emotions were for the good Master. He indeed appeared to me as one of those loving souls who can say with Jesus Christ, they are willing victims, offering themselves to the will of God without a murmur, and remaining peacefully upon the altar, even until the consummation of the sacrifice. The habitual cry of his soul, urging him ever onward in the path of immolation, was : ' What would one not do for God !'"

It was this thought that strengthened his faith, made firm his will, ardent his heart, and even manifested itself in his exterior, rendering his words more distinct, clear, and incisive, his conversations more entertaining. "I saw him quite often about this time," says one of his Polignan friends, "for he used to come to the Theological Seminary, and I still seem to hear those earnest words which were the habitual expression of his joy—the joy of a heart filled with love for Our Lord, and desirous of making others share the happiness he enjoyed in the novitiate. Formerly, I had not perceived that he possessed much vivacity; now I was struck with it." This ardor, however, was full of gentleness and sweetness, which really gave to his countenance a heavenly expression.

"At this period," says his youngest brother, "his whole person was redolent of the sweetest and most penetrating odor of virtue. No one who had occasion to

converse with him could fail to notice it. Hence I am
not astonished that it was this happy, radiant face which,
during this year, captivated and secured for God's service
a young man in the world, who, coming hither to make a
few days' retreat, was thus brought in contact with him—
I mean Father Leonard Cros. Charles attracted this ardent soul as the flower the bee."

Let us listen to Father Cros's account of it. " Whilst
studying law in Toulouse, in 1851, a friend induced me to
make a retreat with him at the Jesuit Fathers'. I was
placed in Brother Sire's charge. Up to this time, I had
scarcely seen a religious, and the sight of that angelic
face, a perfect mirror of innocence and joy, impressed me
deeply ; indeed, it proved for me the source of one of the
signal graces of the retreat, resulting in my vocation to
the Society of Jesus. I said to myself : ' One must be
happy in the religious life to have such a beaming countenance !' After the lapse of fourteen years that picture
and the vivid impression it made upon me are still fresh
in my mind.".

This heavenly joy of which Father Cros here speaks was
even now one of the most salient traits of Brother Charles's
virtue, "and," says one of his confrères, " it softened
for him the rigors of the rule and made easy that strict observance of it which others found so severe. Lively and
joyous at Polignan, he was even more so in the novitiate,
and perhaps this was the reason his virtue appeared less
striking, his conduct being always simple and natural.

" A happy, even-tempered disposition like this could
never be inconsistent. He was true in every relation of life,
and often spoke of his brothers and other members of his
family with such overflowing affection, that one might
have supposed he was living in their midst at Saint-Jory,
instead of in the novitiate."

To avoid any appearance of levity, the natural result of this joyousness, Charles was continually renewing the generous resolution he had taken during the retreat, of living entirely in the novitiate, of never allowing himself to be absorbed in anything, or pre-occupied to the detriment of present duties, but of hourly realizing this motto of a saint: *Age quod agis:* "What thou doest, do with all thy heart." And the better to impress this upon his mind he not only wrote it down, to be read every day before Mass, but resorted to innumerable other plans for keeping it ever before him.

"I remember," says Father Sénac, "noticing several times when he came to visit us at the Theological Seminary that he had in his hands a blessed medal, which he would occasionally look at with visible emotion, and then gently raise his eyes towards heaven. Upon my pressing him to know the meaning of this, he told me it was a sign to remind him of the presence of God. He also said, in connection with this subject, that in the novitiate, during his recreations and walks, he was accustomed, once in a while, to withdraw from his companions for the purpose of recollecting himself in God's presence. Seeing him nine years later, at Bordeaux, I found that his faith and his fervor were the same—he had not deviated in the least from these pious practices."

Another great source of spiritual advancement to him, after the retreat, was the examen of conscience according to the method of St. Ignatius, the abundant fruits of which exercise inspired him with such regard for it, that subsequently he took advantage of every opportunity to persuade his friends to practise it themselves and teach it to others.

And finally, prayer was Brother Charles's one continual staff of support, the means *par excellence* by which he preserved the graces of the retreat. "My progress," said he, "the peace of my soul, depend upon my fidelity to the spiritual exercises, in which respect I try to be very exact, convinced that the man of prayer is all-powerful with God. Fully impressed with this thought, I will strive earnestly to nourish within me the spirit of prayer, consecrating to this holy exercise a considerable portion of each day, and often raising my heart to God, even during my usual occupations and in recreation. The fervor imbibed from meditation being the soul of a Jesuit, I will employ all possible means to make my meditations well." How faithfully he kept this resolution, we shall learn later on.

To facilitate his approach to the Throne of Grace, the generous novice took good care to remember the exalted intercessors whose powerful aid he had in the past so often and so successfully implored. Hence he prayed more habitually in union with Jesus, Mary, Joseph; oftener invoked his holy patrons, as well as St. Stanislas Kostka and the monthly patron. But of all his devotions the dearest to his heart, and beyond a doubt the most salutary, was that to his guardian angel, and likewise that especial form of veneration he practised towards the Blessed Virgin.

How great soever might heretofore have been his devotion to that blessed angel God had given him as a protector and guide through the desert of life, it is certain that not until he entered the novitiate did it develop a character wholly exceptional. Then, indeed, sprang up in his heart such warm love for and confidence in this holy spirit, as excited his fears, lest these pious manifestations lack the solid foundation of true piety; but re-assured on this point by his director, he abandoned himself without scruple to the divine impulse, and towards the end of his novitiate this amiable devotion had become one of the most beautiful ornaments of his soul.

Twice every night, at an appointed hour, his good angel, granting his desires, awakened him, that he might raise his heart to God a few moments; for he found the night too long to consume entire in sleep, without thinking of his Master and testifying his love for Him. During the day he was accustomed to charge his angel with numberless commissions for heaven, and "never," said Charles, "never did he fail to execute them." Every morning, on awaking, he saluted this good angel, and every night, ere seeking repose, he invoked his protection, confiding to him his soul, heart, and senses.

Tuesday of every week was consecrated to him—the whole day: and, moreover, the rest of his time not especially devoted to him was spent in his presence. Charles took him for the model of his actions, the witness of his promises, the companion of his journeys, walks, and visits. When he had business to transact, some particular homage to offer the Lord, some duty to fulfil towards his neighbor, it was always his good angel to whom he had recourse, this celestial spirit being his strength, light, and consolation on all occasions.

Another pious practice of Brother Charles was to honor and invoke the angel guardians of the places through which he passed, and of the persons with whom he was brought in contact. He experienced such beneficial effects from this that he sought to extend the devotion among his friends, not only by word of mouth, but even by letter. Among other pious devices of his love and confidence in this regard, the following have come to our knowledge.

When retiring for the night, he would charge his good angel to take advantage of this opportunity to watch before Our Lord in the Sacrament of His Love. When, also, the Church was to celebrate a festival in honor of Jesus or Mary, he would, on awaking, beg his angel to wish them a happy feast-day for him, and congratulate them in advance upon the glory they were about to receive. In his meditations, his visits to the Blessed Sacrament, and especially in his Communions, he besought this tender friend and protector to prepare a place for Jesus in his heart; to adore Him and pay Him homage for him, to make reparation for his faults, and obtain for him, by fervent prayer, all those graces and heavenly aids of which he had need.

It is easier to imagine than describe all the consolation, sweetness, and spiritual vigor Brother Charles derived from this confiding love for his guardian angel. Says one of his confrères: " It was truly delightful to hear him speak on this point, and with such simplicity; the enumeration of the favors for which he was indebted to this heavenly guide was endless, and he spoke his praises with charming naiveté. ' Never ! ' he would say, ' never, has he failed to come to my aid when I needed him, and that was often.' "

" One day," says another novice, " when out walking, straying beyond the suburbs of Toulouse, we got lost. The road we had taken led us into the woods surrounding a villa, a glimpse of which was visible through the trees. Unwilling to go farther, my companion and I said to Brother Charles, who headed the band, that we had better return. ' Ah,' he replied, ' here is just the occasion of proving the value of our guardian angels. Let us put the matter in their hands, and see if they will not help us.' We now recited the *Angele Dei*, ' and followed Brother Sire, who walked on with as much confidence as if he were

---

[1] This is a short prayer to the guardian angel, to the recitation of which the Church has attached an Indulgence of one hundred days. The words are as follows:

> Angel of God, my guardian dear,
> To whom His love commits me here,
> Ever this day be at my side,
> To light and guard, to rule and guide. Amen.

at home.   At length, reaching a dwelling, we rapped at
the door to inquire of some one our way, but not a living
soul could we find.

"Brother Charles was greatly amused at our fears.
'Now,' said he, 'since our good angels have left us to ourselves, we must see what there is, if anything, interesting
about here.'   Looking in a little building with colored
windows, we perceived that it was an oratory.   After a
short prayer on the threshold we continued our investiga-
tions, and found some statues hidden under the bushes, at
which we laughed heartily.   However pleasant all this
might be, we could not remain here, but must needs find
our way out.   Brother Charles struck boldly into the first
path opening towards the end of the garden, and in a few
minutes we found ourselves upon the well-known road,
after a little adventure, simple, indeed, but full of interest
for us.

"Brother Charles now told us that he had placed our
walk under the protection of our good angels when we
left the novitiate; and he took advantage of the occasion
to turn our hearts towards these holy spirits, by culling
from his own experience agreeable and edifying anecdotes
concerning them.   I fully believe that my devotion to my
guardian angel dates from this day."

And others who read these lines will make the same
acknowledgment.   We can even assert with confidence
that thoughts the most consoling and delightful, resolutions the most generous, have been for some of Brother
Charles's imitators the immediate fruits of their invocations to the guardian angel.

And what shall we say of his favorite devotion, his
devotion to the Blessed Virgin ?   We have already cited
many anecdotes of this, and here are some additional ones
furnished us by his brethren in the novitiate.

"Every one acquainted with Charles," says Father Martin Carrère, "was perfectly aware that one of the distinguishing features of his piety was a very tender and filial devotion to Mary. This mark of the predestinate was his in an eminent degree. He told me, one day, that whilst at the Theological Seminary he had had a strange scruple—he feared that he loved our Blessed Lady more than he did Our Lord. But his director, he said, re-assured him on this point, telling him that the love of a soul for Mary was never in conflict with that for her Son, but was always referred to Him; that she had no greater desire than to see Him loved; that she was all-powerful in obtaining for those who called themselves her children the grace to love Him; consequently, to love Mary was the shortest road to the true love of Jesus. Tranquillized thus, this pure soul abandoned itself unreservedly to this attraction, and it was with truly child-like confidence it had recourse to Mary in its least necessities.

"Being a novice at the same time as himself, I was, one day, the happy witness of an incident proving his boundless confidence in the divine Mother, and her promptness in responding to it. He had been granted permission to repair to Saint-Jory for a family reunion; but as his time there was very limited, he did not wish to go until assured of the arrival thither of all his brothers, and he was in doubt respecting two of them—when they would be there. We went out to make inquiries about it, but no one could enlighten us.

"Brother Charles seemed quite perplexed for a moment, for the carriage he must take would leave in an hour. Suddenly his face brightened, and he said to me with a joyous air : 'Come with me to Our Lady of Good News, and I promise you we will soon have an answer.' 'Willingly,' was my answer, although I must admit I was far from sharing his confidence. We now directed our steps towards the basilica of St. Sernin, and after a short prayer at the foot of this venerated altar we turned to leave. On going out of the church, we inadvertently took the wrong way, which brought us face to face with one of his brothers, who happened to be passing at the time, and who was the very person that could give the desired information—that the two brothers (so the family had just learned) would be at Saint-Jory in about a week. As soon as we were alone, I expressed my surprise at the promptness with which his prayer had been answered. Looking at me with a smile, he said, ' You are astonished at that, are you ? It is no matter of surprise to me, for it is nothing new ; frequently have my prayers been answered thus. I come very often to Our Lady of Good News, always asking some especial favor, and never once has she refused to hear me. Try her yourself, and your experience will be like mine, provided the subject of your petition be something you really need, and not a mere caprice. After this, have confidence in Our Lady of Good News, she will always hear you, she is always ready to bestow her favors.'

" Even amid the distractions of college life he ever cherished a grateful remembrance of this sanctuary, and whenever any one was going to Toulouse Brother Charles would charge him with some commissions to Our Lady of Good News. He spoke of it frequently, and with the affectionate warmth with which one would speak of a native land he could never forget.

" I shall always remember the angelic joy with which, meeting me on the road as he was returning to Toulouse, ere starting on the foreign missions, he announced the latter fact to me, and added almost immediately, ' I shall see Our Lady of Good News again, and I will not forget you '

" He seized every opportunity to speak of Mary, and his words, always simple and natural, were at such times truly charming. His manuscripts furnish proofs innumerable of his filial tenderness of manner towards the Mother of God, as he was accustomed to note down the graces received ; and these, according to his own testimony, were abundant. Other friends of Father Charles may have much that is far more interesting to relate concerning him on this point. As for myself, I can vouch for the strict fidelity of the above.

" Father Martin Carrère."

III.—Brother Charles's Conduct during the Second Year of his Novitiate. He is appointed Monitor.

The day after the touching family festival to which Father Carrère alludes, Brother Charles, who had edified every one at Saint-Jory, gladly returned to his dear retreat, eager to enter upon the second year of his novitiate. And God, desiring to try his virtue, and crown his first labors, sent him the cross of suffering, but accompanied by a superabundance of graces that fitted him to accept and bear it lovingly.

Really exhausted by his voluntary penances and the continual efforts he had made, since the retreat, to vanquish nature and his temperament, Brother Charles's strength was gradually so impaired that his friends began to feel seriously alarmed about him ; and it was only by the most assiduous care, and complete rest towards the end of this vacation, that the impending danger was averted.

He was still a convalescent, when Father Desmoulins, who had been in charge of the novitiate some months, appointed him to the delicate office of *monitor*. He who fills this post must transmit to the other novices the especial orders and instructions of the novice master regarding all points of exterior discipline, and likewise see that they are observed.   Twice a week he must examine the rooms and call the Brothers' attention to whatever he perceives amiss therein.   Hence, the monitor is the novice master's right arm, his confidant, and the intermediary between himself and the novitiate.   His office is also the first and most important dignity of the novitiate, presupposing in him who is clothed with it the authority of example, good sense, prudence, zeal, and fraternal charity.   The manner in which Brother Sire acquitted himself of this duty contributed in no small degree to maintain and increase this year in the house that spirit of peace, unity, and joy, which makes the charm of the novitiate and assures its fruits.

His first care, on entering upon these functions, was to give good example ; hence his vigorous efforts to overcome his least faults.   Some of the rules regarding modesty, especially that of the eyes, cost him much, but this was only an incentive to greater circumspection on this point; and to insure fidelity herein, he consecrated to self-examination on this subject the first three days of each month, and a reasonable time after each walk into the city, always imposing a penance upon himself when he had failed in the least.

He likewise made it a duty to edify his brethren by observing punctually and to the letter all the rules of the society, all the counsels of his superiors, and even the least advice given him by his confrères or assistants on occasions when, no matter what the motive, he was bound to obey them.   But above all it was the simplicity with which he acquitted himself of his *experiments* [1] that gave

---

[1] Thus are designated certain tests, ordinarily imposed upon every novice, and which are very trying to nature.

such lustre to his virtue and such irresistible force to his example. The following letter, dated March 14, 1852, to his brother Vital [1] gives us some insight into this portion of his life.

" On the 15th of October, I was named sacristan for the second time. At the beginning of December, I was charged with two *experiments* at the same time—that is, for a month I, assisted by another Brother, had the care of all the lamps in the house ; and as I was first lamp-lighter, my duties were heavier than his. During the period of my *experiments* in connection with the lamps, I was obliged to go five times a week, frequently through snow or rain, to the two public hospitals of La Grave and Saint-Jacques, in the exercise of my apostolic work among the sick.

" Towards the end of January, I was put in charge of the refectory, and was separated from the rest of the community the greater part of the day, taking my recreations and making my spiritual reading with the Brothers co-adjutors, being under obedience to one of them. Two weeks later, I was sent to the kitchen, to wash the cooking utensils, grind the coffee, prepare the salt for the table, and obey the orders of the Brother cook in all matters whatsoever, and this the whole day, except on the eves of holy-days. From the kitchen I went to the sacristy, and I am now first sacristan, and that for the second time since last October.

" I have also, since that period, been teaching catechism at the Minims, as before my sickness, that is, every Sunday; but not with the same companions, for they have been changed three times, many of our Fathers and Brothers having left for their respective missions. We now num-

[1] M. Vital Sire. Charles's second brother, was then professor of theology at the Theological Seminary of Rodez.

ber but twenty-nine in the house. I am the sixteenth in seniority, but not in virtue, to my shame be it said.

"Besides teaching catechism at the Minims, I give religious instruction to two young men, each aged about twenty-two, and a man of forty-five, the latter extremely defective in hearing and speech, and understanding only the *patois* of Saint-Girons; I have also kept a retreat for a postulant.

"With all these occupations, I have never once dreamed of weariness. Had the thought occurred to me, I should have had no time to dwell upon it, and even if I had the time, the many delights of the novitiate would have banished it from my soul; for nowhere else have I ever known such happiness, such uninterrupted peace, as I enjoy here. Not that I have made great progress in the path of perfection, but that I rest quietly in the paternal hands of Providence, Who will supply all my wants. . . . From this happy solitude, I send you a fraternal kiss. Adieu."

One of the Brothers, who was undergoing his probation at the same time as Charles, and who left the novitiate precisely because he could not stand these trials, thus recounts the admirable manner in which Charles bore them.

"He performed all these humble duties with an evenness of temper truly unalterable, and an unwavering spirit of faith, entertaining himself continually whilst thus engaged with holy thoughts appropriate to the occupations.

"One day, as he was blacking his boots, I picked up the brush to perform the same office for myself, but my manner showed plainly that it was most distasteful work. Courage, brother, courage !' said he, we must pay attention to our feet no less than to the rest of our being—even more. 'Bethink yourself that your feet are those of a missionary ;' and then he quoted the text, *Quam pulchri pedes*, "How beautiful are the feet of them that preach the

gospel of peace." [1] I could not refrain from saying, 'Oh!
tell me your secret, that secret which makes you so happy
amidst those vile employments that exasperate me ! I have
seen you contentedly cleaning the lamps, dressed up in an
old greasy cassock, and your fingers full of oil. If they
were ever to put me at anything like that, I couldn't stand
it !' ' You astonish me,' he replied ; ' the *experiment* of the
lamps pleases me better than any other. *Unxit me Deus
meus oleo lætitiæ*— "my God hath anointed me with the
oil of gladness." [2] Whilst thus employed, I think of all
the symbolisms of oil ; I meditate, work, and pray at the
same time ; behold the secret of my joyfulness.' I could
not help smiling at this cheerful answer, and it was without demur or comment I accepted the charge of the lamps
immediately after him.

"Another day, I had given me an *experiment* far more
disagreeable even than the above-mentioned, at which I
really stormed, declaring I could hold out no longer ; so,
leaving my work, I went to my room, ready to give up the
whole thing. The good angel of my soul and vocation
found me there and divined the cause. ' Rough, isn't it ?'
said he. ' I should like to see you at it,' was my answer.
' Well,' he replied sweetly, 'I will do it for you. You
imagine it worse than it is. Moreover, were it far more
difficult, I should not hesitate ; we cannot do enough to
prove our love for Him who deemed no sacrifice too great
to make for us.' ' No, don't go,' was my answer; ' I will
return and finish it myself,' and I did."

The longest trial imposed upon Brother Charles during
his novitiate was that of catechism at the Minims. For
the majority of the novices this was only an ordinary trial,
lasting, like all the others, about a month; but for him it
was a work, and an important one, of a year's duration,

---

[1] Rom. x. 15.   [2] Ps. xliv. 8.

proving his apostolic zeal, and attended by the happiest results.

"Every one here still remembers gratefully," says M. Bonnal, present curé of the Minims at Toulouse, "Brother Sire's untiring efforts, zeal, and charity when he taught catechism in this parish, then a mere experiment; our only chapel was a very humble one, the old sacristy of the Minim Fathers prior to '93."

It was in this modest building, situated a little more than two kilometres from the novitiate, that Brother Charles, a few days after the grand retreat, began to display his apostolic zeal, teaching the children catechism three times a week, presiding over the evening Offices on Sundays and feast-days, preaching the word of God to this congregation eager to receive it, and, during the whole month of May, conducting the exercises, edifying the faithful here assembled, no less by the charms of his virtue than by his innumerable pious devices to honor Mary.

"This humble sanctuary was to him," says a confrère, "the image of those improvised by our missionaries in the forests and deserts of strange lands, and whilst we found it hard not to complain of the rain, the heat, the cold we endured, according to the season, in our long walks to and from the novitiate and the faubourg of the Minims, he seemed to regard them as pleasant promenades. He loved his children and that explains all. *Ubi amatur*, says St. Augustine, *non laboratur* : 'Love lightens labor.' "

"During the fourteen months this holy religious exercised among us the first fruits of his apostolate," says one who attended these exercises, we could not but admire his modesty, mortification, cheerfulness, and love of poverty. [1]

---

[1] Mme. Chaulet, who had charge of the little chapel in which Charles taught catechism, and who kept the key, was thus brought in frequent contact with him. "And yet," says she, speaking of him since his death, "we could never prevail upon him to accept the least favor. How often, amid the heats of summer, did

I see him now, with his dress somewhat worn, and his broad-brimmed hat. Instead of blushing and complaining of it, he seemed to joy in this livery of poverty, believing apparently that it was really too nice for him, whilst it excited, if not our pity, at least a smile.

" What struck us most in him was his true, solid piety, his love for the Blessed Virgin, and his apostolic zeal. We remarked it especially during the month of May, when he with one of his brother novices conducted the exercises, and preached to us, in virtue of an Indult accorded the Jesuit Fathers, and with the express permission of the diocesan authorities."

Brother Charles really surpassed himself this month, his tender affection for Mary inspiring him with such burning words as inflamed the hearts of all his hearers. He says himself, in his notes of the novitiate, that this congregation was so earnest and fervent in honoring the august Queen, adorning her altar, embalming her with the odor of flowers, chanting canticles of love and thanksgiving to her name, the little boys and girls consecrating themselves to her service in the most solemn manner, and, after their example, the young men and women offering her their hearts, and presenting her an elegant banner in token of homage. What he did not mention, but what was nevertheless well known, was the fact that whilst all hearts were filled with enthusiasm for Mary, they lauded him to the skies—him, the young apostle, whose piety and zeal had thus brought down upon them such showers of grace ; and when he left them the children even could not restrain their tears. Adds one of his brother novices: " It would be impossible to estimate all the good he accomplished here by his lessons in catechism, his

he not reach our house, dripping with perspiration and parched with thirst, notwithstanding which neither my husband nor myself could ever induce him to take the least refreshment, not even a little sugared water, his invariable response being, ' *Our rules forbid it.*' "

other religious instructions, and the consultations he generously accorded every one. He was indeed the father of
that precinct. All knew him, loved him, and regarded him
as the fervent apostle whose zeal was indefatigable. I accompanied him only too seldom, for I was always greatly
edified."

This zeal devouring his heart Brother Charles exercised
everywhere, in the hospitals amid the sick, in the Theological Seminary among his friends and fellow-students, in
the novitiate with his brethren, and even in the short visits
he sometimes made to his parents. It would exceed the
limits of our narration to mention here any detailed incidents of this zeal so characteristic of him, and we shall
content ourselves in ending this long chapter with a glance
at the fruits of his novitiate, and the retreat of the first
vows ending the novitiate.

IV.—Brother Charles's Conduct towards the End of His Novitiate. His First Vows.

All these works of piety in which Brother Charles was
engaged outside of the novitiate, far from distracting his
attention from the fundamental object within—the sanctification of his soul and his advancement in perfection, allied
him but the more closely thereto, by reason of that spirit of faith and recollection, that purity of intention ever
animating him. This is the flattering testimony of his
brethren, and the very natural conclusion to be drawn
from his account of conscience set forth in writing every
fortnight for his director, a paper depicting clearly the
state of his soul, its faults, its defects, its virtues, its progress, all its dispositions. We feel, in reading it, that our fervent novice was ever in spirit within the novitiate, that his
all-absorbing thought, of which he never lost sight for an

instant, was to advance in the path of perfection, aiming ever at the highest.

He writes as follows in June, July, and September : [1] " The farther I proceed the stronger the attraction for my vocation. God sometimes gives me most ardent desires of perfection. In the course of the present year I have made perceptible progress. I love poverty, chastity, obedience ; I observe the rules very strictly, and conform my will and judgment to that of my superiors, for God's sake. Sometimes, but rarely, have I found it hard to obey, and then only because the thing commanded was painful. Ordinarily I obey with joy, seeing God in the person of my superiors. Likewise do I behold His hand in all that happens to me.

" I have also made some progress in patience, humility, and love of my neighbor. Perceiving that I was sometimes annoyed and out of humor at the simplest request made of me, I resolved to correct this fault ; and now my tone and manner on such occasions are invariably gentle. I likewise discovered within me a tendency to contradict whatever certain Brothers would say; now, as soon as I am aware of this feeling, I restrain it, keeping silence, and being pleasant with them. I am especially watchful on this point as regards my relations with God, for I saw, in my grand retreat, that lack of cheerfulness in His service had been the obstacle to my obtaining from the novitiate all those fruits of benediction I had expected.

" I like mortification, both exterior and interior. In this connection, I must say I would prefer depriving myself of much at supper, but there are some evenings when I believe it a duty to eat to compensate for a scant dinner, or seek refreshment from fatigue. I sometimes feel a certain natural repugnance for what is troublesome, but that

[1] Account of Conscience of June 20 and 30, July 12, and September 13.

is of slight account.   What disturbs me most are the slight
faults I commit from time to time against charity, the
distractions and negligences I carry with me in spiritual
things.   I never experience any sensible sweetness or consolation in meditation or holy Mass : all is aridity and desolation overwhelming.   Although I have used every means
to overcome this wandering of my ideas and torpidity of
mind, none has succeeded.   It may proceed from need of
sleep and bodily fatigue ; likewise, it may be a trial from
God ; but I fear lest the *entire* application of my soul be
wanting.   The exercises in which I succeed best are spiritual readings, exhortations, the particular examen, and
above all Benediction of the Blessed Sacrament.   If permitted, I should be delighted to spend an additional half-
hour a week at the feet of Our Lord in His tabernacle ; it
is there I find my joy.   Never even does a Communion
speak to my heart like a Benediction.

"Zeal for souls predominates with me.   The first step
herein is difficult for me, but in the depths of my heart
there are great devotion to this work, affection for it, and
purity of intention regarding it.   This devotion I bring to
the exercise of my duty as monitor.   I pray much for the
community, for the older members as well as for the new
ones.   I am grieved when the conversations do not edify
me ; I would like my morning meditation or my Communion to furnish the subjects of them, but, alas ! I am so
sterile in spirituality !   My greatest aid herein is devotion
to the Sacred Hearts of Jesus, Mary, and Joseph.   Pious
conversations are very beneficial to me, exciting in me a
holy desire to emulate the fervent example of others.   I
find no difficulty in conversing with strangers thus, even
myself introducing the subject; but with certain of my
brethren I have an exceeding repugnance to do so ; nevertheless, even at the risk of displeasing some of them, I will

discourse on pious subjects, for in so doing we are but obeying our rules and our superiors. To please Jesus, we must
sometimes contradict His servants." [1]

After so faithful an exposition as the above of the pious
sentiments animating Brother Charles towards the end of
his novitiate, there remains for us, in finishing the sketch,
but to relate briefly the preparations for his departure and
an account of the retreat of the first vows. His own journal
will furnish us the details.

As the time approached, he resolved neither to make nor
express any conjectures as to what college he would be sent
to, or to what position assigned, but to abandon himself entirely into the hands of Providence, and make every moment
of these last days of the novitiate available to his spiritual
profit. To this end he offered the novice master his resignation as monitor; then, making a meditation upon this
maxim of the saints, *Age quod agis:* "What thou doest,
do with all thy heart," he gave himself up to recollection
and piety.

"Doubtless," says he in his notes, "I should prepare
for my departure by placing all my affairs in order, and
making an ample provision of literary knowledge ; but the
dominant idea during these last days shall be that of edifying my confrères, and benefiting my mind and heart. I
leave an important post : I, one of the oldest of the novices,
who am on the eve of my departure and of taking my vows.
I have a past to repair, a monitor to instruct, a whole community to edify and form to the rule by my example. And
oh ! what graces have I not received during the novitiate !
Sacristan four times (and with whom?), regulator, monitor,
the grand retreat of thirty days, and now, a simple novice—
what favors !

[1] To insure fidelity on this point, Brother Charles often read over the list from
which the children of St. Ignatius are advised to select the subject of their conversations to render them edifying.

"If the Reverend Father Rector were to say to me, ' Brother, you must re-invigorate the community by your zeal, charity, gentleness, your firmness, your conversations, I should really undertake it in good faith, it seems to me. And if Jesus were to say to me : *Deinceps ut vera sponsa, meum zelabis honorem,* ' Courage, my son, you must, henceforth, like a true spouse, labor zealously for My honor '—oh ! what would I not do ! What charity should I not have for my brethren ! The soul of any man is of infinite price, but the soul of a Brother should be far more precious to us than that of another ! Hence, I will strive to edify my brethren, especially the new ones ; I will make them love the novitiate by my amenity, my edifying conversations, my exact observance of all the rules and customs. At any cost, I must leave in the community a germ of edification.

"If Jesus wishes me not to see my parents, I conform in advance to His desires. To do otherwise would be to love them more than Him. As He is my model, He it is I should imitate. He bore the cross: I should bear it after Him."

On the evening of October 4th, Brother Charles, on going to his cell, found in it a pair of new shoes : it was the signal of his departure. Next day, in fact, he received his mission. He immediately went to take leave of Our Lady of Good News, asked and received her blessing, and that same evening set out for Bordeaux, or rather for La Sauve, the seat of a Jesuit college.

"As Saint-Jory was on the route, and the carriage in which he was travelling relayed about twenty steps only from his father's house, he could easily have embraced his parents and stopped a few minutes with them. But reflecting that these moments of joy for his mother would be followed by the keenest sorrow, he deemed it more perfect to impose upon himself the sacrifice of not seeing them, happy to inaugurate thus his first mission.

Installed at La Sauve on the 7th of October, he entered, on the 9th, into the retreat of his first vows, and on the 17th, the octave of the feast of St. Francis Borgia, one of the saints and most illustrious generals of the Society of Jesus, he pronounced, with transports, the vows of chastity, poverty, and obedience, in the presence of Mary, his good Mother, St. Joseph, his three patrons, all the holy apostles, and all the saints of the society.

The following, from a letter to his parents, dated the day of his vows, is a description in his own words of this solemn act. " Figure to yourselves, my dear father and mother, a young man, aged twenty-four years, in the habit of a Jesuit, approaching the sanctuary steps. . . . It is your son. There is nothing extraordinary in his surroundings ; the chapel is poor and scant of decoration, and there are present only two or three priests and some Brothers. The Reverend Father Rector of the college takes the ciborium from the tabernacle, and, just at the moment he distributes the sacred particles, I kneel down, and holding a written paper in my hand, pronounce my first vows.

" Addressing myself to the omnipotent God, and pronouncing all my names, I declare that, in spite of my indignity, I dare, resting upon the Lord's infinite goodness and mercy, to consecrate myself to this good Master, impelled by an ardent desire of thus serving Him more perfectly. I add: ' In presence of the most blessed Virgin Mary and the whole celestial court, I make a vow to Thy divine Majesty of perpetual poverty, chastity, and obedience in the Society of Jesus, and I promise to enter this same society with the intention of living therein forever, understanding all things according to the constitutions of the aforesaid society. Imploring now the goodness and clemency of the Lord, I conjure Him to grant me, through the blood and merits of His divine Son, grace to be ever faithful to my vows.

"Having pronounced my vows, I received holy Communion as a seal thereon, and oh! then it was I tasted the inexpressible happiness of belonging to God, by a voluntary sacrifice of earthly goods, sensual pleasures, and my liberty.   Oh! then could I exclaim with St. Teresa, 'May Jesus give me His life! May He reign, and I be His captive!   I aspire to no other liberty!'   I was happy indeed.

"In a little while the Father Minister came to tell me to go into a room adjoining the community chapel.   I obeyed and was received with open arms by the Reverend Father Rector, who said to me: 'You now belong to us; we possess you.' I replied, 'God possesses me.'

"At half past eight the bell was rung for recreation, which lasted an hour and a half.   It was then I saw, embraced, and conversed with all the Fathers and Brothers of the house.   At noon we dined.   My place at table was ornamented with flowers, and a crown of dahlias was upon my plate.   Everywhere, to-day, I was the king of the feast, everywhere I occupied the seat of honor.   In the evening we had Exposition and Benediction of the Blessed Sacrament, with a canticle for the vows.

"Oh! congratulate yourselves on having given a son to God; for the promises of the Gospel are as applicable to you as to me.   We read in that of to-day: 'And every one that hath left house, or brethren, or sisters, or father, or mother, or children, or lands, for My name's sake, shall receive an hundred-fold, and shall possess life everlasting.' To-day I have proven the truth of these words, for I realize that no one is so rich as he who leaves all things to follow Jesus, Jesus, his dearest friend, his brother, the spouse of his soul.   I am happy indeed; and likewise will you be happy on earth, by the protection of Heaven over your family and your goods, and by the abundance of graces vouchsafed you to work out your salvation;   and happy in eternity, by the tranquil possession of the Sovereign Good and surrounded by your children, who will form your crown. Enter into these sentiments, my dear parents, and then will the sacrifice of your children be infinitely profitable to you.

"Your most loving son,

"CHARLES SIRE,

" Of the Society of Jesus."

CHAPTER VI.

FATHER CHARLES'S REGENCY AT THE COLLEGE OF LA GRANDE SAUVE, NEAR BORDEAUX.

THE college of La Grande Sauve, where Brother Charles made his regency, is situated thirty kilometres from Bordeaux, in the country styled *des deux mers*, upon one of the lofty eminences overlooking the valley of the Garonne. It was one of the first colleges the Jesuit Fathers opened in France in 1850, after permission to teach had been restored to them by the government. That family spirit which has ever animated it makes this one of the most delightful and happy establishments of the society.

I.—General Idea of Brother Charles as Regent.

When Charles entered La Sauve, the household was composed of twenty-two religious, nearly all still very young, and a goodly number of brother novices.

Says Father Ayroles: "Perfect harmony and the most cordial gayety reigned among us; and although truth no less than modesty obliges me to make an exception in the following point, I can say that all were full of joyful devotion, zeal, and charity. We were so happy at being reunited again; Brother Charles, in coming among us, assimilated marvellously with his surroundings, and although, at that time, neither I nor any of the other members of this religious family believed that we possessed in him a saint, whom God was to glorify later by miracles, we all loved him as a good, pious religious, and an excellent confrère.

" By turns professor, sub-prefect, vigilant, assistant to the procurator or the prefect of discipline, he acquitted himself of these divers employments with exactness, skill, and punctuality. I spent five years with him at La Sauve, and during all that time I could not but admire his devotion to duty, his abnegation, his fraternal charity, and the care he bestowed upon the children. He ever enjoyed the confidence of his superiors and the esteem of his scholars. There was nothing extraordinary in his exterior life, nothing unusual or calculated to attract attention; all was regular and conformable to the rules. Truly, his merit was great before God.

" One fact alone, far better than details, will prove Charles's great virtue: he passed the whole period of his regency, that is, seven years, in the same college; which is equivalent to saying that he always pleased his superiors and confrères, and was himself pleased with them."[1]

" During the four years," adds Father Tourel, " that I was at La Sauve, one year as prefect-general and three years as rector, this excellent and perfect religious was continually under my eyes; and I can safely declare that of all those whom Providence placed under my charge during that period, Brother Sire was, in my opinion, the most remarkable, the most regular, practising with scrupulous fidelity all those virtues that constitute the true son of St. Ignatius. I used frequently to ask myself this question : ' What is there defective or reprehensible in this dear Brother ? ' ' Nothing, nothing,' would be my invariable conclusion; and I could but admire in him the riches of divine grace.

" A saint being the greatest of all treasures for a college,

---

[1] He was, indeed, the only Jesuit who ever remained so long at La Sauve, either before or after ordination.

in begging God to prepare me for the trials His love might send, I earnestly implored Him to leave us dear Brother Sire, and He deigned to grant my petition.

" Humility, angelic modesty, unvarying gentleness, most exemplary obedience, unremitting fervor and regularity— such were Brother Charles's striking virtues, the mould, as it were, in which God's goodness had cast this beautiful soul.

" Asking nothing and refusing nothing, he was always in readiness for whatever might be required of him ; and no one ever asked his assistance in vain.   He was indeed beloved by all.   The amiability of his virtue was an irresistible magnet, attracting even the most exacting natures ; and those selfish characters whom others failed to please, through lack of patience, gentleness, and forbearance, were ever the conquests of Brother Sire's unvarying kindness and self-abnegation.

" In a college, especially where the number of students is considerable, every day imposes personal sacrifices, often very painful ones ; and more particularly is this the case on solemnities or other extraordinary occasions, the general excitement increasing one's natural love of enjoyment. To console the sick at such times, to have charge of those who need restraint, to be a faithful sentinel at some obscure but important post, one must needs know how not only to renounce his own will, peace, and pleasure, but even to contradict that of others ; he must be a man of good will, that is, of profound self-abnegation.   And such was Brother Charles, as was evidenced by his offering himself to the superior for the above-mentioned heroic duties, which he always performed most cheerfully and with angelic simplicity.   How I admired and blessed him !   What edification was wrought within my soul, at sight of this religious, a model of perfection, far surpassing the most advanced of his brethren !

" In this beautiful life, so regular, so perseveringly faithful in the least things, one could catch a glimpse of what a St. Aloysius Gonzaga or a St. John Berchmans must have been. What struck me especially in him was the sweetness of his modest face, his charming look of respect and charity for others, his amiable yet thoroughly religious bearing, his evenness of temper—all truly a part of his identity. The only signs—I will not say of impatience—of emotion I ever noticed in him during the four years he was under my eye, were some rapid changes of color in his face, either of pallor or the contrary, or the silent suffusion of his eyes with tears, under circumstances the most trying. And even these involuntary expressions, I discovered, were the oftener due to his timidity, so admirably in unison with that sweet nature made perfect by virtue, or to his having been misunderstood by his superiors or others—yes, it was plain, they were not movements of impatience.

" As to the various duties intrusted to him, he brought to each and every one of them an intelligent and indefatigable zeal. He never did things by halves, and God, to Whom he gave himself entire in his works, rewarded his efforts, Brother Sire being noted for his success in imparting instruction, for his watchfulness, his material order, his system. His talents were not naturally brilliant ; and, in my opinion, he found his work difficult, but he brought to it such application, docility, judgment, and tact, as must needs have accomplished great results. I was especially struck with this during these four years, and more particularly as regards his instruction of the lower classes, in which capacity of instructor he formed the hearts of his dear little scholars to piety, whilst keeping them up to the level of their ordinary studies. His greatest aptitude was for order, discipline, material administration. Brother Sire was a man of order *par excellence.* Had he been given some disordered machinery to regulate, a chaotic mass of work to arrange, ill-kept books to balance, or any duty whatever requiring him to cope with confusion, soon indeed would one have seen the admirable result of his efforts in a complete change and the substitution of what was desirable.

"Hence, his superiors selected him in preference to others as assistant in those offices, whether of discipline or administration, which demanded heroic fidelity and perseverance (rare and precious talents in the practical routine of college life), and good order in details, these constituting the greatest element of solid and brilliant success in the grand work of education. Brother Sire was eminently what is styled a college man. His great zeal as an apostle was such as to obtain for him the privilege of being called to the foreign apostolate ; but oh ! what good might he not have accomplished in our colleges, had God deigned to leave him there; also, what good in our dear missions, had he not, at an early age, been ripe and worthy of a crown prepared by the consummation of all merits !

"Yes, I cannot help saying, because firmly convinced of it, that in the death of Father Sire we have lost an amiable Brother, whose exalted virtue had been a powerful assistance in our works, ever directed towards God's greater glory and the salvation of souls.

"The above is all my restricted time permits me to say of that blessed memory, piously embalmed in the depths of my heart. Would that my written contribution were comparable in richness to the religious virtue of Father Sire."

To this double testimony of superiors and confrères we shall add but a few details furnished by the scholars, reserving for a more extended Life of this holy man a collection of incidents and facts which, depicting him more perfectly as professor and sub-prefect, may induce those filling these offices to take him for their model.

II.—Brother Charles as Professor.

1. *His zeal and success.*—Speaking of him as a professor, the children of La Sauve never weary of sounding his praises—the good order he preserved, his paternal kindness, his zeal not only in imparting instruction, but also in training their intellectual faculties and inspiring them with a taste for study. They have much to tell of those innumerable charming devices to which he resorted for maintaining life and interest in his class, and exciting a truly Christian emulation.

" Although Father Sire," says one of his scholars, [1] " was eminently a *religious,* it was not precisely in this character he made the deepest impression upon me. What I beheld in him at first, I, a mere child, so lately snatched from the maternal caresses, was the professor, the instructor of my childhood, my first initiator into those serious studies which commence with the development of the faculties.

" His angelic countenance attracted me ; his wise indulgence won me—I could not but give myself up to him who appeared so lovable; and this spontaneous, irresistible affection was fraught with good for me, inspiring me with the strength to walk courageously in a new path. It was as a beneficent ray of light illumining and warming my infancy. He was my professor. Although the class was large, we all loved him with an affection and confidence far different from that we had for any other. There was nothing he could not arrange for us ; his kindness always put us at our ease ; severity was not in his nature, and even in those paternal corrections a teacher is often obliged

[1] M. Joseph Beaune, now a magistrate. He was a scholar of Brother Charles whilst in the fifth and sixth classes.

to administer we could but perceive his ever-watchful
affection.

"And what shall I say of the progress to which he
incited us in our studies, through those many ingenious
expedients he disdained not to employ, knowing thus,
after the example of Our Lord, how to render the truth
accessible to all? His brethren in religion, who perceived
his great talent for exciting emulation, often begged him
to reveal his secret to them. The secret? Ah! it was
his heart, his goodness, an artifice natural to him, and not
feigned, that aroused such generous rivalry among his
scholars. I still remember that more than once several of
us, excited by his voice, his influence, allowed our ardor to
get the better of our control. Ah! he knew how to inspire
emulation for the laurels and for honor!

"As for me, I feel convinced that the whole of my
college life, and, consequently, my subsequent course, has
its foundation in those holy counsels he lavished upon me,
on occasions when the apostle's zeal was constrained to
pierce the professor's robe. How often did he not present
to my disheartened imagination glimpses of triumph which
imparted renewed courage! And this was another secret
of his heart—that gift of inspiring others with the tranquil firmness so inseparable from his own nature. Nothing was too much for his devotedness; he would interrupt
his labors, notwithstanding their regularity, his prayers,
so recollected and fervent, to fly to me, if needs be, and
console me in discouragement, or excite me to emulation
in the classics. Had I not been blessed with a professor
like this, I am sure my advancement would have been far
otherwise than it was, for the least contradiction or failure
would have arrested my strongest intentions, and paralyzed
my most courageous efforts."

And M. Beaune's experience was that of many others;

for, full of solicitude for all intrusted to his care, Brother
Charles neglected no one, but gave to each and every one
the especial assistance he needed, the instruction suited
to his capacity, exciting the capable to renewed efforts,
sustaining and encouraging the timid, awakening the interest of all—such was his ambition, his happiness, his life,
to succeed in which no sacrifice was too great for him.
And then, how clear his explanations of the lessons! how
admirable his illustrations! what interest and animation
in his classes! Convinced that the distaste for study, the
discouragement, weariness, and lack of conformity to rules
so prevalent among school children ordinarily originate in
ignorance of them, or a forgetfulness of the principles of
education, he was constantly reminding the scholars of
them, for this purpose resorting to innumerable pleasant
devices, the remembrance of which, even after the lapse
of forty years, is still fresh in their minds.

"The first year," says one of them, "we were but nine-
teen in the seventh class, all very young and backward in
our studies. To very ordinary capacities nearly half of
us joined a natural indolence, anything but encouraging
to our teacher; yet Brother Charles triumphed over all
these obstacles. His kindness, gentleness, his ever-cheer-
ful countenance excited our will; his firmness, prudence,
and tact were an antidote to our inconstancy; his clearness of expression opened our minds to receive that
instruction which his patience made take deep root therein. He knew so well how to introduce variety into his
method of teaching that we all went cheerfully to his class-
room. We were much interested in declamation, partly
because it afforded us grounds for merriment; yet Brother
Charles never allowed our hilarity at these times to be
such as might wound the feelings of the declaimer. He
wished his class to be in all things a school of respect and

charity, every member of it enjoying the esteem of his fellow-pupils.

"Thanks to his pains, our success this year exceeded all hopes ; and the two following years were still more brilliant, when Brother Charles, now professor of the sixth Latin class, saw his efforts crowned by the most gratifying and solid results. And again, especially in the third year, during which period the classes were re organized, with the intention of making the course of study more thorough, the success of the sixth class was truly remarkable. Brother Charles had, nevertheless, no superior intellectual gifts—it was his industry, his engaging qualities of heart, his indefatigable zeal, his means of exciting emulation, that accomplished such wonders. I can say truly, without fear of exaggeration, that of all the professors who taught my classes (and I had many excellent ones) none could compare with Brother Charles in interesting, and consequently advancing, his scholars."

A Christian teacher has other duties to his classes besides teaching them Latin and Greek ; hence, Brother Charles, in cultivating the minds of his scholars, labored assiduously in moulding their hearts, thus completing in these young souls God's own work. Wishing to make them men in the highest sense of the term, he ever endeavored to incline their wills and hearts towards duty, striving to make them love and choose virtue, that is, the just, the true, the noble, the beautiful. Then, going a step farther, he strove to make them Christians—serious, practical, enlightened Christians, employing those efficacious means the Society of Jesus has established for that purpose, and which are either of obligation or precept for the professors. Adopting them all from a spirit of obedience, that of zeal actuated him in applying them with ardor, constancy, and wisdom not to be excelled ; hence the success attending his efforts.

"The sixth Latin class," says one of his scholars, [1] "became, under his charge, the model class of the college, the father's dispositions being communicated to the children ; so true is it that the good teacher makes good scholars. Had a stranger come into our midst, he might have supposed we were brothers, so great was our thoughtfulness for one another ; the children had imbibed the father's charity. What a happy family was this sixth class ! When studies were over, we would collect in the court for recreation, and if our good Father's duties permitted him, he soon joined us. It was one of his greatest pleasures. 'Come,' he would say, 'I have ten minutes to stay with you, so let us make the most of it and have a good time running, laughing, playing !' And behold him become a child again, taking part in all the games and sports our young imaginations could invent. When the ten minutes had elapsed, he would say: 'Continue your innocent pastimes, dear children ; as for me, I must now leave, and go pray for you.' So saying, he would turn away, and we would interrupt our amusements to look after him until the door shut him from sight, so dear was he to us.

"He treated us as a tender father. In class he was always kind and even-tempered, full of solicitude for his scholars, especially the most backward, striving ever to improve both mind and heart, and setting before us an example of piety which implanted in our souls the precious germs of virtue.

"Were it necessary to reprove a scholar, he did so, with the authority of a good father, but likewise with a gentleness which could not fail to recall us to a sense of duty. And we understood him, this dear Father, whom we sought

[1] M. Raymond Follardeau, now a landholder in the Gironde, and the father of a family.

to please, frequently anticipating his desires, and in our success sometimes exceeding his hopes.

"And how, indeed, could we have helped loving him? Did not his many amiable traits of character win all hearts? I knew him several years at La Sauve, both as professor and vigilant, and I always found him the same—that is, always holy, no matter what his employment; and among the Fathers, as among the scholars, his praises were on every tongue. I do not believe he had an enemy, the tenor of his life was so even, so gentle. He went about doing good; these few words describe more clearly and eloquently than studied phrases what he was—a man of good will *par excellence,* a saint.

"And now, dear Father, having paid, though feebly, my tribute of gratitude and praise to your memory, let me beg your intercession. Oh! remember in your abode of glory that sixth class, once so dear to you, and obtain for each of its members benedictions abundant, that the germs of virtue you implanted in their hearts may ripen, and we all, one day, rejoin you in heaven."

2. *His virtues as professor.*—Brother Charles's zealous efforts in forming the hearts of his scholars to piety and virtue would have met with but moderate success, had they not been sustained and fructified by that union of Christian virtues which wins the Christian teacher the esteem, confidence, veneration, and love of his pupils. Being fully aware of this, he sought ever to edify them by good example.

"In which lesson of edification," says one of them, "he succeeded so well that, in scanning my recollections of his character, I cannot discover the least fault, not even those slight imperfections so often found in teachers, for their task is a most trying one, and the strongest virtue will sometimes succumb to the burden. My memories of him are embalmed in affection and gratitude, and I know not one of my schoolmates whose sentiments are not identical with these." Another of his children exclaims : "It is an admirable fact that the more I question my memory, the more I am convinced that he who most closely observed Father (then Brother) Sire will be the one to praise him most and relate the greatest number of edifying anecdotes, for all his actions merited praise."

So great the perfection he had attained, that truly might it have been said, all the virtues made their abode in his heart. We shall merely allude here to some of those which shone most conpicuously in him as a professor, consequently, those his scholars admired most, and which exercised upon them the happiest influence.

"He was justice itself," says one of his scholars. "and never did he unjustly punish any one whomsoever. Moreover, in punishments as in rewards, in praises as in censure, it was all meted out with equal weight and measure. Never was there the slightest partiality, never the least regard to condition of life, fortune. or exterior qualities. Neither, in this matter, did he ever listen to the voice of flesh and blood, and his brother at La Sauve was treated by him just as one of us, perhaps less leniently, insomuch that we were accustomed to say, ' No one can accuse Brother Sire of showing partiality to his brother, rewarding him unmeritedly,' which really meant that the latter met with less consideration than ourselves.

"This impartiality and justice towards all his scholars individually was observed most scrupulously towards them as a class, for never were we burdened with too many or too difficult restrictions or lessons, Brother Charles always calculating in advance the time each study would be likely to demand of a pupil of ordinary capacity, or even of one below the average. And, as some unforeseen event might interfere with one's study hours, he told us always to inform him, at the beginning of class, whenever such had been the case, that thus no one might be exposed to unmerited punishment. And in this he was ever consistent; hence, it is no wonder that he gained the esteem and love of all.

"As to patience and gentleness, none could exceed his merits in these. We had some very indolent scholars in the seventh class, likewise a few in the sixth, all of whom tried him severely; yet he never seemed vexed, never betrayed the least sign of anger, even on occasions when it was evident that only angelic patience could have restrained him. To be sure, he reproved the delinquents, he punished them, but always with moderation and dignity, and never exceeding the bounds of justice. He had too much respect, both for himself and his pupils, ever to wound them by angry or injurious words. We could but feel that the teacher who corrected was also the father who loved. He was always willing to listen to our excuses; he pardoned readily, and when one acknowledged his faults all the extenuating circumstances were taken into consideration.

"He greatly preferred preventing evil to remedying it. Persuaded that a well-behaved class is ever a diligent one, and that the most effectual means for keeping it thus are firmness and gentleness, with these two aids he maintained discipline among his pupils; and that wise, mild, uniform discipline which commands respect, exerts an irresistible influence over the will, and banishes all spirit of criticism or censure. Never in his dealings with us was there the least trace of anything capricious, arbitrary, or severe, wisdom and moderation characterizing all his actions. Hence there was very seldom any occasion for his resorting to severity in punishing; his well-known firmness restrained the most giddy, and his kindness did the rest."

After justice and gentleness, patience and firmness, the

most salient virtue in Father Charles's character was his kindness, a kindness thoroughly supernatural, and which took a strong hold upon the confidence and esteem of all who knew him, manifesting itself as it did by a tenderness, charity, and devotion truly extraordinary. We relate a few incidents relative to this point, from the many which have been sent us by various of his scholars.

" I was very young, but nine years old," says M. Joseph Jacquemet, of Bordeaux, " when I left the paternal roof. Having been indulged by a father and tender mother and all the other members of a large family, I was a long time, I must confess, getting used to college life. Assigned to the sixth class, after an examination as to the little I already knew, it was here I had the good fortune of having for teacher the excellent Father Charles Sire, at that time pursuing his studies, previous to ordination. I shall never forget his kind attentions to me during those days of sudden transition from one mode of life to another. Of a somewhat sensitive disposition, it was no easy matter for me to bear those little jests thrust upon the new-comer, pin thrusts, as it were, wounding deeply those yet unaccustomed to them. I confided all these juvenile sorrows to Brother Charles, whose words of consolation soon dried my tears ; and thanks to his good counsels, ere long I was at ease with my companions."

" How often," says another of his pupils, M. Joseph Beaune, of Lévignac (Lot-et-Garonne). did not his touching solicitude speak to my young soul the language of affection! how often did he not dispel the little vexations of my childhood by that holy and innocent joy with which his heart was full—the joy of the elect! O memories of youth, ruins of La Grande Sauve, reveal to the world those mysteries of humility, simplicity, and devoted affection within your keeping! On that last supreme day, what revela-

tions will ye not make of all that is beautiful and admirable
—of noble sacrifices, of acts of generous immolation!"

"What struck me most forcibly in him," adds a third,
M. Louis Béraud, of La Rochelle (Charente-Inférieure),
"was his earnest endeavor to soften the rigors of college life
without deviating from the rules—rigors often most keenly
felt by children separated from their families and seeing
them but once a year.

"In thinking of all this now, I realize what courage, what
self-abnegation must ·needs have been his in devoting his
time, his zeal, his strength, his service even to the utmost,
to children who seldom suspected these sacrifices. No, for
one of his greatest merits was the spontaneity of his devotedness. It was always so natural and so joyous that one
might readily have supposed he really took pleasure in the
sports, preoccupations, and cares of us boys of twelve.

"The details of these precious memories are somewhat
indistinct by reason of time; but never can I forget that
inexhaustible kindness and goodness which so often calmed
and consoled my childish vexations and griefs.

"It was especially during the period he had charge of
the sixth class that I tested to the full his excessive devotedness. Our relations as teacher and scholar brought
us in daily contact; hence, I had constant opportunities of
observation, the result of which is that, in my opinion, the
most salient points of his character—judging by what I saw
of him in class, in his room, and by the many little talks
we had with him—were a goodness and kindness unparal-
leled, a fund of cheerfulness inexhaustible. Ah! God
grant that the especial affection he had for me during his
earthly career still be warm and undiminished, now that
he is in heaven."

"When a new scholar came to join our circle," adds a
fourth, "our amiable professor would always receive him

with a smiling countenance and a kindly word of welcome, and introduce him in recreation to gentle and agreeable comrades. Did he perceive a child in tears or apparently in trouble, he would instantly go to him and propose a game of ball or some other boyish sport, taking part therein with such zest and animation that his object was soon accomplished—the tears were dried, and smiles lit up the little scholar's face.

"Oh! how we loved him, this good Brother! and how happy we were to be under his care on holidays, and when we went out walking, knowing well what a delightful time we would have! He was accustomed to come among the little ones during their Sunday recreations. Occasionally, he would pass through our recreation grounds or hall at other times, saying a few pleasant words to one or another, and telling us all to enjoy ourselves. His visits to us, as I have said, were generally on feast days or in the winter, when the inclemency of the weather or the shades of night obliged us to take our recreations in a room not much to our taste, and where we were too crowded to indulge in such sports as we wished.

"Scarcely had he entered ere he was surrounded by the scholars, disputing among themselves for the place nearest him, like little birds over choice food. Even the wildest and giddiest, when speaking of him, would say: 'Oh! what a good child Brother Sire is!' an expression which was frequently on the scholars' lips, especially the younger scholars,' and which he forbade, both because it savored of too much familiarity, and also because he was unwilling to receive so many more testimonies of affection than the other teachers in the house. On this point, however, he was obeyed rather reluctantly.

"One day Father Matharan, having taken out for a promenade some of his scholars, nearly all of whom had

Brother Charles for one of their professors, said to us:
' Write, each one of you, on a piece of paper, a few words,
in whatever signs and characters you wish, and I promise
you that I can read it.' They did so, and Father Matharan soon read aloud the following which, with one accord,
although without any preconcerted action, each had written, *'Brother Sire is good.'* "

Charles's affection for his scholars was always actuated
by principle, that is, founded on a religious sentiment and
the spirit of faith.

"He loved us," says one of these children (M. Joseph
Beaune), "not on his own account or for our natural qualities, but for God and the benefit of our souls, striving thus
to win his way into our hearts, and fashion each one of us
into the living image of Jesus Christ. He loved us and
brought himself down to our level, because he looked with
an eye of admiration on the children of God destined for
that heaven he now enjoys."

This same motive inspired him with true respect for his
scholars, whom he regarded as young souls made to the
image of God, redeemed by the blood of Jesus Christ, and
still wearing their baptismal robe of purity and innocence;
it was thus he ever thought of them, and this consideration
was apparent in his words when he spoke of them. On
the day of their First Communion, not content with
assisting at all the Offices of the Church with them, he
even took his meals and all his recreations in their company; and if the next day were a holiday, he would take
charge of them during the morning and evening walks.
Appointed vigilant in 1855, during the recreations of the
retreat, he availed himself of the opportunity to enkindle
in the candidates for First Communion a little of the fire of
divine love that burned within himself, which he did by
his words of fervor and anecdotes calculated to impress

them. And when the God of the Eucharist, having descended into their hearts, had transformed them, he eagerly embraced these young souls, as so many living tabernacles, but with such profound, religious respect that they have never forgotten it. Ten years later, M. Béraud, one of this number, and now a lawyer at La Rochelle, speaks thus of this event:

"Of all the souvenirs of La Sauve which I lay before you, there is one far more vivid than any other, partly by reason of circumstances connected therewith—it is that of my First Communion. When Brother Charles embraced me on this occasion, his manner was so serious and grave that I involuntarily showed my surprise. Remarking it, he told me of the deep, holy respect with which he was filled for the child whose heart had just become, for the first time, the abode of the Eucharistic God. The action and words, at once so simple and natural, betokened such lively faith, such profound piety, that the impression made upon me was ineffaceable, and second to nothing of the kind I have ever received since, not even through the many sermons I have heard."

Innumerable incidents similar to the above-mentioned, whilst revealing the beauty of his soul, could but gain his scholars' hearts, their esteem, confidence, and religious respect " to a degree," says one of them, " approaching veneration. We were always delighted to see him, to hear him, to be loved and esteemed by him. We joyfully went to his class, morning and evening, and considered the time thus spent as the most agreeable part of the day. Our veneration and love for him were the principal motives urging us to industry in our studies and the observance of the rules. If any one forgot himself in point of conduct, the whole class assumed an attitude of protestation against him. We loved our professor, and seeing his gentle care over us, the

pains he took with us, we could not feel indifferent towards
pleasing him, or take pleasure in worrying him, a not un-
common thing among boys at school. Even those who, on
account of their extreme youthfulness or levity, sometimes
lost sight of their good resolutions of giving him no trouble,
generally came to him, expressing the deepest repentance,
begging him to forget their misconduct, and promising to
prove themselves less unworthy of his kindness in the
future."

We would be guilty of great injustice to his pupils if
we did not add to these testimonies of affection bestowed
upon him when living, the many subjoined since his
death. In reading the letters innumerable written on the
occasion, we perceive on every page evidences that the
affection dictating them was no ordinary one; it was more
than esteem, respect, devotion: it was veneration such as
one accords a saint he has known and loved on earth—a
veneration full of confidence and tenderness. To the joy
of speaking of this good Father and expressing a most
grateful remembrance of him is nearly always joined the
desire of bringing thus a modest flower to his crown of
praise, a grain of sand to the pious monument a fraternal
hand is striving to raise over him. And let us not omit
mention of the astonishing fact that several of these pupils of his, impelled to invoke him, have experienced the
happy effects of his intercession.

III.—Brother Charles as Sub-prefect.

1. *His zeal for his pupils.*—Every one at La Sauve
being struck by the reciprocal affection between Brother
Charles and his pupils, Father Maurin, who was prefect of
studies, believing this pleasant feeling might be rendered
conducive to the well-being of the whole house, asked of
the superiors that Brother Sire be appointed sub-prefect,

which request was the more readily granted, as his health, somewhat impaired by teaching, needed for its re-establishment a more active life. He received his nomination in the beginning of October 1855, just at the time of his annual retreat. To consider before God his new duties, imploring His assistance in the proper fulfilment of them, and to adopt means calculated to insure success therein, making good resolutions in this regard, were at once the most natural, important, and fruitful of his works during these days of recollection. The following is the line of conduct he traced out:

" 1. As regards my superiors. I will ever adhere strictly to authority, sustaining it under all circumstances, and frequently consulting those who are placed over me, especially in reference to my duties and studies, observing to the letter the regulations laid down for me and the advice given me by the Reverend Father Rector or the Reverend Prefect.

" 2. As regards my scholars. My manner towards them shall be uniformly dignified, gentle, and modest; and whilst striving to be ever kind and thoughtful, and ever preserving a cheerful countenance, I will, on the other hand, sedulously guard against all those familiarities forbidden by the rule, and which serve only to diminish authority. In recreation I will not avoid such scholars as are uncongenial to me; on the contrary, repulsing immediately any unfavorable thought regarding them, I will endeavor to show myself especially kind and considerate towards them.

" I will not only be very exact myself in keeping every point of the rule, punctual in obeying the first sound of the bell, but strive my utmost to have my scholars do the same. I shall pray much for them, and not recoil from meting out adequate punishment, when necessary, to such delinquents as fail to profit by the admonitions previously given them.

"3. As regards the Brothers. I will always be kind and gentle, particularly when my office obliges me to transmit to them disagreeable orders.

"4. As regards every one. I will faithfully follow the practice of St. John Berchmans—avoid the evil and imitate the good perceived in others.

"I will strive to be very circumspect in my behavior towards every one, more especially the music scholars and their teachers. There are some things naturally requiring secrecy, which secrecy I will guard inviolably, both as regards my confrères and the children. When I have to suffer anything, a reproach for example, I will not excuse myself, neither will I speak of it to another—such conduct would be unworthy of a religious.

"5. As regards myself. Activity, fervor, sacrifice; to live in the present, to be energetic in all things, *age quod agis;* to mercilessly eschew all reading prompted by mere curiosity.

"6. Finally, as regards God. Love, generosity, confidence. Without Thee, O my God, I can do nothing; with Thee, I can do all things. Should I fall, I will arise, saying, 'the Master is here,' *Dominus est.*

"I will make frequent visits to Our Lord, exposing to Him my needs; and in all my necessities I will have recourse only to Heaven and those divinely appointed to assist me, the spiritual Father, for example, the Reverend Father Rector, or the Father Minister. But especially will I address myself to Jesus, Mary, and Joseph, as well as to my good angel and the good angels of all with whom I have any transactions.

"I will read these resolutions and a chapter of observations on them, together with the instructions and rules of my office, at the beginning of each commentary, that is, every morning; and if needs be, I will consult the divers notes of my retreats, without waiting until the monthly retreat."

To understand all the wisdom of these resolutions and the merits of Brother Charles's fidelity thereto, a thorough acquaintance with the details of this office of sub-prefectship, which he filled for four years, would be necessary. In lieu of this (an impossibility) we present our readers the following extract from a letter to his mother, dated February 28, 1856, which will give us an insight into his many and various duties.

"I cannot, it seems, relieve your anxiety regarding my health, my dear mother, although I have told you times innumerable that you must not suppose I am sick because I do not write. If you do not believe me upon my word, and still remain incredulous and anxious, notwithstanding my assertions, what is the use of them? And, if you do believe me, why worry so when there is a longer interval than usual between my letters? I beg you to lay aside all these doubts and cares, for if I were sick I would not fail to let you know, and an indubitable proof of my being in good health is the fact that I am at my post of sub-prefect. To give you some idea of my daily employments, let me lay them before you in detail, thus satisfying, at the same time, your maternal yearnings to hear from your children, even those who have bid adieu to the world.

"*First of all, I am sub-prefect*, that is, I take the place of the Father Prefect, during his absence, everywhere and in all things, throughout the house, especially in maintaining discipline. This first duty begins when I arise in the morning, and ends only when I lie down at night, since it imposes upon me the office of second *vigilant* in the large dormitory, in an alcove of which I consequently sleep.

Secondly, I am præfectus atrii—vigilant over the corridors and courts. In this capacity, it is my business to accost every boy I see strolling around and ask him: ' Where are you going? Where have you been? What are you doing? Who gave you permission to be here?' and similar questions, that frequently bring to light a violation of the rules, which must be punished. As *præfectus atrii*, I must be always on the alert to see that silence is maintained at the appointed times, and all other stipulated regulations of the house observed.

" *Thirdly, I am prefect and vigilant of music.* This places me in charge of the music teachers and their scholars. I must select and announce to them the chants and music for the various feasts, both social and religious. I give the signal for the hours, or rather half-hours, allotted to the music lessons. The orchestra, band, and choir are also committed to my care, it devolving upon me to procure all the sheet music and instruments for these. This duty is one of my most fatiguing.

" *Fourthly, I am store-keeper*, that is, I must procure and sell to the scholars whatever they need in the way of paper, pens, games, and similar articles. In this, however, I have two trustworthy assistants, two of the larger scholars, who themselves sell these goods, sometimes in my presence, sometimes when I cannot be present.

" To these four principal duties add those innumerable little ones of the day, either fixed or arising from circumstances, which consume more time really than the above-mentioned, and you will have a fair idea of my occupations. Thus informed, you will excuse me, I know, for not writing oftener; you will also thank God for the duties He has given me in this house, and likewise rejoice with me that I have thus every facility for keeping up my health and strength, imparting energy to my character, and thereby fitting me to work later more efficaciously for God's glory and the salvation of souls."

We readily perceive from the tenor of this letter that of all Father Sire's offices at La Sauve the most onerous, difficult, and delicate, was that of sub-prefect. Without diminishing his close connection of the past with certain pupils, it brought him in contact with the whole school, and placed him in authority not only over a few who, by reason of their similarity of age and other circumstances, perhaps required usually the same mode of government, but also over youths of widely varying ages and the greatest diversity of disposition and character, thus necessitating a study of each, and consequent adaptation of his plans of discipline to their individual requirements, as he passed incessantly from one division to another—certainly, a most fatiguing and trying duty. His principal difficulty lay in his having to cope with the self-love, pride, and irascibility of the young men of rank, who could ill brook a check upon their will. Oh! what wonderful prudence, self-control, and tact must needs have been his in preserving his soul in peace under circumstances like these, and at the same time faithfully carrying out the rule.

" Yet," says one of the most distinguished of these scholars, Señor Ignacio de Lardizabal, of Irun, in Spain, " it may safely be said that this office of sub-prefect was that of which Father Charles acquitted himself best, with equal ardor and success watching over the observance of the rule and winning the affection of the scholars—at first thought two apparently contradictory things. The secret of this lay in his own excellent disposition, which herein proved a bond of union between two almost opposing interests. The subsequent experience of my college days has made me value him in this at his true worth, and appreciate the wonders he accomplished in this respect, for it did not strike me at the time.

" How many sub-prefects, both before and since then, have failed at this most difficult post, in spite of their good will, for it must be said that of all the duties constituting the organization of houses of the Society of Jesus there is none placing him who fills them in so disagreeable and annoying a relation to others as this—it is the vigilant eye from which escape were impossible; in proportion as you flee do its glances seem to penetrate still farther; Pascal could have said of it what he did of the Infinite.... Hence, to fill this post and be beloved by the pupils at the same time were to work a prodigy, and this Father Charles did."

" Yet his kindness and tenderness," adds M. Beaune, " possessed no element of weakness. Thanks to the salutary effects of obedience, he knew how to clothe his beneficence with that character of authority befitting it; and he who must needs be always on the alert throughout the college, watching whatever went on, detecting the least disorder to remedy it, and seeing that all was in harmony in the workings of this living machinery, once appointed to the duty of maintaining order in the house, most scrupulously fulfilled it.

" His manner, however, was not that rigid, forbidding one in which virtue frequently loves to appear, and which repels instead of attracting. No, it was clothed in amenity. Doubtless, it had its thorns as well as roses, but the thorns were for himself alone; those who were brought in contact with him perceived but the roses, that is, his tenderness and goodness. One was always sure of that gentle, amiable reception which made him forget the master, and see only the beloved friend. His kindness recalled to one a tender mother, to another, a good father, no longer on earth; and his counsels, sweet and wise, often brought back to the path of duty those who had strayed from it. Many and many a time did we say of him: 'Oh! how good Brother Sire is: we can never forget his kindness!'"[1] All the scholars, even those who had least to do with him, were impressed by his politeness, his unvarying kindness, and his angelic sweetness of temper.[2]

To these natural qualities, adding great weight to his authority, he joined the true zeal of an apostle. Like the Christian mother who caresses her child only to render it more docile to the corrections she is often obliged to give it, he insinuated himself into our hearts by all the ingenuities of love. A slight service gracefully rendered, a friendly smile, a word of praise, a kindly look, became with him so many instruments of zeal, wherewith he gained his pupils' hearts only to turn them to God. When once their affections were his, what pains did he not take to accomplish this latter object; what paternal admonitions and friendly exhortations, what reproaches, tender but firm! Nothing was spared; the most generous efforts, the most painful sacrifices seemed trifling to this heart so inflamed with charity and zeal.

"I can never forget," says Señor de Lardizabal, "the especial marks of esteem he lavished on me. Though apparently insignificant when related to others, they were very grateful to me at the time, and the memory is dear indeed. The relations existing between us, so cordial and warm, furnish another proof of that goodness one read in his face at a glance, for they were founded upon his compassion.

"On entering La Sauve I was quite young, nearly the only one of my nationality, and utterly ignorant of the language of my companions. I tell it reluctantly, but few of them seemed to feel for my situation, and, indeed, I

---

[1] M. Joseph Jacquemet.
[2] M. the Marquis Amédée du Lyon, of Mont de Marsan (Landes).

experienced from some vexations and annoyances, which their subsequent behavior however caused me to forget. Indulged and spoiled as I had been at home, even the warmest welcome from all at my new abode could scarcely have softened the rigors of the sudden transition from the family circle to college life. The Fathers evinced great interest in me and showed me many kindnesses; but of all persons none could have been more thoughtful and considerate of me than Father Charles. The sadness, melancholy I might say, which really took possession of me, owing to all this, naturally touched his sensitive heart. Divining how much I suffered, he promptly took measures for my relief, showing great and constant interest in me, protecting me more than once from the pranks of my little comrades, making efforts innumerable to divert my mind from the sad thoughts that oppressed it, striving to render the rule easier, and assisting me to follow my class in studies.

"Even later, when these first clouds were dispelled, I found him always disposed to grant me any privilege not opposed to scholastic discipline; although, being a true, sincere friend, having my real interests at heart, I often experienced the less agreeable but equally salutary effects of his friendship in the various admonitions, gentle or otherwise, the severe reproaches and even punishments he gave me, in his untiring efforts to correct my faults, which I remember with gratitude.

"And especially with the sweet memory of my First Communion is he associated in my heart. He took a great interest in it far in advance, showing me untiring attentions, which were redoubled as the time of the important event approached, in the happiness of which he shared largely, as he had certainly contributed much thereto. I was too young then to appreciate his cares at their real

worth, as I do now; and it is my regret never to have
expressed to him, during his life, the debt of gratitude so
justly his due. However, I have still left me the language
of prayer, the best of all, no doubt, which cannot but
reach him in heaven, whither he has gone."

Señor Lardizabal's experience of Father Charles's kindness was identical with that of many others, for the heart
and zeal of this holy religious were far from exclusive, every pupil, from the mere fact of being a member of the
household, having in his eyes the same claim upon his
solicitude and devotion; and his great desire was to make
every one in the college happy.

. His duty placing him in the midst of the pupils, he
never lost sight of them for an instant; in the dormitory,
the chapel, the refectory, the corridors and passages, during their recreations and walks, his eye was ever on them,
kind and watchful like that of a tender mother following
the little child to protect it from harm.

"And how many dangers," says one of these children,
"did not his wise vigilance ward off from his charges,
the commission of how many faults did it not prevent, even
on occasions the most likely to lead us astray: for instance,
on grand holidays, when we all went out to enjoy ourselves, our youthful natures bubbling over with exuberant
spirits, what was it but his gentle solicitude, acting as a
salutary check, that restrained us within bounds and forbade our participation in those disorderly outbursts, not
unfrequently ending in disobedience and accident or dis-
aster of some sort?"

We must say that his tenderness and devotion for his
scholars was boundless, and even among the Jesuit Fathers,
where such is proverbial, it could not but be remarked.

Says M. Ernest Lafond, of Bayonne, Basses-Pyrénées,
now a doctor of medicine, formerly a student in a hos-

pital of Paris : " I was very young at the period of my
entrance into La Sauve; indeed, I was scarcely thirteen
when I left there; consequently, my acquaintance with the
excellent Father Sire was at an age when impressions are
not deeply graven in the heart and very soon effaced, especially if one's surroundings are completely changed.   In
leaving La Sauve, I entered the Lyceum in Paris, where I
spent four years, and I can say with truth that, notwithstanding the fickleness and thoughtlessness of youth, many
and many a time did my thoughts turn gratefully towards
this holy religious, whose innumerable kindnesses have
made his memory imperishable and dear.

" He was not an ordinary man, who complied with the
strict requirements of duty, but who went no farther.   Each
one of us felt that he had in him not only a teacher, a vigilant over his conduct and manners, but a veritable father,
protecting and encouraging him by the most affectionate
counsels—counsels which his experience and profound
knowledge of the human heart rendered salutary and
precious.

· " His affection and kindness to me have left a deep and
lasting impression, abiding with me for the good of my
soul.   How often did he not come to console me when I
was smarting under some merited and perhaps grave punishment! How often did not his feeling heart show its
kindly interest in me by words of gentle counsel!

It was not by punishment he endeavored to bring his
scholars to repentance and acknowledgment of some fault
they had committed.   No, he used means nobler and
more worthy of him.   Taking the culprit aside, he strove
by gentle, affectionate words to make him realize the gravity, greater or less as it might be, of his offence—a most
effectual method indeed, for none left his presence on
these occasions but with softened and thoroughly solaced

hearts, his truly paternal admonition making a deeper impression than the severest punishment he could have inflicted. He certainly possessed, in the highest degree, the inestimable gift of knowing how to admonish or encourage children, and of instilling into them the love of virtue and duty.

"His disposition was cheerful; there was always a smile upon his countenance, and never for an instant did his amiability forsake him. And thus it was he gained the affection of his pupils, who all loved him not only as the earnest, austere religious, but also as the enlightened professor, the good, kind vigilant and prefect. Of all the priests I have known, none have ever made such an impression upon me, and I can never forget him."

The above testimonies, and others of a similar nature, which we have received from many of the former pupils of La Sauve, prove not only how much Father Charles loved and edified those under his charge, doing everything in his power to make them happy, but also the good he did their souls, aiding them to correct their faults and to form themselves, even at this early age, to the character and habits of a true Christian life. We regret that the limits of this biography do not permit us to dwell longer upon a point so interesting.

2. *His zeal and success with strangers.* The apostolic zeal consuming Father Charles embraced not only his scholars, but also their parents, the employees and servants of the house, the assistant teachers of music, drawing, and painting, indeed, all with whom his duties of sub-prefect brought him in contact, and these were many.

He it was who ordinarily received the scholars' parents at the re-opening of school, and conducted them to the Father Prefect or Father Minister, doing them the honors of the house, and, in their presence, installing their children in the dormitory, the refectory, or even amidst their companions at recreation ; he would welcome them in the parlor on feast days, at the distribution of prizes, and at the academic exhibitions, and assign them their places in the hall. Frequently, too, he saw them in their houses, for instance, when he went to bring the pupils back to college at the re-opening of school, or conducted them home on holidays or for the vacations. And under all these circumstances his affability, gentleness, politeness, but more especially his simplicity, modesty, and piety, struck every one.

"Of the many Jesuits I have known and esteemed," said, one day, a mother whose child was under his care, " none have pleased me like Father Sire. Kind, simple, frank, and courteous, he was indeed most estimable." " All my children," adds M. Dupuy of Bordeaux, " sound his praises, and their affection for him was truly extraordinary. When they spoke of him, which was frequently, it was always as the *good Father Sire* or simply the *good Father*. As for myself, who often saw him and even accompanied him several times from La Sauve to Créon, as he was taking the scholars out walking, I can say without the least exaggeration that he always impressed me most favorably, and that the moments spent in his society were delightful ones."

And the experience of other parents whose children were in his care coincides with this; likewise does that of persons who merely saw him casually. Grateful for his kindness to their children, they could not forbear admiring, esteeming, and praising him. " What a most estimable person this Father is! " they would exclaim; " he is a saint. Are all the others like him? " They were delighted to seek him out and converse with him, were it only for a few moments; and on such days as afforded them the oppor-

tunity of doing so, they were eager and proud to offer him
hospitality. Some even went so far as to press him to spend
the vacation with them, urging it upon the plea of the improvement such change would be to his health, and telling
him they would remove all difficulties by obtaining the
Rev. Father Rector's consent thereto. Finding their entreaties useless, they consoled themselves by writing him
letters expressive of their veneration and gratitude, every
line of which bears testimony of the writers' sincerity.

The idea many of them entertained of his sanctity was
such as to cause them to preserve as relics any letters received from him, and deposit them in the family archives, a
precious heritage, henceforth inalienable.[1] After his death,
there were requests innumerable for even the most trifling
objects that had belonged to him, which, when obtained,
were guarded with religious care. Many, too, invoke his
intercession, believing that in him they have for themselves
and their children a powerful protector, a devoted patron,
not unmindful of their interests. The following was written August 25, 1864, to a brother of Father Charles, by one
of these parents:

" Reverend Father, desiring to add our tribute of honor
to the memory of your worthy and venerable brother, the
Rev. Father Charles Sire, we write to express the great
satisfaction and pleasure his friendship (prized indeed by
us as that of a heart rare in its goodness) afforded us during the three or four years we were so situated as to be
brought in contact with him occasionally.

" Madame Laumond and I made his acquaintance during
a short stay at La Sauve, near our young Antony, who was,
at that time, under your honored and estimable brother's

---

[1] The most of these families dwell in the Departments of the Lot-et-Garonne, the
Gironde, the Basses-Pyrénées, the Charente-Inférieure, and the Landes. Some of
them, however, belong to Spain.

gentle care. From the very first, our relations were the most friendly and cordial. We eagerly cultivated his society: his heavenly countenance, his pure heart, his delicacy of manner, all rendered him unusually attractive, and made the shortest conversation with him linger in one's memory, redolent with the odor of spiritual good.

"We have in our possession two autograph letters of his which we highly prize. They were written to our child, and we ourselves have no inconsiderable share in the sentiments of kindly feeling their pages contain. Their wise counsels to our son were invaluable. And here, Monsieur, let me remark how struck we were by the charms of their style: so simple, clear, pure, the beauty and delicacy of the sentiments therein expressed—sentiments always directed towards the same end—justice, virtue, and the fear of God.

"These two manuscripts, which we venerate by so many titles, will pass from our hands into those of our child, with the pious recommendation—our earnest request, indeed—that they be religiously preserved in the family as two monuments of the affection of your venerable brother, through whose intercession we may hope to obtain from the thrice-holy God remission of our sins and the grace of receiving from the abyss of His mercies that eternal felicity for which we were created.

"We henceforth associate ourselves with all those innumerable pious persons who, like ourselves, convinced of this good Father's eminent sanctity, invoke him in their prayers, believing that thus their petitions will be so much the more powerful with God, by reason of the recompense bestowed upon that pious, beautiful, and perfect soul."

Next to the scholars and their parents, those who shared his more important services at La Sauve, and testified the most affection and gratitude for him, were the music teachers. Being prefect of music, everything relating to this branch of studies was under his charge: it was his duty to arrange and organize the orchestra, the band, the choir; preside over the rehearsals and note all that occurred; receive the superiors' complaints and transmit their orders; listen to the professors' requests, moderate, when necessary, their desires, and soothe their vexations; watch also over the pupils, to weigh their faults, and punish their caprices.

If we consider that nearly all these rehearsals of music are especial occasions, on which the scholars are privileged to talk, and that the professors themselves are never allowed to punish them, we can readily form some idea as to what Father Charles's services must have been to these latter, how invaluable his gentleness, firmness, prudence, charity, and especially his spirit of order and peace! What murmurs and rebellious outbursts he stifled during these three years! What scowling looks were dissipated, what disrespectful or hasty replies were daily arrested by those wise counsels his good sense, piety, and affection ever suggested! For these gentlemen, the music teachers, he was never a master, but instead, a friend, a counsellor, a protector.

Hence their feelings towards him were those of respect and veneration. Whilst he lived they praised and extolled him; and when death cut him off in the flower of youth they shed tears over his memory. Many and touching indeed are the tributes of affection they bring to this simple monument erected to his virtues. "I cannot speak of him without tears," said the leader of the orchestra, M. Bader; "never can I forget his goodness, his gentleness, his many acts of kindness to me. Excuse me for not being able to say more, the news of his death is such a shock to me."

"Ah! what a good Father he was!" said another professor of the same college of La Sauve; "what a good

Father he was! He was kindness and gentleness itself.
I could say nothing of him but to his praise. Oh! I loved
him as if he had been my brother; and how kind he was
to me, always receiving me with a smile when I arrived at
the college, or, at the end of my classes, consoling and
encouraging me amidst the multitudinous vexations and
annoyances inseparable from my duties, with all the solicitude and interest of the best of friends. If I was sick,
he visited me, and at his departure from La Sauve he embraced me cordially and expressed the regret he felt at the
parting.

"My mother loved him also, although she had seen
him but once.   When she learns from my lips what took
place at his death, and what has passed since in connection with his glorious transition, oh ! how confidently will
she not pray to him! I have but one letter from him, and
that on business; nevertheless, I shall lay it reverently aside
as a precious relic, to be guarded with religious care. I am
truly happy to know how God has honored him!" With
these last words, the speaker wiped away the big tears that
filled his eyes.

The following touching scene took place on the road from
Bordeaux to La Sauve.   Two brothers of Father Charles,
M. Vital and M. Césaire, ' journeying thither in company
with M. de Krévenkeuil, one of them offered him a picture
of Father Charles. "Oh! how I thank you," he exclaimed, "I am delighted to possess such a memento, but,
if you do not object, I would prefer receiving it at La
Sauve, on the very spot where I saw that good Father for
the first time."

---

¹ M. Césaire is the youngest of these brothers. Having been three years a scholar
of Father Charles at La Sauve, he was pleased to accompany M. Vital thither in
1864, and point out to him the scenes of the various incidents herein related of
Father Charles whilst there. M. Césaire is now a Sulpician and professor of theology at the Theological Seminary of Puy-en-Velay.

Reaching the village, the three gentlemen directed their steps towards the college, and scarcely had they crossed the threshold when M. de Krévenkeuil, throwing himself into the arms of M. Vital, said with emotion, "Here it is, Reverend Father; permit me to embrace you, for in doing so here I can imagine that I see and embrace Father Charles." He immediately turned aside to hide his feelings, and disappeared, wiping away the tears.

After this scene, so consoling, what new sources of emotion awaited M. Vital and M. Césaire within the portals of the college! Every step they took, every person they met, gave them reason to believe that Father Charles had left there a memory imperishable. Workmen, tradesmen, servants—*all* spoke of him with a spontaneous enthusiasm and love that was most gratifying to hear.

"Oh! yes, that is he! how like him!" exclaimed an old servant, to whom they showed his picture. "It is the good Father who loved us servants so much, and who used to preach to us! I can assure you, he told us many beautiful things." "When he taught us catechism," continued another servant, "he spoke to us of God in such a manner that we were charmed. I remember his one day filling us with admiration and wonder at God's grandeur and power, by telling us of the inconceivable distances between the earth, the sun, the moon, the stars, etc."

The pastor of the parish, M. Daverat, happening to be at the college whilst these gentlemen were there, said to them: "Oh! how blessed you are in having had such a good brother! I knew him here for four years, that is, during the period of his sub-prefectship, and I can say in all sincerity that of the many religious I have seen at the college he it was I loved best, and whose departure I regretted most. Moreover, every one who knew him at La Sauve (and his office brought him in contact with many) esteemed him. His goodness, his affability, his gentleness, attracted all hearts to him. One was happy to see and converse with him. Many a misunderstanding with his confrères have I been spared through his mediation."

One of the business men employed by the Jesuit Fathers at La Sauve, having learned that two of Father Charles's brothers were in the college, hastened to seek them. Going confidently up to them, he said : "And you are brothers of Father Charles! Ah, you are happy to have had such a brother. He was such a good, holy religious, it would be impossible to find another man as pious and amiable as he was ! For a time he filled the position of spiritual Father to the poor, a work of charity for which he was admirably fitted, acquitting himself of it with fidelity and zeal. His words, his very expression, his smile, all told them how great a share they had in his love and esteem, and that it was his happiness to assist them. He never betrayed the least weariness or annoyance at their presence, but was invariably kind, beneficent, gracious; no wonder the poor loved and praised him as they did.

"When he left La Sauve, every one regretted it, for it could be said of him as of Our Lord that 'he went about doing good.'"

CHAPTER VII.

FATHER CHARLES'S SCHOLASTICATE AT VALS, NEAR PUY-EN-VELAY.

AFTER the seven years of regency we have just glanced over, Charles was sent by his superiors to the house at Vals, there to finish his ecclesiastical studies and to prepare for ordination. September 12, 1859, receiving his orders to set out, and to go by way of Saint-Jory, on the following day he turned his face homewards; and after a few days in the bosom of his family, proceeded towards Puy, taking the route and complying with all the directions marked out for him by his superiors. Several incidents worthy of note that occurred during this journey, we will relate in a more extended Life [1] of him.

The vacation at Vals not yet being ended when Charles arrived, he profited by these few days of repose Divine Providence accorded him in striving to invigorate his health, also in visiting Our Lady of Puy, that through her intercession the most abundant blessings of Heaven might descend upon his scholasticate.

Too mistrustful of self to rely entirely upon his own prayers, he begged his parents and friends to unite with him in invoking the Blessed Virgin's assistance. "Often visit Our Lady of Good News," is his request to one of his brothers, "and ask her to obtain for me intelligence, judgment, memory, together with the greatest taste and aptitude

---

[1] The religious side of Father Charles's life at La Sauve and Vals is the most abridged of any portion of the present Biography.

for my theological studies, especially during this first year;
also, unbounded generosity in her Divine Son's service, and
a renewal of fervor, that I may profit by the many shining
examples of virtue in this house."

This request was frequently repeated, and when writing
to the younger brother, who then was in Toulouse, he
urged him to entreat Our Lady of Good News to bestow
upon him the spirit of a perfect scholastic of the Society
of Jesus.   He likewise made the same request of Catherine
and of his parents, but more especially did he address himself on this point to his brothers who were already priests.
"Ah! if I were now like you a priest, and could offer daily
on our altars (it was thus he wrote to M. Dominique, professor at the Sulpician Seminary in Paris) that holy Victim
priceless and all-powerful, what weight would not my petitions have before Heaven!   But, alas! such happiness
for me is far in the future, and whilst awaiting it, my
voice is feeble, my prayers inefficacious.   Let me therefore conjure you, Dominique, also Marcel and Vital, to
make use of your power in my behalf and that of all who
are dear to you.   Recommend especially to Our Lady of
Victory my first year of theology, that, if it please God,
I may pursue these studies with ease, relish, and success."

Striving earnestly to touch God's heart by every means
in his power, Charles asked his brothers to let him know
the exact hour at which they were accustomed to celebrate
Mass, that every morning he might unite with them in
supplicating this good Master to enrich his soul, through
the merits of Jesus Christ and the all-powerful prayers of
the Church, with that abundance of graces he so desired.
Thus imploring God's help, the pious scholastic had but
one desire, that of corresponding to it, and the following
pages prove his fidelity in doing so.

I.--His Zeal in the Acquisition of the Ecclesiastical Sciences.

The first object engrossing his attention was his studies. Says Father Bascourret, who had been his professor of philosophy the preceding year: "Without having what is usually termed quickness and clearness of perception, or even a very ardent love of knowledge, Father Charles was capable of success in the more serious studies, and he had really an especial aptness for philosophy and theology, by reason of his sound judgment, good memory, and truly practical mind, which never sacrificed the main object to what is merely accessory, nor sought to entangle itself in systems. Yet, to attain this success, effort was necessary, and innumerable were the obstacles to energetic and continuous study on his part."

"Mental labor," so he expresses himself to the Reverend Father Rector, in his accounts of conscience at Vals, "has always been wearisome and fatiguing to me, so that I cannot apply myself seriously, any length of time, without feeling it. It is thus especially in the evenings, when I find I have little relish for Dogmas and Hebrew. During the winter, I suffered from cold, headaches, and, for several days, from violent palpitation of the heart, and in Lent it was the same. Add to these obstacles the difficulty I have with Latin, my deficiency in the philosophy course,[1] a lack of clearness in the lessons of one professor, of precision in another, the weariness and fatigue consequent upon a perusal of the class notes, some of them rather puzzling, and you will have an idea of what efforts and sacrifices study costs me.

"However, I am content, and my general health is good, thanks to my endeavors to avoid all unnecessary exposure of it, and my not imposing too many privations upon my-

---

[1] Seven years devoted to duties incompatible with application to serious studies rendered the first labors of the scholasticate most arduous to Charles.

self at meals, or neglecting my usual walks. I feel that it is an imperative duty for me to labor assiduously if I wish to be a useful member of the society."

To stimulate himself to this, Father Charles noted down in a little book, and read over daily, the various thoughts with which he was most deeply impressed on the subject, and the motives urging him to renewed efforts and perseverance in his studies, which motives nearly all referred to God's glory, the honor of the society, and the good of souls.

"Why, Charles," he writes therein, "did you come to religion? Why make the sacrifice of honors, pleasures, riches? Was it not to procure God's glory and the salvation of souls, to prepare for the priesthood and the apostolate, to do penance for your sins, to imitate Our Lord, to render yourself useful to the society, at least to protect its honor, especially in the eyes of the brethren?....And is not study, the study of the ecclesiastical sciences, one of the most effectual means of accomplishing this end so desirable? And when, therefore, you have such facilities for study as are now yours in the agreeable position wherein it has pleased God to place you, should you not form yourself to habits of study?....Do not your age and almost total lack of resources for the pulpit and the confessional urge you to continuous, unremitting study?

"What was Our Lord doing at the early age of twelve years? Increasing in knowledge and wisdom, He interrogated the Doctors in the Temple, listening to their answers and profiting by all they said—behold the model for the scholastic. Following His example, let me avail myself of every opportunity of instruction, endeavoring during these two years to make up the deficiency in my theological studies. Let me live in my cell, leaving it only when duty compels me, and ever returning to it with pleasure. Let me also accustom myself never to lose a momemt, and to cultivate carefully a love for study, but study of a grave, religious nature. Energetic in action, mindful of brevity in what I write, I will studiously prepare my allotted tasks, observing perfect order in all I do, and scrupulously adhering to the rule marked out for me and approved by my superiors."

These resolutions once made, Brother Charles kept them faithfully; " so faithfully," says one of the Fathers of Vals, " that during the two years I passed with him in the scholasticate he proved himself there as hard a student as he had been at La Sauve a diligent professor and devoted vigilant."

Convinced that a young student, to prepare himself worthily for the priesthood, must work seriously to attain perfection, at least as far as is compatible with human weakness, he endeavored to adorn his mind with all those human sciences that not unfrequently help a priest to win hearts to God, by attracting to himself the respect, esteem, and affection even of those who do not practise virtue.

Hence, not satisfied with pursuing those studies marked out for him in common with his brethren—Dogmatic and Moral Theology, the Holy Scriptures, Canon Law, the Sacred Liturgy, Church History, the art of preaching and catechising, Greek and Hebrew, he added some others, not of obligation, but which, forming the complement of those already mentioned, filled his mind with an agreeable fund of varied information. It was a maxim with him to neglect nothing, but to value all the gifts of the Lord according to these words of the Holy Spirit: *Particula boni doni non te prætereat.* [1] Hence, he appropriated mentally all that he heard or read in the house; nothing escaped his attention, not even things the most indifferent apparently,

---

[1] " Let not the part of a good gift overpass thee."—Ecclus. xiv. 14.

as Reviews, Annals, and those pamphlets innumerable·
which seldom claim more than a glance or a cursory perusal.

During his sójourn at La Sauve, he had collected from
publications of this sort a fund of edifying anecdotes,
which he was accustomed to relate during catechism class,
recreation, or when out walking. Continuing this work at
Vals, his journal and note books there were filled with
most valuable and beautiful extracts and anecdotes from
the contemporary Annals of the Society of Jesus, from
other of their annual publications, and even from the private letters to himself from his superiors and confrères—
all which matter of instruction he had carefully classified
and arranged.

" He was so well posted as regards the rules of the society," says one of his room-mates, " that every few moments some one was knocking at the cell to make inquiries
of him. He would always answer them pleasantly and without the least sign of impatience, but likewise as briefly as
possible."

" If any of us," says the Reverend Father Rouquayrol,
"wished to recall some point of our regulations we remembered but indistinctly, we were accustomed to say, Brother
Sire can tell us that, he knows; and seldom was he referred
to in vain, his memory or notes being rarely at fault.   To
understand to what lengths the true, zealous aspirant to
the priesthood could go in his love for work, employment
of his time, and his ardent desire of thus advancing by the
acquisition of knowledge God's glory and the salvation of
souls, one needs but look over his note books."

II.—His Zeal in Acquiring Priestly Holiness.

Another most important object engrossing Father
Charles's attention during the scholasticate was the ac-

quiring of the especial holiness of his state of life. Christian sanctity he already possessed in an eminent degree, for according to the testimony of his brethren, his heart was still that of a little child, and he was even ignorant of anything that could tarnish his purity, although now thirty-one years of age. Says one of them: "He often astonished us by his innocent questions. Sometimes he spoke of his conversion, which took place when he was very young, and of the great crime which had preceded it, a crime well known to us all, and which we relate in his own words : ' One day our neighbor's hens,' said he, ' having come into our garden to scratch and ravage as usual, I threw a stone at them, and killed one ! ' This hen had quite a reputation among us, for we heard of her whenever the good religious accused himself of the greatest sins of his life."

He also possessed religious sanctity, since his superiors and brethren declare him to have been, during the whole of his novitiate, one of their most fervent and edifying members; and, moreover, according to his own written words, he had ever aspired to the most perfect.

As to sacerdotal sanctity, which consists in the daily and hourly immolation of self for God and souls, or, at least, the desire to keep one's self in these dispositions, Charles did not wait until his ordination ere striving to attain it. Sacerdotal zeal, say his friends, was always one of his distinguishing characteristics. "I first knew him," says Father Maupomé, "at the period of his entrance into Polignan, where I lived with him on terms of the closest intimacy for some years, and during all that time never did I hear or see words or acts of his not stamped with the imprint of Christian virtue, later, of religious virtue, and always, after his fourth year, of zeal for God's glory and the salvation of souls."

Nevertheless, on beginning his scholasticate, he seemed to feel the need of laboring yet more diligently in order to acquire the sanctity of the priesthood, thus to increase his usefulness in the exalted sphere of duty to which God had called him. " Yesterday evening," one reads in his notes of the first retreat he made at Vals, " yesterday evening, during recreation and the visit, I shed tears, in thinking of my coldness for the God of love, and the sterility of my life, and I made the resolution of giving myself to Him unreservedly. ' Wherefore,' I questioned my soul, ' did you come to religion ? wherefore make the sacrifice of all things? Was it not to progress daily in priestly virtues, to labor seriously at your own perfection, and spare yourself nothing in laboring for the salvation of others? And is not zeal the instrument with which we accomplish this?'

" Hence, let me strive to become a saint, with this intent practising, at first, almost continual interior mortification; let me fight incessantly against my nature, trying to overcome myself in all things, even the most difficult, doing, if needs be, what is most trying and repugnant to me. Let me renounce all affections, even the most legitimate, if I perceive they are too strong. Far from extending my worldly intercourse, let me, on the contrary, seek to diminish it, occupying myself much less than formerly with the exterior affairs of the college. Let me go still farther, and to make continual and wondrous progress in virtue, let me sanctify every moment, every action, living more in the supernatural. All that displeases me in others I will avoid; all that I see good in them I will imitate. Especially will I apply myself to the practice of the solid virtues: humility, charity, obedience, and perfect modesty, thus contracting habits befitting the priesthood, and most useful to me therein. Should my courage begin to fail, I will excite myself to fervor by these words of the good Master: ' It is I, fear not.' '

" God's glory and the salvation of souls being henceforth the sole end of my efforts, I will endeavor to exert my apostolate everywhere, and principally through my letters and conversations. As one must be very edifying himself to inspire others with the love of virtue and goodness, I will strive to give good example, avoiding anything that might scandalize in the least, such as speaking of myself or my relations. With the same intention, I will watch over my actions, even the most trifling apparently; for example, I will avoid crossing my feet and legs, I will observe silence strictly, and practise to the letter all the advice given me from whatever authorized source it come, or of how little value it seem. What is commanded signifies not, when the order emanates from God, and the result tends to His glory and our neighbor's salvation."

Charles proved so faithful to these resolutions that his regularity in the house became almost proverbial. He says himself, in his accounts of conscience at Vals, that his love and esteem for the rule were such as left nothing to be desired on that point; that obedience for him was difficult only inasmuch as the things commanded were difficult of execution or painful to nature, and that the one desire of his heart was to be obedient, doing in all things the will of God.

"So efficacious was this desire," says Father Cros, " that during the whole time we were room-mates not once did I perceive him violate the least article of the rule. Never did the second sound of the bell in the morning find him in bed; never did he break silence unnecessarily; and never, when any one came to the door to make some inquiry of him, did he utter four words if

' " Ego sum, noli timere." —St. Luke xxiv. 36.

two would answer. His regularity was such that at the same hour, every day, he varied the subject of his studies. I was with him but a short time, scarcely a month, ere constrained to notice his scrupulous exactness in these matters, which edified me much, and notably increased the esteem and veneration in which I already held him."

These sentiments were shared by all the Fathers and Brothers in the house who had been any length of time with him. "When Father Charles left the scholasticate," says one of them, "to go to Bourbon, everybody at Vals felt convinced that France had sustained a great loss in his departure; and I frequently heard it said that he was ripe for heaven, and would not be long on his mission ere receiving the palm of martyrdom."

The following was written four years subsequently by a former Brother of Vals, who now holds an important position in the library at Paris: "All that I hear of Father Charles rejoices my heart, but does not astonish me. He was, without exception, one of the most amiable and edifying religious I ever knew, and he is enshrined in my memory amid a halo of charms, such as seldom radiates from any but the saints—charms that grow brighter the more I think about him. Oh! what candor, what simplicity were his, what tender piety, what practical love of the rule! Eight years after he had left the novitiate, I saw him at Vals, his exterior perfection, even then, being that of the most enlightened of novices—which is saying everything, men of experience knowing well that this is a mark which seldom deceives. As for myself, I can assure you that no one ever impressed me more, even though in the midst of subjects of edification. His earthly career was short, but full of good works, for he accomplished much in a brief span, and I doubt not the imperishable beauty of his crown."

In his scrupulous observance of the rule, Father Charles had but one desire—that every act of his tend to God's glory and his brethren's salvation. Thus regular to please God, he was edifying to benefit his brethren, avoiding in his regularity whatever might wound or annoy them, and striving to clothe his obedience with that gentleness, simplicity, modesty, and charity which renders it attractive.

There was nothing forced or strained in his actions; and it might have been said that observance of the rule came natural to him, so serene and cheerful was his countenance, so joyous his manner. It was evident that, far from pressing heavily upon him, the yoke of obedience was to him sweet and light. Making himself agreeable to all, he attracted his companions, who in recreation sought his society, thronging around him, but with the veneration and love accorded a saint. The more he endeavored to escape their notice and testimonies of fondness for him, the more attracted to him were they, even as one seeks the humble, hidden violet, whose perfume betrays its presence.

" To comprehend his sanctity," says Father Candeloup, " his zeal for God's glory and the salvation of souls, one needs only to have observed his regularity in the minutest details of his scholastic life. In the refectory, in class, in recreations, and during the promenades, even in the corridors and when taking part in the debates—everywhere and under all circumstances, was he edifying. His modesty was so perfect, his piety so amiable, that one could but admire them.

" Yes, even in his room," adds Father Clavé, " he edified by his bearing, his mortification, his charity. For some time I occupied the same cell with him. It was in the depths of winter, and we felt the cold most keenly, as our room was not only a northern exposure but there was no way of heating it.

" Charles left the best place for me, taking himself that between the door and the window, and trying to protect himself from the draught (that he could not but feel) by wrapping a coverlid around him. Perceiving at length that I was uncomfortable, he immediately informed the superiors of it, and to him am I indebted for my having been removed to another cell. As for himself, he appeared satisfied, and remained there the whole winter, without a word of complaint, although he must have suffered bitterly from the cold.

" It was whilst we were together in this cell he gave me the most touching example of mortification and piety. Never, in my presence, did he allow himself a position in the least undignified or careless. His bearing was ever modest and religious. One felt that he worked always under the eye of God, lived in His presence, and sought above all things to please Him. His piety was tender and ardent, and often in prayer his humid eyes and radiant face revealed the fires of charity burning in his heart. This life, all hidden in God, I feel sure, was most agreeable to the good Master, and though not so brilliant before the world as many others, I doubt not that it has already received in heaven a magnificent recompense."

To procure the two ends he had ever in view, God's glory and the salvation of souls—ends most dear to him, and really bound up with his existence, Father Charles did not rest content with merely edifying his brethren by his good conduct and truly Christian demeanor. No, to the apostolate of example he added that of the word. "That I may meet in heaven those I love," said he, "I must ever strive to turn them towards piety and perfection, especially by pious conversations." Hence he went to recreation with the determination to make it spiritually as profitable as possible to his confrères. If it happened that the companions assigned him by Providence were, like himself, interested in subjects of piety, his apostolic heart would dilate immediately, his face brighten, and the fire of divine love that inflamed him would reveal itself both in his person and words. Quickened and warmed by his zeal, each one of them, as did the disciples of Emmaus, would say when he left them: " Was not our heart burning within us whilst he spoke in the way ? " [1]

But if these first words fell upon souls that returned no responsive echo, he immediately changed the subject, or accommodated himself to his confrères' desires by lending a most attentive ear to what seemed more interesting to them, and this without betraying the least sign of emotion—so much was he master of himself. His expression, always open and amiable, his pleasant smile, and the respectful consideration he cordially gave his interlocutor on these occasions, proved conclusively his perfect self-renunciation and the charity that animated him. Moreover, he never interrupted a conversation; and if (as sometimes happened, although rarely) obliged to contradict what was said, he did so in the gentlest, most amiable manner, or at least (no matter what the circumstances) without contention or anger.

In his intercourse with his confrères he sought only their good, their pleasure; when he could not accomplish the former directly by holy words, he would divert their minds and send a glow of happiness through their hearts by his innocent and fraternal gayety. " How often," says one of them. " was I not indebted to him for the enjoyment of my recreations, for, when spent in his com-

---

[1] *Nonne cor nostrum ardens erat in nobis dum loqueretur in via ?*—St. Luke xxiv. 32.—Testimony of several Jesuit Fathers, but more especially of Father Blanchard, the friend of his childhood.

pany, never did I leave him but with renewed cheerfulness and elasticity of spirits."

He was always careful to avoid any subject that might be painful to his companions or embarrassing, much less disedifying or calculated to make them relaxed in discipline. On the contrary, his conversations tended to bring them nearer God and His holy Mother, to attach them more strongly to the Church and her teachings, to the Constitutions and Rules of the Society of Jesus, its spirit, works, and especially its members. Seldom did one quit his company without feeling improved spiritually, or at least without taking the resolution of being more closely united to God.

The good he accomplished at Vals by his words was considerable, yet that which he realized through prayer was far greater. He says himself, in his accounts of conscience, that, although he had not yet been initiated into zeal for God's glory and the salvation of souls, yet it was already sufficiently intense to devour his heart, and to manifest itself in his soul by fervent prayers, most ardent desires, and the habitual offering of his actions. Heretofore he had doubtless prayed much, as we have said elsewhere, but for himself, his friends, his relatives, and pupils; at Vals he forgot himself, as it were, and thought only of his neighbor.

After the example of St. Teresa, who, it is said, converted nearly as many by her prayers as St. Francis Xavier by his apostolic labors, of innumerable fervent religious communities, whom zeal for God's glory and their neighbor's salvation hold ever suppliant in His presence at the foot of the altar, and especially of Our Lord Jesus Christ, of the Blessed Virgin, and St. Joseph, whose lives were one unceasing prayer, he made of this exercise a veritable apostolate, extending over the world. The missions of Asia, Africa, America, Oceanica—to none of them was he indifferent, and in addition to the prayers in usage among the members of the " Propagation of the Faith" he added especial ones for the conversion of the infidel. He was also associated with a number of pious souls in imploring God to raise up fervent missionaries, and after his death the practices of this association were found among his favorite prayers.

The schismatics of the East, the heretics of the West, and all those misguided Christians of our own country whom error holds enthralled, afar from the bosom of the true Church, were in his eyes brethren in Jesus Christ, and as such having a strong claim upon his affections; hence, the cordiality, the eagerness with which he united himself to those fervent Catholics of the present day, who earnestly implore of Heaven the return of Russia and England to the centre of unity.

But the especial subjects of his prayers were those modern persecutors of the Church, those implacable enemies of the temporal power, those obstinate calumniators of her institutions and her Supreme Head, those unhappy, short-sighted Catholics of France, who, seduced by an anti-religious press, rush ignorantly into the paths of error and rebellion. Though abhorring their doctrines and branding their actions with their true stamp, he cherished their persons, and after the example of the generous, holy Pontiff so wisely governing the Church, he yearned for their conversion, and earnestly besought it of God in prayer—fervent, unremitting prayer.

" Let us unite ourselves," he writes to his parents, " let us unite ourselves with the Sovereign Pontiff, supplicating the Lord to console His Church, and take pity on France—this France, where one beholds the sad spectacle of the deepest miseries side by side with the noblest virtues." Writing afterwards to his brother in Paris, he says:

"Upon what evil days are we not fallen, my dear Dominique! Let us pray the Lord to roll away the dark clouds from the sky of our future. And let us, in praying thus, at the beginning of the year, for the various members of our family, beg the same blessed boon for France, for the Church, and her worthy head, the august and venerated Pius IX. I endorse and extol your happy thought with which you acquainted me, of the little pleasure you are preparing for him, in the offering of the last work undertaken by you."[1]

In nearly all his letters there is some reference to this idea, and during the last three years of his life he made the tranquillity of France and the triumph of the Church the continual subject of his prayers, offering to God for this intention all his daily actions, the Masses he heard, the chaplets he recited, his Communions, his visits to the Blessed Sacrament, his studies, and more especially his works of penance and charity.

On reading over the collection of his prayers one is astonished at the fecundity of his zeal and the purity of his intentions. In this collection he has marked out in order all whom he recommends to God, and the especial works he offers for them—his superiors and equals, both spiritual and temporal; his friends and benefactors, living or dead, those especially who were or who had been united to him by more than ordinary bonds, such as his confessors and directors; all the religious communities and those in charge of them; the clergy, secular and regular; the bishops, more particularly the Sovereign Pontiff; then, in the temporal order, the head of the State, its ministers and magistrates, dispensers of justice; the soldiers both of the

---

[1] Father Charles here alludes to the translation, into every known language and idiom, of the Bull *Ineffabilis*, in which His Holiness, Pope Pius IX., proclaims as an article of Faith the dogma of the Immaculate Conception of the Blessed Virgin.

army and the navy, protectors of order and of the country—
in fine, all who govern or who have any charge over us
were the objects of his solicitude and prayers. And these
supplications, to which he was impelled by duty, gratitude,
and love, were habitually offered with that piety, persevering earnestness, and glowing fervor, which ever accompany the yearnings of a heart striving to obtain from the
throne of grace those gifts and blessings each needed most.

His love for souls went even farther; he recommended to
God all the works for souls: the schools that instructed,
the missions that sanctified, the congregations and socie-
ties that perfected them—his apostolic charity embraced
all. In a word, no want of the Church, be it ever so
slight, found him indifferent—he responded cheerfully to
all its desires and prayers; to the demands made upon
him by its pastors, to those of his brethren, and generally
all persons recommending themselves to his prayers—not
even his enemies or those of the Society were forgotten.

But his fervor and zeal in prayer were most abundantly
poured out upon his double family—first, the adoptive
family to which he had given himself by vow, and to which
he clung with the deepest affection. Loving and esteeming it as he did, incessant were his petitions to Heaven for
its well-being. In addition to the exercises of the rule,
he daily offered up especial prayers for the preservation of
this *good mother*, as he loved to call the society, for the
success of her works, for the various houses of the Order
and their inmates, especially that of Vals, where he was
then living. Deeming his own voice weak and powerless
with Heaven, he borrowed that of the guardian angels of
those dear ones for whom he prayed, of St. Ignatius, the
holy Founder of the Society, and of all holy Jesuits, his
children, conjuring St. John Berchmans, their patron of
studies, to make especial intercession for the scholastics

of the house, "that" (we quote his own words) "walking generously in your footsteps, we may, like you, all make notable progress in our studies, but still more in piety; that, like you, we esteem little things, love the chaplet, the crucifix, our rules; and dying, like you, surrounded by these sacred emblems, merit, like you, to be aggregated forever to the Society of Jesus in glory." [1]

Not only did charity towards his confrères keep Father Sire's heart ever at the foot of the altar, but likewise did filial piety impel him to multiply his good works, especially prayers for his venerated parents and his numerous relatives. His desire to benefit them thus was not merely the ordinary one, but a strong yearning, a veritable hunger and thirst; and it would be impossible to enumerate all that he did in the course of his life towards their spiritual assistance, converting one, sanctifying another, endeavoring to bring all to the practice of the highest virtue, the most perfect sanctity. Later on, we may edify our readers by recounting various incidents of his apostolate among the members of his own family; it suffices here for us to say that he continues it in heaven, and that since his death many and great are the favors, both in the spiritual and temporal order, this good Father's intercession, invoked by them, has drawn upon them.

---

[1] The prayer to St. John Berchmans, as well as that to St. Ignatius, had been copied by Father Charles, and they were found among those he prized most highly.

CHAPTER VIII.

His Foreign Mission.

I.—The Call of God and his Superiors - His Correspondence to it.

IN the Society of Jesus, as among the secular clergy, there are two kinds of apostolate: the ordinary apostolate, which is exercised in one's own country, and the foreign, or that of missions, which some privileged members exercise in pagan or non-Catholic lands. Among these, Madura, in Asia, Reunion Isle and Madagascar, belonging to Africa, are the two posts of honor allotted Toulouse; and it is here nearly a hundred and fifty Jesuits are laboring daily for the conversion of the heathen, sacrificing thus to the Lord their talents, health, repose, and life.

It was to this illustrious phalanx God called Father Charles, about the end of his scholasticate. Says Father Cros: "To appreciate all the merit of his obedience herein, one must understand that Father Sire had never formally requested a foreign mission. During his last year at Vals, the good God had inspired him with the thought of devoting himself to the laborious life of a missionary, and he believed it his duty to make this known to the Father Provincial, in the following words: 'I have sometimes felt a desire to consecrate myself to the missions.' This was all he said on the subject. A few months later he received his appointment. Said the good Father to me, in speaking of it: 'This was very unexpected, and I must confess that it caused a terrible struggle within me between nature and grace ; happily, grace has triumphed, and I can say, not only that I consent to go, but that I am pleased with the call, which evidently comes from God, for I did not ask to be sent on the missions.'"

To sustain him in this exalted state of virtue, and, indeed, to raise him still higher, God so ordered his affairs that he was almost immediately promoted to the sub-deaconship, deaconship, and priesthood—privileges, holy privileges, filling him with such an abundance of graces that he was not able to restrain his transports of love.

"'The day he was made sub-deacon,"[1] says Father Cros, "having been chosen to sing the beautiful Epistle of the Nativity of the Blessed Virgin, he acquitted himself of this duty in so sublime and touching a manner that every one was struck with it. I could but remark it myself ; and finding an opportunity of speaking to him alone that day, I said, ' Brother, I was much pleased with the way in which you sang the Epistle.' ' Oh !' he answered, ' I felt so happy to sing aloud the praises, and such beautiful praises, of the Blessed Virgin ! I cannot keep from telling you that I was almost beside myself with joy.'"

The Bishop of Puy having fallen sick a few days after this ceremony, it was at Lyons, and in the sanctuary of Our Lady of Fourvières, that Charles was made deacon, on the 21st of the same month, feast of St. Matthew. Mgr. Charbonnel, who had just renounced the bishopric of Toronto, in Canada, to become a Capuchin, presided at the ceremony, and addressed Charles in these consoling words: *Accipe Spiritum Sanctum ad robur, ad resistendum diabolo et tentationibus ejus, in nomine Domini:* "Receive in the

---

[1] Father Sire was ordained sub-deacon at Puy, September 8, 1861, by Mgr. de Marthon under the auspices of Our Lady of France, in the chapel of the Theological Seminary, dedicated to St. George, patron of the diocese.

name of the Lord, by His power and for His glory, the Holy Spirit, that you may resist the devil and his temptations."

These words, pronounced over him in that sanctuary of Mary where so many apostolic vocations had been blessed and rendered fruitful, and coming from the lips of a man who had himself left all to follow Jesus Christ, made the deepest and most salutary impression upon Charles's soul. From that day he appeared in the midst of his confrères as a new man, an apostle breathing only the spirit of sacrifice. " Oh! if you could but know," said he to them, " how happy I am, since I have made to God the absolute renunciation of my country, my family, my future, myself !" Says one who heard him on this occasion: " He uttered these words with such joy and enthusiasm, that they have always remained engraven in my heart, as if they had been the last will and testament of a friend, and the more especially, as he was on the eve of departure for a far distant country, whence he never returned."

There now awaited him in Puy a letter from the Reverend Father Provincial, ordering him to Toulouse. Comprehending the meaning of this, he immediately sought his spiritual Father, the Rev. Father Rouquayrol, then rector at Vals; and the following is the latter's account of what passed in this interview:

"The question of Father Sire's departure for the missions presented itself under an especial form, for it is not customary to send on foreign missions (although the rule leaves superiors free in this regard) any except such as request it. Those who are impelled thus by grace mention the subject first to their confessor, in order to make, under his direction, a thorough examination of their dispositions, and ascertain whether the desire is on a solid foundation, or merely a movement of the imagination, not to be acted upon."

The spiritual Father beheld in the present subject a peaceful soul, a generous heart, in a word, all the qualities requisite for this kind of work; but the account the good Brother was obliged to give regarding his physical health and strength induced the former to believe that Charles might be more useful in his vocation by remaining in France, the result of which suggestion was that Charles felt impelled by two opposing forces—his own inclinations urging him to accept the missions, and his confessor's advice to take no step in the matter precipitately. His general health was not what might be called bad, unless one takes into account a great weakness and tendency to fatigue, which he took pains to conceal from all save the depositary of his soul's secrets.

When the young religious left the novitiate his director's last words were these: "Go to the Reverend Father Provincial and tell him everything—your desires to serve the foreign missions, and the fears induced by your rather precarious health, and be governed entirely by his decision. It is thus, the child of obedience, you will neither be wanting in fidelity to the grace which seems to impel you, nor, on the other hand, will you rashly undertake what is beyond your strength." God willed that these desires of the fervent religious be granted, and Father Sire was assigned to the missions.

The following is his own account, in a letter to his brother Vital, of the interview he had just had at Toulouse with the Rev. Father Provincial.

"To the greater glory of God!

"My very dear brother, scarcely am I informed of my superior's intentions regarding myself, ere I hasten to acquaint you with them, knowing your deep interest in me and your pleasure in hearing from me.

"On my arrival at Toulouse, the Rev. Father Provincial

asked me if I wished to go to Bourbon, and of course, you know my reply. I told him he had only to make known to me his desires; I was at his disposal, and I would be but too happy should holy obedience assign me to such a post of honor. I did, however, observe to him that my brothers would, no doubt, be surprised, and perhaps disapprove of this disposition of me. He replied that, being priests yourselves, you would the more readily understand it than others. ' Besides,' added he, ' I am sending you, not to Madagascar, but to the college of St. Denis, on Reunion Isle, where you can prepare yourself for the life of a missionary, at the same time that you are filling some position at the institution; and in the course of a few years we will be the better enabled to judge whether you are to remain there or re-inforce the active missionaries.'

" As for myself," adds Charles, " I am both happy and proud at thoughts of this double elevation to the priesthood and the mission to Bourbon; and I love to believe that, far from opposing my departure (which probably will not take place for a month), you will beg Our Lord to confirm my superior's decisions, and advise me how to prepare our parents for the sacrifice."

Whilst awaiting the answer to this letter, Father Charles was not inactive. The day after writing it he went to Pibrac, and with fervent prayers recommended to St. Germaine his ordination to the priesthood and his foreign mission. During his stay in Toulouse he also frequently visited the shrine of Our Lady of Good News, to whom he had such great devotion. Fearing now lest some negligence or delay on the part of man put an obstacle to God's designs, he wrote to his brethren at Vals and Lyons to send him immediately all the articles needed for his ordination. These reached him October 15th, and the next day everything was definitely settled—the day of his departure as well as of his ordination. From this moment, full of joy and hope, Father Charles had but one sentiment in his heart, one word upon his lips—prayer! In all his visits or other intercourse with his fellow-beings, the cry of his soul was : pray ! pray ! pray ! And his heart was dilated with joy to know that this cry, reaching the farthest circles of his friends and relatives—at Rodez, Paris, Lyons, Vals, Saint-Jory, Toulouse—awakened everywhere a response of fervor, enthusiasm, and testimonials of the tenderest friendship.

It was thus his brethren wrote to him from Vals: " So your lot is to be cast with that of the blessed missionaries, and you set out fortified by the graces of the priesthood! How truly and wonderfully favored you are, so much so that, were you not a cherished Father, whose joys are also ours, we might be tempted to feel jealous ! Go, then, happy traveller! our desires and affections will follow you over the wide waste of waters, whilst our fervent prayers ascend to God in your behalf. May His angel ever protect you!

" All the household of Vals, especially the theological students, regard you with affection, sincere and deep, and whilst grieving over your departure, they will not forget you at the foot of the altar. Adieu, then, adieu. Always and devotedly yours in the Hearts of Jesus and Mary."

These testimonials of friendship, and the fervent prayers, the fruits of such friendship, no doubt filled Father Charles with joy and consolation inexpressible; but how much greater even must not his delight have been on the blessed day that witnessed the double ceremony of his ordination and first Mass, surrounded by his parents, relatives, and friends, all receiving holy Communion! To a heart so tender and loving as his, what a source of the purest joys, the most abundant graces !

II.—Father Charles is ordained Priest.—His First Mass.

It was on the 24th of October, 1861, in the beautiful church of the Jesuits at Toulouse, that this interesting ceremony took place. After the ordination, all the relatives and friends of the newly-ordained, more than forty in number, collected in the parlor of the Jesuit Fathers, and the new priest, radiant with happiness, gave them his blessing. "The Archbishop came also," says one of the assistants, "and after expressing his pleasure at having ordained so holy a religious, and congratulating his parents at having given so many sons to the Church, he related some very interesting details concerning Bourbon, of which place he had once been bishop." The jubilation and enthusiasm filling all hearts appeared upon the countenances. Charles's, as we have said, was radiant—he was overflowing with happiness, and he never wearied of saying that he could not find words to express it.

To describe the impression made upon one by his words, full of zeal and sweetness, were impossible—one must needs have heard them, to have an idea of their effect. Next day, at the appointed hour and place, his friends were again assembled, all desiring to see the young priest again, to receive from his hands the Bread of the Strong, and to gather up some of those words of benediction and life that fell from his lips. His father and mother, transformed by their son's piety, were inundated with joy. M. Marcel speaks of it thus in a letter to one of his brothers: "Charles's ordination and first Mass have accomplished marvels. Our father, our tender mother especially, are enraptured; nothing could be more admirable than their dispositions of heart. They have made their sacrifice, and in a truly Christian manner. No doubt their tears will flow at his departure and even after it, but tears of piety like these dim not the lustre of their offering.

Let us bless the Lord, Who has so wisely ordered all things; and especially, let us fail not to thank Him for the honor He has conferred on us, in selecting one of our number to be a missionary and an apostle; and whilst acknowledging our unworthiness of this favor, let us endeavor to accept generously a cross which must needs draw down upon the family most abundant benedictions."

This prediction was not long in being realized, and amply, as we shall soon learn, in noting the graces and benedictions received by its various members. Father Charles's own share on the day of his ordination, and especially of his first Mass, was far from inconsiderable. At the request of M. Césaire, he made known to him, in the following words, the transports of his heart on these solemn days.

"To the greater glory of God!

"My very dear brother, you already know what great events have taken place in my life since our separation— I refer to my ordination and first Mass. It was in the church of our Fathers dedicated to the Sacred Heart that I received and exercised for the first time the sublime power of the priesthood, amidst quite a large assemblage, including about fifty of the Fathers, to bless me, and all the novices of the *Rue des Fleurs* to aid me by their fervent prayers. Each branch of our family was represented by some one, at least, of its most prominent members; likewise, were friends and acquaintances there, and I had the happiness of giving holy Communion successively to my father, mother, and nearly all the relatives and friends present.

"Oh! those beautiful feasts of St. Raphael (October 24th) and St. John of Canti (October 25th). What graces and consolations they brought, first of all to myself, then to those I love! The day of my ordination impressed me much, but that of my first Mass far exceeded even this in the meed of spiritual joy, consolation, and strength immeasurable it imparted to me. And neither the days that followed have been, nor those to come will be barren, in their measure of such heavenly fruits and blessings. I cannot express to you how happy I have been and still am; but what can be made known to you, and what Vital will not fail to acquaint you with, is the admirable manner in which Divine Providence has conducted this affair throughout. Our parents had made their sacrifice before my ordination, and they tasted the sweets of recompense in the midst of our festivals. Doubtless, these surprising effects of grace must be attributed to the many prayers that have been offered to Heaven in our behalf. I desire now to thank you for your share in these multiplied petitions. Ever yours in Our Lord and for His glory,

"CHARLES SIRE."

"These joys ineffable with which Father Charles was inundated on the forever *fortunate* days (as he elsewhere styles them) of his ordination and first Mass, were not," says one who assisted at the ceremonies, "those transient, fleeting joys of the world, which touch merely the exterior of the soul, and nearly always leave in their train agitation, sadness, and regret; no, these were the deep, lasting, celestial joys, which, penetrating the essence of the soul, dilate it with a participation in the joy of God Himself. He was constantly saying that he was happy, very happy; and there was no need of his trying to convince us of it, for happiness beamed from his countenance. His words, his smile, his manner—all betokened joy, the purest, sweetest, most holy, in which one saw neither constraint nor unbecoming effusion; everything about him was calm, orderly, modest. The prodigies grace was operating in him so absorbed his being, that, like the Blessed Virgin in those most beautiful days of her mortal life, he knew nothing but to praise, bless, and exalt the Lord: *Magnificat anima mea Dominum......quia fecit mihi magna qui potens est.*

"These sentiments were always before him, and he gave expression to them on every occasion, in his intercourse with men no less than when conversing with God: in the church, the parlor, whilst visiting—he was ever the same. It was necessary to see or hear him but a few minutes to be touched to the depths of the soul."

"Never," says one of his relatives, "never can I forget the impression made upon me at seeing him make his thanksgiving after Mass. Alone in the sanctuary, his fervor in prayer was so remarkable that I could not keep my eyes off him. His attitude of recollection alone, revealing at a glance the holy and generous emotions of his soul, was truly a sermon."

"He abridged his thanksgiving," adds another eye-witness, "so as not to keep waiting too long the numerous relatives and friends whom he had taken care to have invited into the parlor and seated. Presenting himself before this goodly assemblage, with many of whom he was unacquainted, he said to them: 'How pleased I am to see you all here! I have just left the good God, to come and share my happiness with you. It is said there is no heaven upon earth. Ah! I can assure you of the contrary, for to-day I feel as if I were in heaven. Yesterday I was between heaven and earth, and my soul was filled with happiness, although I trembled with awe at thoughts of being invested with the dignity and powers of the priesthood and the tremendous consequences involved. To-day I am all for God, and God is all for me; my happiness is unalloyed and perfect. I was, indeed, with the good God in my thanksgiving just now, and I felt as if I could have remained with Him all day; but I shall find Him again, for I left Him but a few moments, and only to share my happiness with you.' Every one was affected to tears at sight of this young, holy priest, whose innocent, radiant face so clearly mirrored the beauty of his soul. ' Ah,' said he, ' why are you weeping? This should be a day of joy. Come now, let me bless you!'—and we all fell on our knees to receive his blessing."

This touching scene made so deep and lasting an impression upon those who assisted at it that even now, after a lapse of twenty-two years, it is still fresh in their memories, and they often speak of it as one of their holiest reminiscences, never to be forgotten, all expressing their happiness at having seen and heard a saint, having been present at the Mass of a saint, and having received, as a memento of it, the picture of a saint.

Deeply touched by this pious enthusiasm of which he was the object, Father Charles, in token of gratitude, gave with his own hand, or sent to each by a friend, a souvenir of his first Mass. Some received a medal, others a chaplet—the majority, however, a little picture with a maxim or prayer appropriate to their needs, and bearing his signature. Though of slight intrinsic value, the recipients prized these articles and preserved them with religious care. After his death, they became in the owners' eyes veritable relics, not to be parted with at any price.

One of his cousins, who had never seen him, being invited by Mme. Sire to her son's ordination and first Mass, experienced, on both occasions, such wonderful effects of grace that she could not forbear speaking of it to her family. A brother of Father Charles, having heard something of this, wrote, asking her in all simplicity to give him an exact account of what he knew merely from hear-

say, and telling her it would redound to the good Father's
glory. The following is her answer:

"If what I write, my dear cousin, concerning your
blessed brother, can be of the slightest service to you in
the manner you desire, I shall be the happiest person in
the world; but, alas! I feel my inability and my unworthiness to use my pen in so beautiful a cause. To speak of
a saint! I am not capable of it! Hence I claim your indulgence whilst complying with your request, which I dare
not refuse, since you tell me the glory of Father Charles is
concerned.

"I begin, then, by telling you in all simplicity that I
was very much pleased to receive your letter of invitation
to these beautiful feasts, as I would thus have an opportunity of seeing this cousin, of whom I had already a most
exalted opinion, although personally unacquainted with
him. On the eve of his ordination I went to confession,
to prepare myself the better for participation in the happiness of the family. Next morning, during the ceremony,
my soul was inundated with joy. To tell you what my
emotions were whilst in the parlor of the Jesuits would be
impossible, for I do not believe I could find expressions
descriptive of them.

"Father Charles impressed me as a great saint, embel-
lished with every virtue. His interior was revealed to me
as clearly as if he had given me his holiest confidence thereof; the purity of his soul rivalled the whiteness of a lily.
The few words he said to us touched me deeply, at the
same time that they showed forth his humility. On leaving the house, I said to my daughter and another person
who was with me: 'What do you think of this priest? I
believe him to be a veritable saint.' They told me that
they thought the same. Nor did these impressions prove
transient—the whole of that day they were before me, and

I often said to myself, ' Why am I so weak and miserable, when there are such holy people as this in the world?'

"Next morning I hastened eagerly to his first Mass, and during the celebration of the divine mysteries I felt impelled to ask of God, through Father Charles's mediation, that my children become saints, my son a priest; also, that, if the latter were ever called, like him, to win souls for heaven, or increase devotion to Mary Immaculate, I might have the grace to make the sacrifice. I likewise prayed to God for the most precious graces for my daughter, and all these favors I entreated through Father Charles, for I could not believe he would let pass the most beautiful day of his life without invoking benedictions on all his family.

"I was especially impressed at sight of him making his thanksgiving after Mass. I seem to see him now, kneeling in the sanctuary, a living, breathing picture of the most profound respect and liveliest gratitude. The scene can never be effaced from my heart.

"Retiring to the parlor, I received with the others there assembled his blessing. He also gave me a little picture, which I preserve with religious care, together with another, bearing his signature, which your mother gave me. I asked him on this occasion if he would be so good as to bless my children before his departure; and he promised me he would. I returned home with this hope; but as time passed, and the day of his departure drew nigh without my having received the promised visit from him, I concluded to go myself to St. Mary's college, where he then resided. This was either on the eve of the Presentation, or the very day of the feast. Though weak and suffering greatly, I took my son (then two years and a half old) in my arms; and such was my eagerness, that I reached St. Sernin's ere I was aware of it. Here I was uncertain which direction to take. After recommending myself to the Blessed

Virgin, whom I never invoked in vain, happening to turn towards the church, I saw a lady just coming out, and on going up to her, to inquire the way, I was delighted to recognize your mother. Learning my desires, she invited me to accompany her home, where Father Charles then was.

"I had the happiness of there spending a half-hour with him, a short time, indeed, but infinitely precious; and both I and my children (for the latter I had especially desired it) received his blessing. At this moment I felt penetrated with the greatest respect and veneration for him, and my joy was beyond description. He seemed to take quite an interest in my son, caressing him and asking me various questions about him. Condescending still farther, he promised, in compliance with my request, ever to remember us in his prayers and even at the foot of the altar.

"This last interview and benediction had a wonderful effect upon my children. From that day we have never ceased to invoke him as a saint. My grief at the news of his death could not have been greater if he had been my brother; and mingled with my grief was the thought of the good he might have done to souls, had he been spared to earth. Resigned, however, to God's will, I said to my children, ' We have now a great protector in heaven.'

"There is no measure to my confidence in the power of his intercession, for I have several times experienced the effects of it, having obtained thereby graces of various sorts.' In sickness we have frequently experienced relief by the application of a piece of wearing apparel which had once belonged to him, and which your mother was so kind as to give me. My husband and I invoke him daily; likewise do Alphonse and his sister Angela, morning and even-

---

¹ This letter was written on December 13th, 1863 ; hence it was in the year following Father Charles's death these graces were obtained.

ing. Alphonse often says to me, 'Mamma, we must not forget Father Charles Sire ; you know he cured me, and he will tell the good God to make me grow and be very good.'

"I have the most exalted idea of your brother's sanctity, so much so that words fail me in expressing it. I was struck more particularly with his detachment for love of God, his spirit of mortification even in those things which are permitted, his life of union with God, his modesty and great humility. Any relic of him would be in my eyes most precious, far exceeding in value gold or the costliest stones."

III.—The Adieus.

If Father Charles had left Toulouse the day after his first Mass, according to previous arrangement, the anguish of the parting had been much less keen. But God does not will to deal thus with His dearest friends. Application not having been made for his passage in time in the packet which was to take him to Bourbon, there was no berth; he must needs wait a whole long month for another packet to sail, forced to contemplate thus at leisure all that was most painful to nature in this separation.

Like Jesus Christ at Nazareth, daily must he renew the sacrifice; and every instant, we might say, he was compelled to utter the most heartrending adieus; sometimes to a friend or mere acquaintance, sometimes to a fellow-student, a teacher, a confrère, a beloved relative. With his heart, as it were, in his two hands, lest it be overcome, he was continually renewing the pangs of separation from nature's strongest and dearest ties. Poor human heart! oh, how it must have quivered with anguish! But strong with the love of God, the happiness of making a sacrifice for His sake re-animated its courage and soothed its sorrows, so that, notwithstanding his sensibility, he ever appeared calm, and his countenance never lost, for an instant, that expression of peace, happiness, gentleness, and affability which were its chief characteristics.

The moment of departure approached; and now began that series of adieus the most painful of all. M. Vital and his eldest nephew had already taken leave of him. His three younger brothers, then in Paris, hastened also to bid him farewell by letter, and oh! how was his heart wrung with anguish at reading each, filled as it was with sentiments of the deepest fraternal affection, for Father Sire loved his brothers most tenderly, and these cordial expressions of sympathy regarding his mission were not calculated to diminish his love for them, or his grief at parting with them. The bitterness of these farewells, however, was nothing in comparison to those he must yet make by word of mouth.

The first from whom he must part thus was that pious peasant at Saint-Jory, who played so important and touching a rôle in his childhood, and who re-appears, like a spiritual mother, at all the grand epochs of his life.

When he was about to become a Jesuit, Father Charles and Catherine had made a pious contract, in virtue of which they were to live united by prayer. During his noviatiate and regency, this compact had been scrupulously observed, but his correspondence during this period being limited, they seldom heard from each other. During his scholasticate, however, these pious relations resumed their former character, through the mediation of Mme. Sire, the pious peasant often recommending herself to Father Charles's prayers, confiding to him her troubles, asking his advice, and promising him the feeble assistance of her prayers; [1] whilst, on the other hand, he, warmly interested

---

[1] Mme. Sire writes thus to her son, February 28, 1861: " Catherine offers up the most

in Catherine, never passed a day without praying for her, and always spoke of her in the most grateful manner.

Knowing all this, we are not surprised to learn that he went to see her ere leaving for Bourbon, and that, renewing their pious compact with new clauses, they promised mutual intercession—that, united in spirit before the Lord, they would ask of Him for themselves and families complete detachment from the world, great love of God, and a holy death, adding that the one who died first (Father Charles or Catherine) would redouble his or her entreaties to obtain for the survivor the graces just mentioned.

Father Charles, moreover, desired Catherine to share in his apostolate, requesting her, in view of this, to beg for him two especial graces—first, that he might convert all souls confided to him; secondly, that he might never deny his faith, but generously and unflinchingly bear testimony to it, even amidst the greatest torments, should Our Lord see fit to subject him to such.

Thoroughly in unison with these desires, Catherine promised Father Charles to receive holy Communion for him ten times a year—a Communion on each recurring anniversary of the ten days he called his *most fortunate* ones;[1] and he, in turn, promised her four Masses a year.

fervent prayers for you, praying especially, according to your desires, for your perseverance in the Society of Jesus, your progress in science, and your preparation for the priesthood.

"She has several times said to me that she felt more and more impelled to pray for your intentions—that frequently, when about to offer up a Communion for another, the good God would say to her from the depths of her heart, ' *no, it must be for Father Charles.*'

"And her husband, too, remembers you daily at the feet of Our Lady of Garaison. When you write to me, be sure to enclose a little invocation or short prayer of some kind, were it only three words, for this excellent family. Catherine and her daughters will be most faithful in saying it every day."

[1] These ten *fortunate* days were: those of his birth, his Baptism, his First Communion, his Confirmation, of his receiving tonsure, minor orders, sub-deaconship, deaconship, of his ordination to the priesthood, and of his entering the Society of Jesus.

He now, writing his name on some little pictures representing the respective patrons of the members of this pious family, gave them to Catherine, and at the same time a medal of St. Antony for her husband, whose patron St. Antony was. It is needless to say with what respect and joy these articles were received and distributed, or how carefully preserved, for Catherine's children had for Father Charles a love and veneration second only to that for their pious parents.

The hour of separation approached, the final adieu must be said. "Every one was in tears," said Catherine, "myself among the number. I wept bitterly, for I really felt more keenly on this occasion than at the death of my father and mother.

"Father Charles, on the contrary, was cheerful, or at least feigned to be so. 'What is the matter with you, Catherine, that you are crying?' said he. 'Come, cheer up. It is God's will that I go, and you should strive to rejoice in its accomplishment. It is so sweet, so beneficial, so necessary to do the will of God.' Then he added, 'Catherine, you must bear the cross; the good God requires it of you; He desires you to be immolated like Jesus Christ. Receive, then, the cross[1] from His hand and bear it generously.' Too overcome by emotion to reply, I took his right hand, and kissing it respectfully, my tears falling fast upon it, I silently withdrew."

If Catherine's grief was so keen, we can judge what Mme. Sire's must have been. The very thought of his departure was as a sword through her heart. "My very dear son (she writes thus to him on the 3d of this No-

---

[1] These words of Father Charles were verified to the letter, Catherine, to the day of her death, bearing a very heavy cross. Frequently in the course of her life had she offered herself to God as a victim for the conversion of sinners; and during the last year of it her offering was fully accepted, for it can be said that for the last six or seven months preceding her death she suffered a veritable martyrdom.

vember), we are on the eve of the feast of St. Charles, a day
memorable indeed to you as well as to myself. Ah! what
will not be my grief when future anniversaries of the day
come round, and you so far away! Looking sadly at your
portrait, I will say, 'Where is my son? where is my son?
You can never understand my anguish, for my heart must
needs break at thoughts of separation from a child so
beloved, did not the good God soothe my pain. I make
this sacrifice, which rends my soul, but I make it only to
please Him.

"It was He Who gave you to me, a sacred trust committed to my hands, and which I was to guard most pre-
ciously. Alas! have I done so? God alone knows. He
alone knows whether I shall merit praise or reproach at
that last great day of reckoning. Pray the good Master
to pardon me if I have failed in my duty.

"O my God, Thou askest of me now the return of
this holy deposit, and I give it to Thee, by the hands of
St. Charles, his patron. It is to this great saint I entrust
him during the remainder of his life, that Thou wilt bestow on him also the grace to be a saint, and on us all the
happiness of meeting in heaven.

"I wish you a happy feast-day, my very dear son. I
will pray for you at the holy sacrifice of the Mass said in
honor of your patron. And now I am going to ask
something of you: that you will do me the favor of spending a whole week with me. I hope you will not refuse me
this consolation, my dear son; it is the last your mother
will ask of you."

In compliance with the request, Father Charles remained several days at home, lending himself to all his
mother's desires, and striving to sweeten for her, as well
as for his aged father, the bitterness of the separation.
Encouraged by his words, fortified by his example, and

sustained above all by those interior graces the holy sacrifice of the Mass, offered daily with this intention by five of her sons, could not fail to draw down most abundantly upon her, Mme. Sire kept up nobly, and when the moment came for the final adieu, she accompanied her son to Toulouse, and participated in his sacrifice. Her lively faith and mother's love carried her even to the point of longing to share his mission and die with him, were it God's will.

Father Charles, on his side, clothed in virtue of his holy office with that strength which comes from on High, took, as it were, his soul in his two hands, and overcoming nature by grace, he said to the Lord, like the Divine Master at the beginning of His Passion: " Father, not my will but Thine be done." [1] Leaving then his aged father plunged in grief, he set out for Toulouse, where, after taking leave of all his confrères there, he repaired to the house of one of his cousins to partake of a farewell repast with his relatives. And now began for him those heartrending scenes which, testing his virtue to the utmost, put upon his sacrifice the last seal of perfection.

It was Sunday, and in the diocese of Toulouse the feast of St. Saturnin, bishop and martyr, who, having been its first apostle, was honored as its patron. He was also the especial patron of the magnificent basilica of St. Sernin, where Father Charles's three brothers had made their First Communion and nearly all the members of the family had received signal graces; and, moreover, where two of his grand-uncles had, as we have already said, watered for thirty years with their sweat and tears this portion of the Master's vineyard. All these circumstances, truly worthy of note, had struck M. Marcel, and inspired him with the happy thought of going to St. Sernin to consummate, under the eye of Our Lady of Good News, that sacrifice

[1] St. Luke xxii. 42.

which, generously made by various members of the family,
could not fail to draw upon it the most abundant benedictions. It was agreed, then, that here, at Mary's feet,
should the final farewells be said, the signal for which, to
avoid all demonstration, should be a picture handed his
mother by Father Charles.

Both mother and son willingly endorsed the arrangement,
and on the vigil of the feast received in token thereof the
body and blood of the Holy Victim, whence the martyrs
derive their strength; the mother seeking at Mary's feet
that courage her soul needed to make the sacrifice of her
son, and the son, forced thus to pierce his mother's heart,
wishing to leave her consolation and support.

The repast being ended, Mme. Sire, weeping bitterly,
fell on her knees at Charles's feet. The holy religious,
deeply affected, yet controlling his emotions, raised his
suppliant hands to heaven, and with a dignity truly celestial, pronounced in a firm voice these touching words:
" May the benediction of the omnipotent God, Father, Son,
and Holy Ghost, descend upon you and remain with you forever." [1] Then, immediately raising up his mother, and, in
turn, prostrating himself before her, he begged her blessing, which, sobbing, she gave as follows: " May the Lord
bless you, my son, and be ever with you! I bless you in the
name of the Father, of the Son, and of the Holy Ghost."

It was now about two o'clock, and they set out for St.
Sernin's, M. Marcel, being the eldest brother, representing
the others, and also, like St. John, whose name he bore,
accompanying mother and son to this new Calvary. Before
entering the church they stopped a few moments at Mlle.
Vabre's, where M. Felix, Charles's youngest nephew, resided, and where a few of Charles's friends had met to re-

---

[1] *Benedictio Dei omnipotentis, Patris et Filii et Spiritus Sancti, descendat super te, et maneat semper.*

ceive his last blessing. Arming himself with new courrage, he blessed each one, and without shedding a tear; " but," said Mme. Sire, whose maternal eye observed him closely, " it was with a great effort he controlled his emotions." Giving his blessing to Mlle. Vabre, he said: " Adieu, until we meet in heaven." This lady was then but forty years of age, and in the full enjoyment of health; but three years later, holding in her hand the crucifix Father Charles had given her, she rendered her soul to God, leaving her memory fragrant with the odor of virtue.

It was now nearly the hour for Vespers, and the moment of separation had come. Entering the church, after a short prayer at Mary's feet, Father Charles, as had been agreed upon, handed his mother a little picture. " At this," says one who was present, " Mme. Sire could no longer control herself, but arose and followed her son, who had not yet crossed the threshold of the church. ' Come, mother,' said he, ' make your sacrifice.' ' I cannot,' was her tearful answer. ' My tender mother,' he replied, ' what are you saying? Would you not be happy to learn, some day, that you had given a martyr to heaven? Pray, then, and make your offering generously—you will be recompensed.' ' Adieu, my dear son, adieu,' answered the mother, embracing her beloved Charles, here under the protection of Mary and St. Germaine, for the last time on earth. The good Father immediately departed, setting out on his journey to heaven at the same time that he turned his face towards the port whence he was to sail for Bourbon."

IV.—The Departure and Voyage.

This sacrifice of relatives and country Father Charles so generously made the Lord must have been most agreeable to Him; for, according to Catherine's words, Jesus and Mary lent him their protection during the voyage and covered him with graces and benedictions. Mme. Sire expressing to the latter a mother's fears for her child's life, exposed to the treachery of wind and wave on so long and perilous a voyage, was answered thus by the pious peasant: "Oh! fear nothing, Madame, for Charles; he is too well guarded not to reach Bourbon safely; Our Lord and the Blessed Virgin are ever with him."

Later Catherine's words were confirmed by Father Charles himself in a very interesting and detailed account which he wrote to his friends of the voyage, describing their route, the imminent dangers threatening their lives, the touching impressions made upon him on setting foot on that distant land, and dwelling especially upon the manifest protection of Providence in his regard. The limits of our present work forbid the reproduction of this narration here; and we content ourselves on this point with a quotation from Father Chanut, his travelling companion, who says that Charles edified all on the vessel by his piety, his regularity, his devotion to the holy sacrifice, his spirit of poverty, his calmness and self-possession amid danger, and more particularly by his exquisite charity for those with whom he was now brought in contact.

"In leaving France," says Father Chanut, "Father Sire was filled with consolation; the joy of sacrifice inundated his beautiful soul. He used often to say to us: 'What a happiness it is to be sent to evangelize the poor pagans! Ah! the missionary is the priest in the plenitude of his vocation!' This thought was ever before his mind, and he endeavored in all manner of ways to inculcate it, especially when he heard our confessions. The good Father! it was thus he hoped to infuse into our souls some of that joy with which his own soul was overflowing.

"His regularity was perfect. Amidst all the perplexities of a life so new to him, amidst the suffering and pain

inseparable from such a voyage, surrounded almost entirely by laymen, for the most part Protestants, he followed,
with heroic courage, the rule marked out for him at his
departure. Every day, at the same hour, he was found
on deck or in the cabin performing his exercises of piety
with the same recollection as if in his cell.

"The Mass was his delight, and he often offered up this
holy sacrifice. It would have been a great consolation to
him to have done so daily, but charity induced him to cede
this privilege sometimes to the Fathers of the Holy Ghost,
passengers like himself on the *Sultan*,[1] and who remember
gratefully not only his kindness in lending them all the
articles necessary for the sacrifice,—articles entirely in his
charge,—but also the delicacy with which he did so.

"Oh! what was not his devotion at the altar, when he
had the happiness of saying Mass! What recollection and
modesty in his exterior! What piety and fervor in his soul!
Hence, what graces did he not receive from this holy action! Yes, this, beyond doubt, was the source whence he
imbibed that lively faith, that boundless confidence, which
never flagged.

"Seeing a storm arising as we drew nigh to Malta, Father Sire, quietly taking me aside, said with the utmost
composure: 'We had better be arming ourselves for the
danger.' 'What do you mean, Father?' was my reply.
'I mean,' said he, 'that I would like to have some holy
water, for it is very efficacious in danger.' Acting upon
this, we took advantage of the first moment of our young
companion's leaving the cabin.[2] Closing the door, Father
Charles, ritual in hand, hastened to bless the water, and
during the continuance of the storm, when the vessel was

---

[1] This was the name of the vessel.

[2] The cabin in which Father Charles was had four occupants: on one side, the
two Jesuits, and in berths above them, a Hollander, and a young interpreter for the

rocked most violently, he would sprinkle the cabin with the holy water, but as quietly and composedly as if he saw no signs of danger.

"In his intercourse with strangers he was always gentle, polite, affable, but very prudent, his conversations having ever but one end in view—the good of souls; and on such occasions as promised no hopes of this he maintained silence. One day I asked his permission for a conversation with Mr. Ellis, the Protestant minister on board, who occasionally gave a sermon on deck to his co-religionists.[1] 'Do just as you please about this,' was his answer, 'but it will be time and pains lost.' The future justified the truth of his remarks.

"And now, what shall I say of those other virtues which shone conspicuously in him during the voyage? What shall I say especially of his love of religious poverty? Truly, that I have rarely seen it in any one in such perfection as in him. He provided in advance for all our expenses, and kept a scrupulous account of them, and whilst his charity supplied our every want, not the slightest amount was spent uselessly.

"Poor in spirit, he was rich in the eyes of God. I see him before me now as he appeared at the moment of our arrival. How great his rejoicing, in spite of his fatigue: for most ardent had been his longing to see that land which was to witness the consummation of his sacrifice, or, at least, which he thought would surely witness it—the great African island of Madagascar. It pleased God, however (Whose holy name be blessed!), to dispose otherwise."

French government, going to China; on the other, four laymen, one of whom did not understand French.

[1] Mr. Ellis was the Protestant minister sent out by England to paralyze France's influence in Madagascar, which had become very great in consequence of the conversion to the Faith of Radama II., king of that island. How zealously he acquitted himself of this disastrous mission, we know but too well, from the journals and Annals of the Propagation of the Faith.

CHAPTER IX.

FATHER CHARLES AT REUNION ISLAND.

LEAVING Marseilles November 28, 1861, in one of the mail steamers, Father Charles reached Bourbon and landed at St. Denis on the 28th of the next month, December. This, our winter season, was mid-summer there, a season of trying heat and rains. St. Mary's college, his first mission, was still having its vacation, and it would not be re-opened until January 23d. Father Sire profited by this interval to rest from the fatigues of the voyage, fraternize with his new confrères, and write to his friends in France, so grieved at his departure and so anxious as to his safety, a full account of the voyage, of his emotions on arriving at the scene of his future labors, and a description of the natural charms of his new country.

Then preparing himself by a retreat of three days for the renewal of his vows, he offered himself anew to the Lord by the vow of obedience, as a victim always ready for immolation, and asking for the sacrifice only the manifestation of His will. Made unreservedly and with all the fervor of a young missionary, this offering was accepted, and the next day would inaugurate for him the era of sacrifices.

I.—First Trials of Father Charles.

The day after Father Charles renewed his vows, his old friend, Father Lacomme, who had welcomed him with open arms, and whose presence near him could have alleviated the pangs of recent separation from friends and country, and otherwise smoothed the ruggedness of the young missionary's new path in life, was sent hence to St. Mary's of Madagascar, to evangelize the Malagassy people, and to be appointed, a little later, prefect apostolic of the smaller islands of the mission. The departure of this confrère was so much the more painful to Father Charles as it was followed, on the morrow, by a sacrifice even harder to make.

Appointed *vigilant,* and sole vigilant, of the first division of boarders, he found himself in consequence completely isolated from his confrères, and forced to spend all his time with these young Creoles, whose characters and dispositions were so little in harmony with his own. The following is his own account, in a letter to his brother, of the trials this position necessarily imposed upon him.

"Our re-opening after vacation took place, my dear Vital, on Thursday, the 23d. On that day I entered upon my duties as first vigilant, or, to be more exact, only vigilant, of the first division of our dear boarders. The Rev. Father Etcheverry, our rector, in informing me that this was my post of duty, told me these scholars were not hard to manage; and my experience with them so far confirms his words; for, notwithstanding my indulgence, they behave very well, and even give promise of continued improvement.

"Being vigilant, I must spend my time, day and night, with the scholars. I have no free moments during the week except when they are in class, nor on Sunday, except when they go to catechism. This sort of life has truly its difficulties and trials, for it keeps me isolated from the rest of the community, and in a state of continual anxiety, because I must be ever on the alert to prevent disorder, which anxiety somewhat diminishes my recollection when engaged in my spiritual duties. Besides, it exposes me to the heat, not only during the day, but also at night, as I sleep in the dormitory, where, too, the mosquitoes are plentiful. You can likewise divine that it is the occasion of many other sufferings and privations. But what are all these in comparison with the laborious life of a missionary? what even with that of our confrères?

" I really esteem myself happy in the duty assigned me; first, because it affords me the opportunity of doing good, according to the measure of my strength; again, because my health is better suited to this sort of life than any other, and thirdly, because it is laid upon me by the hand of obedience.

" I must tell you that we take precautions against the heat which greatly mitigate its intensity, and thus render the climate of Bourbon supportable. Our cassocks, for example, are made of the lightest material; so, too, are our pantaloons, which just reach to our short white stockings. The baretta and hat are also very light, and on going out in the sun an umbrella is always used to protect us from its ardent rays. Our linen is changed frequently, our feet bathed often, and the table is served with an abundance of spices to excite the appetite. With all these precautions, one can live in Bourbon; and, in fact, I have already passed more than a month here without suffering much from the heat.

" Shall I soon leave the college to direct my steps towards a more noxious climate? I know not, but this is an event of continual occurrence, for it is here we are prepared for the mission of Madagascar. And whilst I await my final appointment, do you, my dear Vital, supplicate Our Lord Himself to prepare me for the life of a missionary, by giving me the grace to devote all my energies to the advancement of God's glory and the salvation of souls."

It was thus by the aid of prayer, the spirit of faith, and especially of zeal and charity, Father Charles accepted cheerfully and fulfilled most scrupulously the onerous duties of vigilant: happy to bear the cross, following in the footsteps of Jesus Christ, happier still to lighten, in this way, his confrères' burdens, whilst amassing for himself treasures of merits by this life of humility, abnegation, and obedience.

Pleased with his devotedness, and wishing to augment his merits, God added to these trials a third, which, although apparently trifling, was not so to Father Charles's tender heart—his not hearing from home.

As I have already mentioned, his affection for his parents was of the deepest nature, and so much the more sincere and ardent as it was supernatural. Of this affection he had given them many unequivocal proofs ere leaving France. As the hour of departure approached, it became intensified. On witnessing the anguish his separation from the family caused them, especially his mother, his heart was stirred to its depths; and to sweeten the bitterness of the cup for them, in writing home he not only made his letters vehicles of his ever-increasing love for those distant afflicted ones, but endeavored to convince them that he was happy at St. Denis, and enjoying good health.

He was truly happy there, but his was that spiritual happiness which does not blunt for nature the keenness of grief, as we learn from the following letter, written to his brother Césaire, May 16, 1862. "You ask me, my dear Césaire, if God makes me taste at Bourbon the joys with which He favors those who quit all to follow Him. I answer frankly that, having left all, one feels spiritually disengaged from natural affections, so as to be no longer affected at the privation. This, however, does not prevent one's being pleased at hearing from one's family every month, nor pained, on the contrary, when the mail brings no letter. And the latter has been my lot since the last of April." Writing to M. Vital, two months previously, he said: "I expected, my very dear brother, to receive the New Year's congratulations by yesterday's mail; but I have been disappointed in hearing from the family, and this, I can assure you, revives for me the pangs of separation. I sincerely hope you will not let me suffer in this way much longer, and I pray St. Joseph to bring me, in this beautiful month especially consecrated to him, the longed-for consolation.

"Eleven o'clock in the moring—*Deo gratias!* May God be praised! I have just received a letter from my mother, one from little Pierre, and one in common from Felix and Mlle. Vabre. Oh! what pleasure these letters have given me! I would like to answer them immediately, but it is too late, the mail is going. Tell each one of the above to expect to be amply recompensed next month."

II.—Father Charles's Sickness.

This third trial had scarcely come to an end, ere another, far more severe, was sent Father Charles, to fasten him to his Divine Master's cross. Taken really with a violent attack of the stomach and liver on the 13th of March, a few days after Lent had set in, he did not give up and keep his bed until the 16th. On the 19th, removed from the dormitory to a more comfortable room, he was there so ill, for a few days, that all thought him on the brink of the grave. Skillful physicians and nursing rescued him from this first danger; but at the price of what sufferings and sacrifices, God alone knows. Absolute silence and complete rest being prescribed as essential requisites of his recovery, that patience and resignation he had shown in suffering were even more conspicuous in this forced repose. "When we would go to see him," said one of his confrères, "he would turn upon us his gentle look, and smile in token of gratitude, with that amiable smile so familiar to all. He was never delirious, but oh! how he suffered! The pain never left him, day or night, and he was soon reduced to a frightful state of emaciation." The following is his own account of this illness in a letter to M. Vital, April 26th.

"To the greater glory of God! My very dear brother, in my last letter to you I could acquaint you only with the beginning of my illness and the cause of it ; to-day I will give you a more detailed account.

"Shortly after taking to my bed, the disease reached the crisis, and our Fathers were informed by the physicians in charge that there were but two chances out of ten for my life. A great number of leeches were now applied to me, and four blisters, the marks of which I shall bear for a long time. Since their application I have been getting better. Since April 11th, feast of Our Lady's Compassion, I have been able to receive holy Communion fasting, and at half past four o'clock in the morning (I had not received since March 16th); but I could not say Mass until April 24th, and with the aid of one of the other Fathers. Palm Sunday, the 13th, I had the happiness of receiving holy Communion, and that day brought me also a most unexpected consolation—a visit from Mgr. Maupoint, our Bishop, who came into my chamber to see me, and expressed much interest in me. I showed him the passage in your letter in which mention is made of himself and his friend at Rodez. He seemed quite pleased, and asked me to visit him often, promising to come soon again to see me.

"Finding myself much better the next few days, I was delighted to be with our Fathers for a short time at intervals; also, to receive holy Communion with them on Holy Thursday. And all day Good Friday, day of grief and mourning for the Church, I was consumed with fever, which afforded me the opportunity of fulfilling the precept of fast and abstinence. I was very happy at this. On Holy Saturday, glad day of the Resurrection, I began to eat meat again, some chicken—such was my alleluia.

"Since that time I have been gradually growing better; my appetite has returned; likewise can I sleep, and although still very weak, I can call myself convalescent. It is not likely, however, that I shall be able to do anything, or be assigned any duty in the house, for a long time yet, notwithstanding there are so few able-bodied Fathers here. In fact, I really have nothing to occupy me now except the re-establishment of my health. I am in hopes the season of the year, very much resembling the spring-time in France, will complete my cure."

Father Charles's convalescence, or rather the slight improvement of which he writes, continued nearly a month, and the good Father profited by it to write to his parents, to address to the Lord most fervent supplications in their behalf, and to offer daily for some member of his family the holy sacrifice of the Mass. This was the only consolation God gave him; for it was about this time he was much afflicted by the sad news he received from home—several of his brothers were sick, Catherine was in bad health, and his pious mother, though resigned to God's holy will, still grieving over the separation from her son. She writes thus to one of her other children: "My regret at parting from Charles increases instead of diminishing; he is ever before me, and my grief is almost inconsolable. Pray to the good God, my dear son, to grant me a little peace of soul, for my agitation is great indeed. Ah! how anxious I am to see you all during your vacation; never before have I felt so anxious."

This poor mother's heart seemed, in a measure at least,

to have divined her son's sufferings, so continually were they before her. Writing to Charles, she said: "You are ever in my mind and heart. It is in vain for you to say you are well; I cannot be convinced of it, neither can I help feeling a presentiment of some danger threatening you. When my depression in thinking of you is very great, and I scarce know what to do to relieve my afflicted heart, I take your dear picture and kiss it as if it were yourself. Alas! never again on earth shall I have the happiness of seeing and embracing you. One thought alone consoles me—that God wills it thus. May His holy Name be blessed!"

This touching letter was the last Mme. Sire wrote to her son. She was taken ill shortly after this, and despite the skill and care of her physician, never recovered her health. Just about this time, Father Charles had a relapse, falling insensibly into that state of languor which, gradually increasing, brought him to the grave. The following, taken from his last letter to his brother Vital, and written June 3d. 1862, is his own account of the new phases of his malady.

"All our Fathers of St. Mary's college are now having vacation, but they resume their scholastic duties the 11th of this month. I do not believe I shall be able to undertake anything so onerous yet awhile, or really any duty; for since my sickness I am very much changed; indeed, I consider myself a veritable wreck, as a month and a half of complete rest, and following a rule as easy as can be allowed in our houses, have not been sufficient to re-establish my health.

"To favor my convalescence, I have been sent to La Ressource, a charming site, where the air is pure and invigorating.[1] I have been here since the evening of May 7th.

---

[1] This was an establishment where the Jesuit Fathers were educating a number of Malagassy children from Madagascar or some of the small islands near.

At first I was much improved, thanks to the beautiful weather with which God has favored us; my health was really so far restored that I declined going to take the sea-baths which are on the other side of the island of St. Paul, on property belonging to M. de Villèle. But in a little while my convalescence was checked, and I lost in a few days all I had gained. So, now, I am in *statu quo*, which is worse than death. May it please Jesus and Mary that this shall not last very long!"

III.—Father Charles leaves Bourbon to return to France.

Father Charles's last desire was heard, alas! only too soon. The very day he gave expression to it Rev. Father Jouen, his superior, having gone to see him at La Ressource, was so struck by his appearance that he immediately brought him back to St. Denis. Father Charles was then so weak he could scarcely stand, and the least walking fatigued him. His emaciation was frightful, and his sufferings daily became more intense. From the 6th to the 8th of June they increased to such a degree that a consultation of physicians [1] was deemed necessary. It took place at ten o'clock in the morning. After a serious examination of their patient, they all declared that his malady was of too grave a nature to allow any hope of his health ever being re-established in Bourbon, and that he should be sent back to France as promptly as possible.

Father Sire warmly opposed this decision, but fearing lest his opposition proceed from self-will, he went to consult Father Jouen on the subject. And so imbued with

---

[1] Among these physicians was M. Richard, a cousin of Father Charles's sister-in-law. Later, he himself wrote as follows of the patient: " His condition excited our worst fears, but we hoped the voyage would prove beneficial, so that he might reach France greatly improved; this change seemed to us the only plank of safety left for him." This opinion has so much the more weight as Dr. Richard was very fond of Father Charles, and had not yet been selected to fill the position formerly occupied by Dr. Lhermite as physician to the college.

the spirit of the Divine Master on the eve of His Passion
are his words on this occasion, that we give them verbatim.
" Father," said he, " I would greatly prefer remaining
here, for I feel an extreme repugnance to returning to
France; but let me do the will of God above all things.
What do you advise me in this matter?" His superior
having pronounced in favor of his departure, the pious
invalid thought only of obeying, and next day all his
preparations were made for the voyage.

By a remarkable dispensation of Providence, there was
at this time at St. Denis a government vessel, returning
to France with troops that had been in China, and which
was to leave in a few days. Father Jouen hastened to procure a passage thereon for Father Sire, which the governor
granted gratuitously, and a seat at the officers' table, in
consideration of his being a missionary.

The departure took place June 14th. It was so sudden
that Father Charles had not time to see his confrères at
La Residence, much less the Vicar-General of St. Denis,
who then governed the diocese, Monseigneur being on his
way to Rome. This was no inconsiderable trial for a gentle,
loving heart like Charles's. He also regretted his inability
to testify his gratitude to Father Jouen, whose kindness and
attentions had been those of a mother. But the most painful of all sacrifices was that of his departure itself. Happily
for him, by reason of circumstances, the adieus must needs
be in haste, for in Father Sire's weak state a prolonging of
his departure would have been almost beyond his strength.
To quit this post of honor, after which he had so long sighed,
and to quit without having gained for Jesus Christ the
soul of one Malagas! To return to France a wreck in
health, and without even a travelling companion,[1] at the

---

[1] The precipitation of his departure was the reason Father Charles had no travelling companion.

risk of dying on shipboard, without the last consolations of religion, without a friend near to whom he could confide his sorrows and weaknesses! To bid adieu to cherished brethren, trusted friends, who had welcomed him so affectionately,—oh! what a trial, what a sacrifice was not all this, especially to a soul like Charles's! The hour of departure was truly a heartrending one to him.

Says one of the companions of his first voyage: "I can never forget that moment of parting, when, accompanying him to the college door, I embraced him for the last time. His eyes were filled with tears. 'Alas!' said he, I did not think I must leave so soon. I hoped to live and die here, and instead, I am going away without having done anything!' 'Ah! Father,' answered one of us, 'although you have worked little, you have suffered much; and suffering is not one of the least powerful means of saving souls.' 'Ah! well, may God's holy will be done! pray for me,' he replied, as, averting his face to conceal his emotion, he turned to go, leaving us filled with grief. Poor Father! he had fought the good fight, and although very young, he had accomplished much in a short time : *Consummatus in brevi, explevit tempora multa.*[1] All unite in the belief that he truly merited the crown, for his sufferings were great."

All the details we have been able to collect from Bourbon confirm the above testimony, and assure us that Father Charles was already ripe for heaven and worthy of the crown the Blessed Virgin (as we shall soon learn) placed on his brow, at the hour of his death. In sending us, April 6, 1863, some little articles that had belonged to him, his superior, Father Etcheverry, wrote to us as follows : "I send you, M. Abbé, these cherished relics of our good Father Sire. The package had been left by him with the Father Minister of the house, who was absent when Father Charles left.

[1] Wisdom iv. 13.

",What will interest you especially is his little collection of letters.   I also enclose his favorite pictures and the prayers and devotional exercises in which he took most delight.   These will reveal to you our friend's true piety, and the multiplied bonds of love uniting him to Jesus and Mary.

" The memory of this dear Father remains with us as a sweet perfume.   We feel that he is in heaven, whence he smiles upon us, and even more sweetly than he did when on earth, ever charitable and gentle as he was in life."

In order to give a more complete idea of his interior life whilst at Bourbon, we add to this testimony that of Father Richard, his confessor.   Requested by his confrères to contribute his mite of information regarding this fervent religious, Father Richard replied : " I scarcely knew Father Charles except in the confessional, but I can declare that I was deeply struck with his wonderful recollection and serenity of soul.   He accused himself of his slightest faults with perfect calmness, clearly, and in order.   Never did I perceive in him the least precipitation.   He appeared so completely master of himself that I could but be convinced that this profound peace was the fruit of his union with God.

" Such wonderful composure was so much the more surprising to me as I knew what Father Charles's exterior life was—one of constant activity and anxiety, by reason of his onerous office of *vigilant ;* but his lively faith elevated him far above all the tumult and storms of earthly surroundings, and his spiritual atmosphere was unalterable peace.

" I could but observe that herein he was always the same, whether in good health or in sickness, on his arrival in Bourbon, as at his departure. He regarded only the will of God, and esteemed himself too happy in fulfilling it.

" Whenever I met him in recreation I found his con-

versation amiable and agreeable, and generally on pious subjects.   At first I judged him to be somewhat cold and
reserved in disposition; and this may have been the case,
so far as nature goes, but so completely had he mastered
self that only gentleness and humility prevailed.

" It is a source of regret to me not to have enjoyed more
of this venerated Father's society; and I would be happy
indeed could I contribute to his glory by more ample details.   May the story of his life make known all the treasures of grace adorning so beautiful a soul!   I pray him to
remember in heaven his former confrère and friend, who
to-day offers you, in Our Lord, services and devotion unreservedly."

CHAPTER X.

FATHER CHARLES'S LAST DAYS.—HIS DEATH AT SEA.

IT was on Saturday, the 14th of June, 1862, about nine o'clock in the morning, that Father Sire embarked on the *Rhin*, a French mixed transport ship, carrying a hundred and fifty persons or thereabouts, including the sailors and seven officers. After the sad partings which had just taken place at St. Denis, one can readily imagine the weight upon his heart. However, master of himself in this as in everything else, he sat down to table with the officers an hour later, with, if not a gay and smiling face, at least a gentle, kindly manner, that greatly prepossessed them in his favor.

That very evening there was a slight improvement in his appetite—he felt less distaste for his food. After dinner, M. Aiguier, the commandant of the vessel, taking him aside, had a long conversation with him, in which Father Charles gave him much interesting information regarding Madagascar. From this hour the officer paid our young missionary the most delicate attentions, ordering the very best and choicest of his provisions for the good Father, whilst the commissary, on his side, showed equal pleasure in giving the sick man whatever might be of benefit to him.

The first night on ship he passed tolerably well. Next morning, which was Sunday, brought Father Sire a great privation—no Mass to say, none to hear. To console himself, he went on deck in the morning, and there spent several hours in prayer. In thinking of Bourbon, the summits of whose highest mountains were still visible, oh! how often during these holy exercises did he not raise his heart to God, and fervently renew the sacrifice he had just made! The rest of the day he spent in various parts of the ship, assisting at the inspection, and thus getting a general idea of the crew.

The sea and voyage being moderately calm on the 16th, 17th, and 18th of the month, Father Charles profited by it to become acquainted with the officers of the *Rhin*. His acquaintance thus formed with Lieutenant Galtier was an especially pleasant and cordial one. This officer, returning from Asia, had in his possession many Chinese curiosities, which he took pleasure in showing Father Charles. On the other side, the commandant, having noticed among the good Father's effects some very complete maps of the railroads in France, asked the loan of them, with which request Father Charles was delighted to comply.

These pleasant relations which he had the happiness of establishing between himself and the officers of the *Rhin* during these five days, proved for him an especial providence; for, from the 19th he was never able to leave his state-room again, and these gentlemen, of whom he had made friends, came daily to visit him, striving by their kind attentions to alleviate the sufferings and weariness his sickness entailed upon him. Their charity carried them still farther. Perceiving from the very beginning that his sickness would be of long duration, and that his condition was now so precarious as to require constant and skillful care, they asked an Indian from Pondichéry, who was a passenger on the *Rhin*, to nurse the sick man, promising him a suitable recompense for his services.

This young Indian, who had lived at Bourbon, and was now on his way to Nice to rejoin his master, M. Langau-

din, accepted the offer; and immediately installing himself in the good Father's state-room, never left him, day or
night. The infirmarians of the *Rhin*, and especially the
sailor infirmarian, Labé by name, were also assiduous in
their kind attentions; but the principal cares of nursing
and watching devolved on the Indian. In consequence,
Father Charles grew fond of him, and even gave him
touching marks of affection, hoping thereby to gain his
heart and thus open the way to his conversion. This he
had undertaken at the beginning, but his ever-failing
strength prevented his continuing the good work. On
his side, the young Indian became sincerely attached to
Father Charles, and in gratitude for his gentleness and
kindness devoted himself unreservedly to his service. It is
from the lips of this humble friend, and from M. Delmas,
the chief surgeon, we have obtained nearly all the details
of this second voyage; for Father Sire's journal finished
June 24th.

On the 19th, the pain having concentrated itself in the
side, a blister was applied to the left arm. On the 20th, the
sea being very rough, the rolling of the ship was frightful,
in consequence of which the patient kept his bed nearly all
day. Next day and the three following days the disease
having gained upon him, and insomnia likewise, to obtain
a little rest he was obliged to resort to opium.

From this date until the 15th of July he was not able
to get up except three or four times, and then only for a
few hours. Nevertheless, he still recited his Office, until
at length this pious exercise, heretofore so full of charms
for him, gradually became so fatiguing that he saw himself forced to renounce it. He supplied its place by the
frequent recitation of the Rosary, and occasionally he made
the Way of the Cross, by the aid of a crucifix indulgenced
for that purpose. According to the marks left in his Brev-

iary, the last office he recited was that of the Seven Brothers, Martyrs, July 10th, and we note as not unworthy of our attention the singular coincidence that there were then in his family seven brothers living.

"From the 15th of July," says M. Delmas, "Father Sire never left his bed. He had still a little appetite, however; although it was weak and capricious, it never entirely forsook him until a few days before his death. I must here remark that I cannot too highly praise the liberality of the commandant, who placed his wines and provisions at my disposal, to aid me in varying as much as possible our dear patient's nourishment.

"Father Sire was also on most friendly terms with the ship's crew. Even to the last, he conversed willingly with all who came to see him, and the subordinate officers, no less than the commandant, full of respect and esteem for him, went frequently to inquire of him how he felt. I myself had some pleasant conversations with him. Sometimes the subject would be Bourbon, sometimes the various members of his family. Again, we often spoke of our voyage,—the length of it, the little progress we had made so far, and the great distance yet to be gone over. Occasionally he would express a desire to see his family, and speak of the advantage it might have been for him to have gone by way of Suez. ' My embarkation,' said he, ' in that case, would have been retarded several days, as I would have had to wait at Bourbon until the departure of the mail boats, but their route consuming but twenty-eight days, I would thus have arrived much sooner and with less fatigue: yet the will of God above all things!'

"From the 15th of July he spoke no more of his return to France, neither of the distance we had already come, nor of that still to be traversed, which inclines me to believe that he had begun to realize the danger of his situation; especially as, just about this time, a large sore appeared on his back, in consequence of his great emaciation and his long confinement to bed. This, however, is but a supposition on my part, his silence on these subjects resulting, perhaps, from the violent pain he endured rendering him indifferent to them.

" His sufferings, really severe ever since his embarkation, continued to increase, and likewise did his admirable patience in supporting them; for during those long, weary days when he had not one moment's respite from pain, his Christian serenity was truly remarkable. He sometimes spoke to me of his sufferings, but with such resignation as I had never before seen in any one. His consideration for his infirmarians, even when the disease was at its worst, was incomprehensible to me otherwise than by referring it to its true heaven-born source—those hopes of religion which can extract joy from the greatest trials and sufferings of life.

"This example was to the officers far more edifying than all the sermons he might have preached. To the very last, there was ever on his face that kindly smile, so like a reflection of something angelic, when seen at that final struggle, when, for the most of us, the instinct of self-preservation alone remains, and absorbs all other thoughts."

The *Rhin* being delayed at the island of St. Helena from the 23d to the 27th of July, the commandant profited by these four days to visit at Longwood M. de Rougemont, who, in the name of France, there took care of the lodgings formerly occupied by the Emperor Napoleon. On one of these visits, meeting Father McCarthy, Catholic chaplain of the English troops stationed there, he told him they had on board their ship a Jesuit Father, seriously ill. This news the worthy ecclesiastic, who had been

on the island ten years, seeing a priest during all that
time only at rare intervals, was delighted to hear; and
next day he went to see Father Charles.

He spent two hours with him, and profited by the opportunity to make his confession.   He tells us that he
received many wise and edifying counsels, among others
that of always recommending himself to the guardian
angels of the various places to which he might be sent.
Being convinced from the sick man's conversation that he
hoped to regain health and strength to return to his mission,
and being persuaded himself that there was no immediate
danger of death, Father McCarthy believed it advisable to
refrain from speaking to him of the last sacraments.

Later, when requested by M. Vital to give him all the
details of this interview, Father McCarthy related in two
letters, one dated from George, the English colony of the
Cape of Good Hope, the other from British Caffraria, what
we have just recounted above, and added: " I was particularly edified at your brother's patience. During the two
hours spent in his company I heard from him no word of
complaint, either of his physical sufferings or want of attentions from those around. He appeared to me, on the
contrary, a striking model of patience and resignation.
After hearing my confession and giving me absolution, he
talked to me with much simplicity and candor of his
condition and of his interior dispositions, especially of his
confidence in Mary Immaculate, Star of the Sea, in his
good angel, and all the saints. We conversed afterwards
on other subjects, and when I left him he thanked me
very cordially for my visit. It is needless for me to say
how greatly I was edified, or how deep was my regret on
hearing of his death at sea, an event I had never appre-
hended."

After four days in port, the *Rhin* again set out to sea,

going towards the equator. Father Charles, now grown very weak indeed, rapidly grew more so, in proportion as they approached the line, for the heat, already scorching, soon became almost beyond endurance. Besides, delirium, from which he had hitherto been free, now made its appearance, leaving and returning at frequent intervals.

"In this delirium," says M. Delmas, "or rather these transient aberrations of mind, which at night assumed the form of fatiguing, fitful dreams, Father Sire had perfect consciousness of these phantasms of his disordered imagination, and made an effort to control them, but in vain." The good Master he so loved, and Who had tenderly watched over him during the voyage, did not, however, permit him to be continuously deprived of his reason, until just before the end. On the contrary, He gave the pious sufferer moments of complete lucidity, that he might converse with Him, his God, accept his sufferings, and uniting them to those of Our Lord Jesus Christ, drink even to the dregs the chalice offered him.

Hence, during the eight days preceding his death, oh! how lively his faith, his love for God how tender, his piety how ardent! He now conversed little with men, but continually with God. Seeing the rapid approach of death, he prepared himself to meet it by prayer the most fervent, aspirations of the heart unceasing. When we consider that the only words which fell from his lips during his delirium were, as the young Indian tells us, those of faith, hope, desire, "My God! my God! .... The sacraments! the sacraments!" we can readily imagine the transports of his heart when returning consciousness permitted him to converse with God! How he sighed to be with the good Master! How that heart sent forth aspirations of love, resignation, confidence, and holy abandonment into the hands of Jesus and Mary!

We are certain of the fact that he knew full well that he was dying, all alone, far from that native land so dear to him, and just as he was on the eve of seeing it again; far from his family, who would be crushed with grief at the news of his death; without a priest, the representative to him of heaven and the Church; without even a confidant to whom he could unburden his heart. "Poor Charles!" writes one of his friends, "oh! how he must have suffered, for his heart was one of the most loving and tender I ever knew! And yet, notwithstanding all these physical sufferings, these trials of mind and heart, he ever preserved that serenity of countenance, that sweet, amiable smile, indicative of peace of soul! Oh! what a magnificent spectacle it must have been to the loving contemplation of the angels, and especially to Jesus and Mary—this soul so pure, so simple, so upright! Here, indeed, was the death of the just, that death so beautiful, so precious in the sight of God Himself: *Pretiosa in conspectu Domini mors sanctorum ejus.*" [1]

In this state of abandonment and suffering the only human thought that preoccupied him was that of his mother. He saw her—this poor mother, transpierced with a sword of grief at hearing of his death on a vessel in mid-ocean, without even the succors of religion. Like Jesus on the cross, Father Sire, forgetting his own sufferings to think of his mother's, made various efforts to help lighten the stroke when it must needs fall upon her; and taking his pen, he would attempt to write to her, but in vain; overcome by weakness, he would fall back upon his pillow, unable to trace a line. This new sacrifice, added to all the others, gave the last blossom to his crown, the final touch of perfection to his merits.

To compensate for this forced silence, he asked a young

[1] Ps. cxv. 15.

soldier, acquainted with his family, to see them on his
return to France, and give them all the details of his last
moments. Willingly promising to comply with this request, which he regarded as a sacred trust, the young
soldier fulfilled this mission with fidelity, if not success.
Having but a few moments to spare in Paris, on his way
to rejoin his regiment, he nevertheless went to St. Sulpice
and asked to see M. Dominique. Unfortunately, the latter was just about to preach a sermon; and already on the
threshold of the chapel where his audience awaited him, he
could not withdraw. He asked his visitor to return after
the sermon, or wait about half an hour. This the soldier
could not do, as a military man's time is not his own, and
he was obliged to acquit himself of his trust in these few
words:

"I have much to tell you about your brother—much that
is interesting, but since time is wanting, I will merely
say that he died in peace, beloved by all around him, and
that ere his death he charged me to give you all the particulars of it." M. Dominique thanked him sincerely, and
it was with deep regret he saw all further information de-
nied him by the fulfilment of an ecclesiastical duty. In
the preoccupation of mind consequent upon this sudden
news, and the fact of having kept his audience waiting,
he entirely forgot to ask the address of the young soldier,
who appeared quite intelligent, and as if he had had much
to do with the pious invalid; and all subsequent efforts
to discover his name or whereabouts proved fruitless.

After this act of love and filial piety, namely, the arrangement to send some one to his family informing them of all
the details of his illness and last moments, Father Charles
thought only of dying, and dying like a holy religious.
Having already given up everything else on earth, his only
desire now was that of self-detachment. For a long time,

indeed, had he daily murmured these ejaculations: " I am all Thine, O my God, and all that I have is Thine: " *Tuus totus ego sum, et omnia mea tua sunt;* and now he repeated them with transports of delight; likewise, those other admirable words so often on his lips in health: " Jesus, Mary, and Joseph, I give you my heart and my soul! Jesus, Mary, and Joseph, assist me in my last agony! Jesus, Mary, and Joseph, may I breathe forth my soul in peace with you! Then, turning towards his Blessed Mother in heaven, whose tenderness he had so often experienced, he would say in accents of triumphant love: " O my sovereign, my Mother, I give myself entirely to thee, and in token of my devotion I this day consecrate to thee my eyes, my ears, my mouth, my heart, my whole being. And since I thus belong to thee, O my good Mother, I pray thee to watch over and protect me as thy property!" When failing strength necessarily curtailed his words, he would content himself with merely a sigh, a glance towards heaven, and the ejaculation, " All for Jesus, through Mary," or even that briefer one, " Jesus! Mary! Joseph!"

Death was now gaining rapidly upon him. " On the eve of that sad day which took him from us," says M. Delmas, " the heat was atrocious; we were almost on the line. Towards noon, suffering greatly for want of air in his cabin, our dear invalid asked me if he might not be taken to the sailors' hospital, where he could have more room and light. This desire, fortunately, could be granted, as there was not one man sick on board this day (an exceptional thing); hence he had no fears that his dying moments would be disturbed by the presence of another sick person.

"When installed in his new apartment, he seemed to experience great relief, and in token of gratitude he pressed the hand of each one who had assisted at his removal, also of the commandant, his lieutenant, M. Tourneur, and myself, who had directed it. Then he said, smiling gently as usual, that he would try to sleep a little. I returned to see him at four o'clock. He was now very pale, and his pulse perceptibly lower, but his mind still clear. He expressed himself intelligently, but in a broken voice. At eight o'clock in the evening delirium set in, and he died an hour after midnight."

" The night of his death," adds the Indian from Bourbon, "there were but two of us with the dying man, the sailors' infirmarian, Labé, and myself, until ten o'clock. At that hour, perceiving that he was sinking, I went for M. Delmas, who remained with us to the end. A little after ten o'clock his agony began."

Questioned as to the details of Father Charles's last moments, the infirmarian related that during the two hours immediately preceding his death the dying religious held in his hands a crucifix, with every sigh mingling some words, but so feebly articulated they were scarcely intelligible, although, from time to time, he thought he could distinguish the names of Jesus and Mary; whence it is easy to conclude that his death was most peaceful and edifying, truly a falling asleep in the Lord. " He quit this world," said one of the ship's employees, " as we all would desire to quit it. His death was the sequel and consequence, as it were, of his devotion; it was a sort of martyrdom, worth more before God than any other preparation that could be made."

It was on the 4th of August, at one o'clock in the morning, this precious death took place. Singular coincidence! On this day, the Church honors St. Dominic, principal patron of one of Father Charles's brothers, and of two of his uncles who were priests; also *secondary* patron of three of his other brothers, beside being, this year, monthly patron for a fourth brother not bearing the saint's name.

As soon as Father Charles expired, lighted ship's lanterns were placed around his bed; and until the burial, which took place at five o'clock in the evening, a man was stationed to guard the body. The clothing in which he died was left on him, as well as the crucifix, medals, and scapular he wore around his neck. Then a cloth being wrapped around the body, it was placed in the mortuary sack[1] and reverently carried on deck. Here the last sad honors were rendered it, in the presence of the commandant, the other officers, and the whole crew, all in an attitude of mourning and respect, silent, and with uncovered heads.

The commandant read the accustomed prayers, and at the usual signal, accompanied by the words, "May God protect thee!" the body of the deceased was gently committed to the sea, amid a salvo of fire-arms. God wished, it seems, that this *vessel*, image of what is passing away, should be for Father Charles the calvary on which to consummate his sacrifice, and the bosom of the sea, image of the bosom of God, the tomb wherein to take his last, long sleep.

It is, then, in this tomb his virginal body, purified by suffering, and so often sanctified by the body and blood of a God, awaits, with those of countless other martyrs, buried like himself beneath the waves, the blessed day of resurrection, to sing forever with the elect the canticle of eternity: "To Him that sitteth on the throne, and to the Lamb: benediction and honor and glory and power forever and ever."[2]

[1] This sack, ballasted with sand, takes the place of a coffin in burials at sea.
[2] Apoc. v. 13.

CHAPTER XI.

Extraordinary Events that took place at the time of and after Father Charles's Death.

1.—Revelation of the Death of Father Charles and of his Entrance into Heaven.

AT the precise time of Father Sire's death, which took place at one o'clock in the night, Catherine Beillard, the pious peasant of whom we have frequently spoken, then nearly two thousand leagues distant from him, and totally ignorant of his illness or his embarkation for France, was transported in spirit to the vessel, and saw the good Father dying, holding a crucifix, and murmuring these words: "All for Jesus through Mary." "Two persons," said Catherine, "were beside him." One of these, whom she supposed to be Our Lord, was arrayed in vestments similar to the priest's when giving Benediction of the Blessed Sacrament. The other, the Blessed Virgin she thought, was a lady clothed in white, with a black veil thrown over her head. This lady, standing at Father Charles's left hand, placed a crown of white roses on his brow.

Two or three hours later, Catherine was aroused from sleep by a man's voice calling her by name and in the idiom of the country, the only tongue she spoke. She had already opened her eyes and raised her head when she heard a second call. Perfectly awake, she now sat up in bed and listened attentively. A third time was the same voice heard pronouncing her name in a loud, distinct tone, whilst an interior voice said clearly: "Father Charles is dead; he is in heaven." Deeply impressed, she inquired of her husband if he had heard nothing. On his answering in the negative, "What!" said she, "did you not hear some one, just now, call me three times?" Her husband having assured her that he did not, Catherine tried to calm her agitation, and to go to sleep again.

Arising at break of day, she said her accustomed prayers, and after attending to some domestic duties, took her way to church, to hear the seven o'clock Mass. Going thither, she was stopped three times. "It seemed," said she, "as if an invisible hand struck me on the breast, and prevented my walking. Each time I asked Our Lord what He desired of me, and each time I felt myself impelled to make one of the three pilgrimages of which Father Charles had so often spoken to me, but which I had heretofore neglected, because I had not clearly understood him: the first (thus Catherine expresses it), through the mysteries of Our Lord Jesus Christ; the second, through the mysteries of the Blessed Virgin; and the third, through the life of the saints. In speaking to me of this last pilgrimage, Father Charles had strongly recommended it, saying it was an excellent practice, because thereby we honor all the saints, the majority of whom are unknown and consequently little honored—a practice never failing to draw down graces innumerable upon those who are faithful to it. Heretofore I had neglected it; but as God Himself has deigned to enlighten me upon the manner of making this triple pilgrimage, I am happy to perform it, and the fruits thereof in my soul are abundant."

Arriving at church, Catherine heard Mass, and approached the Holy Table with the intention of offering her Communion for M. Dominique Sire, as she had two days

previously promised his brother, M. Césaire, she would do.
(It was her invariable custom to offer a Communion for
each of the Sire brothers on his respective feast-day.)
Scarcely had she knelt at the altar rail, ere she felt irre-
sistibly impelled to change her intention, and offer this
Communion in thanksgiving for all the spiritual favors a
beneficent God had bestowed upon Father Charles in the
course of his life. Remembering now her last night's experience, she redoubled her fervor. Imagine, if you can,
her astonishment when, placed upon her tongue, the Sacred
Host, three several times, assumed the form of a cross, and
especially when, returned to her place, she beheld herself
environed by rays of light far surpassing those of the sun!

This wonderful brilliancy lasted during all the time of
her thanksgiving—about half an hour: and Catherine says,
likewise, that these moments were most precious to her,—
filled with such spiritual consolation as she had never before experienced. Especially astonished and grateful was
she at receiving, in a very considerable degree, the two
gifts of detachment from all things and love of God—
graces Father Charles had promised he would beg earnestly for her, should he die first. Acknowledging her great
unworthiness of such signal favors, and doubting not that
she was indebted for them to Father Sire's powerful intercession, she spent her half-hour allotted to thanksgiving
after Holy Communion in humbling herself profoundly,
begging God to pardon all her weaknesses, thanking Him
especially, and imploring Him to grant her still greater
detachment from the world, and to re-unite her with that
holy friend who had obtained for her these inestimable
graces. Henceforth she felt but disgust for the things of
this world; whilst her ever increasing love of God made
her hunger and thirst for the blessed hour of deliverance
from the bonds of the flesh, that in heaven, with the friend

she esteemed and loved here, she might praise Him eternally.

Returning from church, Catherine told her husband the singular events of the past night, and said she knew Father Charles was dead. As her husband professed incredulity as to the import of what he called a dream, and counselled her not to speak of it, for fear of being laughed at or deemed foolish, much less to attach any consequence to it, she followed his advice, and mentioned the circumstance to no one, save her daughter, a discreet, pious woman, and one who, like herself, held Father Charles in veneration. To prevent any betrayal of these events to the Sire family, she visited their house less frequently; especially after learning that Father Charles had been very sick in Bourbon, that his health was seriously compromised, and that his superiors had decided to send him to his native land as a last resource. And when stopping casually to see Mme. Sire, as she sometimes did, if the conversation turned upon Father Charles, she would suddenly become very reserved. M. Césaire, a providential witness of these visits,[1] thus gives a detailed account of them to his brother Vital:

"Leaving Paris, very unexpectedly, towards the end of July for Saint-Jory, under circumstances with which you are acquainted, I had the pleasure of a visit from Catherine, soon after my arrival home. On this occasion, which I remember well, she expressed a wish to send some messages to Father Charles through me. Her words, which

---

[1] M. Césaire was, at this time, at the Seminary of Issy, near Paris, where he had three brothers. This fact, together with that of its being their vacation (which commenced July 18th), had induced him to ask permission to spend the first three weeks with them. Towards the end of the month he was much surprised to receive word from his superior, M. Carrière, to leave for Saint-Jory the next day, which he accordingly did, to his especial satisfaction, when later circumstances proved how providential was this change, in view of the great sorrow then hovering over the family.

I give as literally as possible, were these: 'I have something I would like very much to say to Father Charles; I do not wish him to think I forget him. Will you not attend to it, M. Césaire, as soon as we have time? We never know what may happen—one might die;' and immediately, seeming to reproach herself for having spoken thus in the presence of my mother, who was always anxious about our dear missionary, she added: 'You know, I am old; consequently, not likely to live so much longer.'

"All the circumstances of this visit are fully impressed upon my memory. In the course of our conversation I requested Catherine to offer a Communion for Dominique on the following Monday, August 4th, his feast-day, and she promised me she would. This was on Saturday morning, August 2d, at the latest.

"Before the 7th of the same month, probably the 4th or 5th, when as yet no one at Saint-Jory had heard of Charles's embarkation for France, Catherine came to our house again, but so preoccupied was her manner, so quiet and reserved was she, that I could but be struck with her demeanor. Hoping to cheer her a little, I remarked that I had time now to write a letter for her to Charles, and would willingly put on paper whatever she might dictate regarding the matter she had referred to in her last visit. She replied that *henceforth it would be useless.* Much surprised at this answer, I hardly knew what to think, except that I was unworthy of knowing her communication to Charles, because of my great desire to hear it.

"A short time after this, Sabin,[1] having gone to Toulouse, learned there casually from the relatives of M. Richard, a physician in Bourbon,[2] that Father Charles, by

---

[1] Sabin was the brother in the Sire family who remained a layman. In age he ranked third of those then living.

[2] In a letter his family had just received, M. Richard mentions among other items that a Jesuit Father of Toulouse, named Sire, had just embarked for France by rea-

medical advisers, had been sent back to France. On his return to Saint-Jory, he hastened to tell us the news, which gave me great pleasure at thoughts of seeing Charles again. Seeing Catherine soon after, as she came out of church and was passing us with a mere salutation, he stopped her and told her, in my presence, that Charles was on his way home from Bourbon. To our great astonishment, she expressed no surprise, but replying coldly, ' *So much the better,*' passed on, without even inquiring how we heard the news. Her conduct appeared to me inexplicable.

" All these events took place during the week in which Charles died.

" On the last day of this same week, Saturday, August 9th, having gone to Toulouse, on the occasion of Clara's [1] holiday, I took advantage of the opportunity to pay the Jesuit Fathers a visit. They confirmed the news Sabin had brought, and said that Father Charles was already on the way home, or soon would be. They could not give me any more definite information.[2] Returning to Saint-Jory, I profited by the first spare moment to go to see Catherine, and have a little talk with her about Father Charles, and our pleasure at thoughts of meeting him so soon again. Telling her in her husband's presence what the Jesuit Fathers had told me about his return, I ventured several conjectures as to the probable time of his

---

son of failing health. M. Richard's friends learning that the gentleman they met bore the same name, inquired of him if he had any relative, a Jesuit, in Bourbon : and on being answered in the affirmative, they informed him of his brother's embarkation for France.

[1] Clara was Father Charles's niece, then at a boarding-school in Toulouse.

[2] Father Roucanières, of St. Mary's College, whom I visited that same day, offered to say a Mass for my intention, which offer, the first of the kind ever made me, I heartily accepted. Learning, five weeks later, of Charles's death, I could but believe it was this dearly loved brother who had inspired Father Roucanières with the thought of saying a Mass for me, thus to compensate me for that he himself had promised me on the feast of the Sacred Heart, and which his illness prevented his saying.

reaching France. To my great surprise, she appeared little interested, and made no reply, except to ask me, at two different times, what was done with persons who died on the ocean. On my telling her their bodies were cast into the abyss of waters, she wept a little, and then inquired if there was a chaplain on all vessels—a question I was unable to answer satisfactorily.

"I remember well that these questions and her whole conduct, the reason for which I never suspected, appeared to me very strange. Until we received the official news of Charles's death, Catherine's manner, on coming to see us, was a most preoccupied one; she had little to say, and if the conversation turned upon Charles, she was evidently ill at ease. She would, at such times, speak of him, but in a most reserved, cautious way, as if fearing to trust herself, so utterly unlike her former simplicity of demeanor. It is also worthy of note, that, although our mother during all this vacation was much distressed about Charles, not receiving any letters from him, Catherine made no effort as heretofore to dispel her fears, but always endeavored to console her by saying, 'We must ever place all our confidence in God.'"[1]

To give the necessary weight and authority to the above testimony, M. Césaire took oath to it. So, too, did Catherine and her husband, to each and every thing related herein (especially the contents of the present chapter) of Father Charles with which they were in any way connected. All was carefully read to them; after which, in the presence of three witnesses, they swore upon the Holy Gospel that their deposition had been strictly reproduced, and they themselves had been scrupulously truthful in making it.

[1] Catherine's conduct singularly augmented Mme. Sire's alarms, and filled her with the most painful forebodings, which not all the repeated efforts of those pious persons to whom she frequently opened her heart in confidence could succeed in dispelling.

II.—Favors of all kinds accorded Catherine.

During the five weeks elapsing between the death of Father Sire and the official notice of his death received at Saint-Jory, Catherine Beillard was the only person who invoked his intercession; and innumerable, indeed, were the favors granted her during that precious interval. "Everything I asked during that time," she afterwards told me, "I obtained; and Father Charles's liberality went even beyond my requests; for, in addition to all that I asked, he accorded me many favors that I would hardly have dreamed of receiving.

"On the day of his death, for instance, the feast of St. Dominic, and several times during that August, he suggested to me the thought of becoming a Dominican. I had never heard of the Third Order of St. Dominic, much less did I know that a married woman could, with her husband's consent, be admitted to religious profession. One day, when Father Charles, then a young seminarian, was discoursing most beautifully about Our Lord and the Blessed Virgin, I exclaimed, 'Oh! how blest you are in being a priest, thus belonging to God entirely, giving all your time, your thoughts, to Him alone, or what relates to Him! It would be my greatest happiness to be a religious, living in holy solitude with God, and devoting myself to Him—but this is out of the question for me, as I am married.' 'Many have become religious after having been married,' he answered; 'there are even some who, being married, live as religious; so, why might not you one day?'

"It was doubtless this desire, expressed on the occasion above mentioned, the good Father wished to satisfy in inspiring me with the thought of becoming a Dominican; and although, at the time, I never dreamed of the possibility of my being received into the Third Order of St.

Dominic—I, a married woman, living with my husband—
or that I could so easily fulfil all the obligations, wonderful to relate, just one year after Father Charles's death, in
that same month of August, a Dominican Father, contrary
to all expectation, came to Saint-Jory to receive me as a
postulant, and on the 4th of August following, anniversary
of Father Charles's death, I was admitted to profession in
the Third Order of St. Dominic, with my husband's consent and my director's express approbation. God grant
this inestimable favor tend to my increase in sanctity and
His greater glory!"

The day of Catherine's profession was for her one of happiness inexpressible. Despite her shattered health, and
the fatigues of a journey, made fasting and on foot, to
Toulouse, a distance of more than ten miles, she remained
in the Dominican church there from half past seven in
the morning until noon, so absorbed in God as to be ob-
livious of all that was passing around her. "I thought
no longer of earth," said she; "I was in heaven!"

From that time, indeed, she seemed to be weary of earth,
and to aspire only after heaven and the blessed society of
that friend to whose powerful intercession she ascribed the
favors and privileges innumerable accorded her during her
sojourn on earth. "I am very anxious," said she to me
one day, "to read Father Charles's Life, but I am more
anxious to be with him; and if one were to promise me,
on the one side, all that the sun shines on in this world,
and on the other death, with the certainty of rejoining
Father Sire in heaven, my choice would soon be made."

Until her death, Catherine lived in an almost uninterrupted union of soul and heart with Father Charles,
thus performing all her actions, especially her prayers, exposing to him all her wants, and recommending herself to
him under all circumstances. And her confidence was re-

warded; for, during the nine years she survived, innumerable were the temporal as well as the spiritual favors she received through this means, both for herself and others—nothing, it seems, being refused her. She would often say, particularly towards the end of her life: "When I think of the favors and graces showered upon me since Father Charles's death, I am filled with awe, and shudder at the mere thought of having, one day, to render an account of them to God. Far from being uplifted thereby and glorying in them, I annihilate myself before Him, and humbly beg pardon for having profited so little by them. Ever looking upon myself as a vile instrument in His hands to reveal Father Charles's glory to the world, I dread nothing so much as placing any obstacle to this design; and I beg Him most earnestly and perseveringly for perfect fidelity to all His graces.

It was this sentiment of fear and humility that sealed Catherine's lips, and prevented her mentioning these favors to any save the director of her conscience and Father Charles's brothers who were priests. The public was kept in utter ignorance of them, and likewise would the Sire family have been, had not God impelled her to offer the afflicted ones consolation, by making known to them these wondrous things, especially the revelation regarding his death. Wherefore should we now keep silence concerning favors not less signal, received by others, and which, giving additional weight to our narration, will edify our readers, and inspire them with renewed confidence in Father Charles's intercession?

III.—Wonders wrought by God to establish Devotion to Father Charles.

The first prodigy God wrought to bring about and increase devotion to Father Charles is that supernatural, almost irresistible impulse urging so many pious souls to venerate, praise, invoke, and take him for a protector.

Scarcely was his death known in his native village, ere these words of veneration and praise were on every lip: "He is in heaven! He is a saint!" And when, five days later, a solemn Mass was celebrated there for his soul's repose, no one would pray for him. "It is unnecessary," they all said; "we should rather invoke him and take him for our protector."

After the services this day, M. Vital, in the presence of a large assemblage of the relatives and friends, disclosed the revelation made to Catherine [1] concerning Father Charles's death. It was received with delight, and, from this moment, many pious souls felt urged in spite of themselves to address their petitions to him. These speedily obtaining the desired favors, the result has been a strong and steadily increasing current of devotion towards this good priest for the last twenty three years, his numerous clients having recourse to him in all their necessities, and never, say they, in vain.

Two months later, Catherine's account having been examined, and its accuracy confirmed by the testimony of those who, on the ship, had been providential witnesses of Father Charles's death, M. Vital, whom the Jesuit Fathers had urged to prepare a Notice of his holy brother for publication, [2] wrote these Fathers a long letter on the subject. This missive, though containing very little save a few de-

---

[1] Catherine Beillard died October 27, 1871, aged sixty-five years, leaving behind her, throughout the country, an established reputation for solid virtue and great piety. The biography of this pious peasant woman will soon be given to the public.

[2] When M. Vital. September, 15, 1862, announced to the Rev. Jesuit Fathers his brother Charles's death, the first words that fell from the Rev. Provincial's lips were, "You must write a Notice of it;" and when M. Vital excused himself on the plea that he had seen so little of Father Charles since the latter's childhood and youth, Father Studers, the Provincial, replied positively: "You must write the Notice; I assure you, he was one of our most holy religious."

tails of the last year of Father Charles's life, and Catherine's revelation concerning his death, produced everywhere the most salutary effects,[1] not the least remarkable of which was that spontaneous outburst of devotion to this holy man—a devotion characterized by such tenderness, veneration, love, and confidence, as could but make it amiable and popular.

Soon after this, at the request of Mgr. Maupoint, Bishop of St. Denis, a little Notice of sixteen pages was prepared at Rodez, and printed by his orders in the religious almanac of Bourbon. It, likewise, contained little matter except an account of the revelation made to Catherine, and a very abridged summary of Father Charles's life; yet the salutary effects thereby produced, both immediately and ever since, are almost incredible.

Having read the manuscript, Mgr. Maupoint wrote to his correspondent at Versailles: "This Notice is excellent. Be very careful to change nothing therein. If the facts related are veritable, Father Charles will, one day, be canonized—truly, a great honor for the diocese. I visited this dear Father on his sick-bed, before he left St. Denis, and was much edified by him. I shall be happy to insert the Notice in *Les Fleurs spirituelles de Bourbon*"[2]

Wherever this little pamphlet found its way, it was read and re-read with vivid interest, especially at Toulouse, every one wishing to have a copy, that, reading it at leisure, or lending it to others, all might be led not only to honor and

---

[1] Father Studers had autograph copies of it made at Vels, and sent to all the houses of the Order, accompanied by a circular requesting the Fathers and Brothers who had known Father Charles to give his biographer any information he might desire of them.

In answer to this appeal and his successor's, the Rev. Father Rouquayrol's, more than eighty Jesuits furnished M. Vital with much very interesting matter regarding his beloved brother.

[2] *Les Fleurs spirituelles de Bourbon* is the name of a charming little volume in 12mo, consisting of interesting notices of persons of Reunion Isle who died in the colony leaving a memory fragrant with the odor of their virtues.

invoke Father Charles, but more especially to imitate him. [1]

However efficacious the impulse given to devotion to Father Charles by these pamphlets, it is certain they never could have invested it with that character of permanence and universality God seems to desire it should have. For this would be necessary a divine action more manifest, which, clearly revealing God's intentions therein, should thus protect Father Charles's devoted clients from all illusion or reproach. In a word, the devotion must needs be confirmed by miracles, veritable miracles, clearly set forth and proven. This, then, is the second means God has used to propagate and establish the devotion to Father Charles.

The first of these miraculous events, in the order of time, took place at Rodez, only five months after this good Father's death. M. Vital, who was one of the happy witnesses of it, thus gives the account:

"When, in quality of Father Charles's universal legatee, I received at Rodez, November 16, 1862, all the effects of this beloved brother, my first care was to examine them and assure myself that everything was there according to the list sent me. Moreover, I wished to behold, to touch, and to press to my heart objects so dear to me, destined, one day, to .be held most precious, and which already furnished me with an easy means of making others happy. I could but perceive that every time I handled these articles something of a divine virtue escaped from them, which, penetrating my soul, filled me with a happiness indescribable. I was moved to tears, but they were tears of love, tenderness, and joy. Likewise have I been receiving daily and hourly the graces I most needed, all which favors, I feel, come to me through Father Charles.

---

[1] M. Vassen, canon of Prato, in Tuscany, had this Notice reproduced in Italian, at his own expense; and until the time of his death he continued to circulate it with a zeal inexplicable, except upon the supposition that he himself had been much benefited by it, and that his devotion had been rewarded by numberless favors.

" What impressed me especially with a joy beyond expression was the following marvel God deigned to operate under my eyes, for the glorification of these relics.

" Among the shirts Father Charles had worn in his last illness were three which on the right arm, or in that portion of them that had been near his liver, the principal seat of the disease, showed large spots of blood. Asked by the laundress of the seminary, Mlle. Hérail, to let her wash these garments, because they had belonged to one of my brothers, I assented; and she washed them, first (as is usual for removing blood stains) in cold water, but finding the spots bright as ever, she put the shirts in the hands of a person who washed them in lye. Even this was in vain, the spots resisting every effort to remove them, which fact so astonished this second laundress, that, in returning the garments to Mlle. Hérail, she could not forbear saying: 'During the twenty years I have been using alkalis, never have I known anything like this, never have I returned my wash in such a condition. What is the matter with those shirts? there must be something extraordinary about them.'

" Informed of these facts, the importance of which I immediately comprehended, to assure myself of the exact truth, I went to Mlle. Hérail, and there, in the presence of six trustworthy witnesses, it was clearly proven: 1. That all soil on the linen, blood stains excepted, had disappeared in the first water; 2. That these, on the contrary, had resisted two consecutive washings, and even the action of the alkali; 3. That, submitted to a warm iron, they had become the color of fresh blood; 4. That they had resisted the action of oxalic acid even, an infallible recipe for removing blood stains. [1] Anxious to ascertain now if the

---

[1] These lines were not given to the printer until they had been submitted to the four surviving witnesses of the fact.

phenomenon were not susceptible of some scientific explanation, I went to Toulouse, and made known the facts to M.
Filliol,[1] the most celebrated chemist of Southern France.
M. Filliol answered thus: "Blood, Monsieur, always
yields to the first application of water; if, then, as you
say, these spots have resisted not only the water, but the
alkali, and even oxalic acid, it is very clear to me that no
natural cause can account for it.' "[2]

Author of the wondrous conservation of this blood, God
soon confirmed His work by even a more striking manifestation of His agency, the occasion of which was as follows.

Just about this time, the religious of Notre Dame of
Rodez were in great affliction. Their worthy superior, at-
tacked, three years previously, by a grave malady, seemed
now permanently incapacitated for active duty; and although there was no immediate danger of death, her
health was so shattered, her prostration and weekness such,
that the three physicians attending her said: "She can
never be cured."[3]

Almost continual vomitings had so affected her stomach
that it scarcely retained anything now, not even cold water,
although distilled. Her nervous system, too, was in such a
state that the least movement caused her intense suffering,
and the pain in her head was excruciating. At the slightest
unexpected noise she was liable to a fainting spell, or an
attack of vertigo, and it was necessary for one of her spiritual daughters to be always in attendance upon her. Her
mind, however, was sufficiently clear for her to be able to
offer her sufferings to God, and frequently to invoke Him.

---

[1] M. Filliol was then mayor of Toulouse, and professor of chemistry in that city.

[2] It is by the application of a piece of one of these garments that most of the favors
believed to have been received through Father Charles have been obtained.

[3] These three doctors were M. Marion, the attending physician of the house, M.
Rozier, mayor of Rodez, and M. Tissandier, a relative of the patient.

After long months, there being no perceptible improvement in her condition, the community called in another physician, M. Lala, a young man recently established at Rodez, but already renowned for his skill in medicine. He soon had sole charge of this critical case. At first, to encourage the Sisters, he told them he thought his patient might be cured, although the chances in her favor were very few; but a little later, being closely questioned on the subject, he let fall these significant words: "I will do my best for her as long as there is life—more than this, I cannot say."

Bereft of all hope from human source, the community in this great affliction now turned more earnestly to Heaven. Prayers public and private, Communions, good works —nothing was spared to obtain so precious a boon; but in vain, God seemed deaf to their supplications. The very few who were admitted to the sick woman's chamber were really frightened at her condition, and evidently impressed with the hopelessness of the case. This was the propitious moment Heaven chose in which to operate her cure, and thus glorify Father Charles, by manifesting to all the power of his intercession with God.

The following is the account given of it by M. Vital, the providential instrument of this extraordinary grace.

"When, yielding to the entreaties of the Rev. Jesuit Fathers, and impelled by what appeared to me a supernatural inspiration, I began the little Notice of my brother, —which I then supposed was to remain in manuscript— I went, one day, to Notre Dame convent to obtain the assistance of a good copyist, and one upon whose discretion I could rely to keep my secret. This was about the middle of February, 1863. I asked to see the superioress, and urged interiorly to speak with her, I declined to state my business to the assistant, who came to the parlor in the Reverend Mother's place, and I determined to wait awhile.

" About the first week in March I returned to the convent; and although the superioress was in the same miserable state of prostration, and had not been to the parlor for three years, she, with a great effort, complied with my request to speak with her. I was convinced, at first sight, that the statements concerning her condition had not in the least been exaggerated. All bent, her eyes haggard, her face discolored, she seemed to have scarce more than a breath of life. Greeting me, she said, ' The good God has sent you to do me good.' Profiting by these words, I immediately introduced the subject of my visit, speaking to her at length of Father Charles, the sanctity of his life, the still more edifying circumstances of his death, and the powerful effects of his intercession. Nor did I omit mention of the singular fact of the blood stains on his garments resisting all efforts to remove them.

" Deeply impressed at this account, and inspired with the thought of having recourse to him herself to obtain her cure, the Reverend Mother asked me for a little piece of the wonderful linen; also, that meanwhile I would loan her a little medal of St. Joseph that had belonged to Father Charles, and which she had heard me say I always wore about me.

" Returning to the convent a few days after this, to bring the relic, the Reverend Mother hastened to inform me of a great favor already obtained by means of the medal and invocation of Father Charles—the instantaneous relief from suffering of one of their boarders, followed by a perfect cure.

" This sudden cure, together with the perusal of the Notice now copied and ready for me, had so increased her confidence in the good Father, she said, that she wished to make him her protector. That same evening she applied the precious relic to her head: the pains in her head and stomach, heretofore so continual and violent, ceased; likewise the attacks of vertigo. At the end of a week she was able to observe the common rule, and in a month's time so complete was her restoration to health, that all the Sisters, astonished and delighted, declared it a miracle.

"Puzzled at this wonderful cure, which baffled all attempts of the medical art to explain, M. Lala, the physician in charge, expressed himself thus on several occasions. Later, being informed of Father Charles's supernatural intervention therein, he exclaimed: 'Ah! that's the key of the enigma I tried so hard to solve at the time. From a medical point of view there was no hope for the Reverend Mother, her stomach being in such a weakened state that it could retain nothing, not even distilled water. You may well imagine my astonishment at seeing her cured, in a week able to digest everything, and in a month resuming her ordinary duties. I could scarcely believe my eyes.'

"Dr. Tissandier was not less surprised, and said to his pious relative, in a tone of the deepest conviction: 'It is God, not we, who have cured you. All our remedies, believe me, have accomplished nothing.'

"Dr. Marion, of whom I inquired about the Reverend Mother's cure," continues M. Vital, "replied emphatically: 'Cured! And do you believe it? For three years she has been a prey to several mortal maladies, and her cure is impossible! And as I insisted that there must be some foundation for the rumor, he added: 'She will never be well; she is struck with death, and can never resume her duties as superioress.'

"And yet, in spite of all this, she was indeed cured, and had been exercising the functions of her office, which, notwithstanding her advanced age, she still continues, to the great satisfaction of her large community."

This worthy religious had henceforth for Father Charles sentiments of the deepest gratitude, love, and confidence unbounded. Thus invoking him on all occasions, and spreading abroad a knowledge of his sanctity and goodness, many and precious were the favors she received through his intercession.

Six years later, requested to give some account of these, for the extension of Father Charles's glory, she wrote thus to M. Vital:

"Although not of an enthusiastic disposition, and little inclined to make known to the world the especial favors with which it has pleased Divine Providence to recompense my earnest prayer, I could not be so ungrateful as to refuse compliance with the request you have just made in reference to Father Charles. To act thus in regard to this great servant of God, withholding the homage his sanctity and powerful protection merit, would it not be to draw upon me from our divine Master the same reproaches He made to the ten lepers of the Gospel?

"Hence, impelled by gratitude, gladly, Monsieur Abbé, do I bring my little sheaf to the rich harvest of pious souvenirs of praise and thanksgiving you are collecting, in all generosity, for God's glory and for an immortal monument to your angelic brother.

"Since the day good Father Charles was first made known to me I have had the most exalted idea of his sanctity and power with God, a salutary devotion to him, and great confidence in his intercession—sentiments which are ever increasing, by reason of the continual graces I receive from him.

"I have likewise felt constrained to direct others, on seeing them in trouble or in any pressing necessity, to seek his aid; and frequently have they told me what an abundant source of consolation their compliance with my suggestions proved to them.

"Whenever I implore the immediate assistance of Heaven, it is to good Father Charles I address myself, and never in vain. What violent grief have I not seen calmed by invoking him! what favors innumerable, spiritual and temporal, obtained by novenas in his honor! I can say, for my part, that at the time this new celestial protector was made known to me I had been long a prey to cruel physical sufferings, and that invoking him they ceased, and my strength has been restored to me. I cannot doubt his instrumentality in this.

"It would be too tedious to enumerate all the especial favors we attribute to Father Charles's intercession, and I must confine myself to these few lines. May this faithful friend of Jesus and Mary, from his exalted place in heaven (for such I believe is his), deign to accept them as a sincere testimony of my profound veneration for his virtues and merits, as well as a feeble tribute of my undying gratitude for the blessings he has obtained for me." [1]

In view of the above-mentioned and innumerable other facts reflecting glory upon the memory of Father Charles, to say nothing of the countless especial favors various members of the Sire family had received through his intercession during the months of April, May, June, and July, M. Vital was inspired with the thought of closing the year in which Father Charles's death occurred by a novena in common, which would also serve as a preparation for the feast of St. Dominic, anniversary of his precious death.

The end of this novena was to thank God and Mary

---

[1] To avoid wounding the modesty of this worthy superior, we were obliged to omit in this account many circumstances that would have added greatly to its interest.

for all they had done for Father Charles since the 4th of August preceding, and to obtain through the Blessed Virgin's mediation that, if God wished Father Charles to be honored and glorified, He would manifest His will therein by a sensible sign—that of according the especial graces they were going to ask through this holy priest's intercession.

For this double intention each person engaged in the novena must offer at least one Communion during the stipulated time, and recite on the first and last days a *Te Deum* in thanksgiving, in addition to the usual daily prayers, which were a *Pater*, an *Ave*, and these two invocations: "Our Lady of Good News and of Beldon, glorify your devoted servant, Father Charles, by granting the petitions we now address you in his honor and through his intercession!" "Beloved Father Charles, now in heaven, manifest your power with God by casting a look of complacency upon the pious work undertaken in your honor!"

This important novena, to be followed by so many others, was eagerly and fervently participated in by the little groups at Saint-Jory, Toulouse, and Rodez. Father Charles had already, time and again, covered with his benefits and it was crowned with success.[1]

Hence, it was manifest to the eyes of all that God wished Father Charles to be honored and invoked as His friend, and one full of goodness and power. Wherefore Father Charles's relatives and friends began to make him known to others, and consequently (aided by that interior attraction impelling souls) loved and invoked.

God, indeed, disposed the minds and hearts of all to a favorable reception of the wonders related of Father

---

[1] All the wonderful facts herein related of Father Charles have been printed only after endorsement by those persons who were either the witnesses or objects of these wonders.

Charles, inspiring them with a true devotion to him, by a daily increase of the favors obtained through his intercession.[1]

Hearts were first attracted towards him by hearing of the sanctity of his life, the still more edifying circumstances of his death, the happiness and glory God seems pleased to have bestowed upon him in recompense thereof, and also, by the heavenly expression of his countenance as seen in his picture, lately reproduced, most successfully, by a skillful lithographer of Paris. His sweet and gentle virtues, his amiable piety, his persuasive maxims, his resolutions, his delightful practices—in fine, his sincere and unaffected devotion, were all as so many bonds of love uniting others to him, a union which was perfected and rendered unalterable by his goodness of heart, ever inclining him to lend a willing ear to the petitions addressed him, both immediately after his death and continuously since. Ah! countless indeed are the graces, the favors of every nature, spiritual and temporal, obtained from his bounty since his soul sank to sleep in the Lord, just twenty two years ago!

1. *In the temporal order.* Many declare unhesitatingly that to Father Charles's intercession are they indebted:— some, for notable amelioration of bad health; others, for instantaneous and often permanent relief from acute suffering; others, again, for rapid recovery from dangerous maladies, the sudden cure of wounds, and of grave infirmities that had reduced them to the last extremity.

The means employed to obtain these favors were some-

---

[1] What God did at the beginning to initiate and increase devotion to Father Charles He still continues to do; and it is to this divine agency we must ascribe its progress and permanency in every country where it has been established; also, to this, the zeal with which so many humble, pious souls, themselves unknown on earth, have striven to extend it, as well as the facility and joy everywhere attending its propagation.

times a Mass for this intention, a novena in Father Charles's honor, a promise of something spiritual or temporal; or, again, the mere application of some relic belonging to him, or of his portrait; or even a simple appeal to his intercession with God.

In the same manner have numberless young persons of both sexes obtained the desired success in their studies and examinations; childless wives, the cessation of their sterility, together with the preservation of their own lives and those of their children, whence many of the latter have received, in acknowledgment of the boon, the name of Charles or of Charlotte.

Many Christian households declare openly that they owe *everything* to Father Charles—the recovery of health, the re-establishment or continuance of union in the family, prosperity, very perceptible and uninterrupted assistance in various matters—consequently, the happiness they enjoy. He helps them at all times and in all things—such is their widely circulated testimony.

2. *In the spiritual order* the favors obtained are still more numerous. Many, many conversions, often those that had been despaired of, have been wrought through his intercession, and not unfrequently they have been sudden; likewise, numberless spiritual transformations of individuals, families, and even communities, accomplished in a very little while, are attributed to his instrumentality.

And as to those things in the Christian, the religious, the sacerdotal life, absolutely requiring an especial grace, God alone knows the numberless times success therein has been due Father Charles's timely assistance fervently implored. And the same may be said of innumerable works of zeal, beneficence, charity; also, and even more especially, of vocations, professions in religion, and holy deaths.

The various detailed accounts illustrative of the above

summary of graces received have been collected from year
to year, indeed, we might say from day to day. We hope
to be able, at some future time, to lay before our readers
in full many of these occurrences, which bear the manifest
seal of divine intervention; also, to acquaint them with the
circumstances under which they were brought about, the
means employed therefor, the testimonies of love and gratitude they have evoked,[1] and to give them an idea of the
great number of persons, some even living in far distant
countries, who in consequence of these miraculous events,
cures, etc., have been led to invoke Father Charles with
confidence unbounded.

For the present we content ourselves in terminating our
account by some explanation of the means used to obtain
these graces.

The first and most efficacious means has been prayer,
either isolated or collective, of which the most common
form is as follows:—This invocation to Father Charles,
"Beloved or Blessed[2] Father Charles, pray for me and
for all who recommend themselves, or who are recommended to your prayers."[3] Then, in union with him, with
all who invoke him, and with their guardian angels,[4] recite a *Pater*, an *Ave*, and a *Gloria Patri*, etc. The above
prayers have been selected not only because they are the
most beautiful in the Church's Liturgy, but also because,
every one knowing them by heart, they can so conveniently

---

[1] A hundred *ex-votos*, principally hearts of gold or silver, have been offered Father
Charles.

[2] The title of *Blessed* herein applied to Father Charles does not in any manner
imply the invocation of him as a saint, canonized or beatified by the Church.

[3] This invocation, besides having the advantage of uniting in prayer all who invoke Father Charles, thus giving greater efficacy to the petition, moreover admits
to participation in his mediation innumerable dear souls, who, unconscious of their
spiritual necessities, of course never dream of praying therefor.

[4] As has been already stated in this Biography, Father Charles had great and
special devotion to his guardian angel.

be recited, at all times and under all circumstances, even when one is exteriorly employed otherwise, and far more so when engaged in a formal exercise of piety.

Whilst thus reciting these prayers, at least once a day, each one must have the intention of uniting them to all novenas made in his honor, thus contributing to his glory and to the greater power of his intercession in heaven.

To the preceding prayers one often adds novenas, private or made in common,[1] in honor of Father Charles, or of the Blessed Virgin, or St. Joseph, by the intercession of this good Father. The three elements of these novenas are frequently: 1. The above-mentioned prayers; 2. The daily morning offering of all one's good actions, whether direct acts of piety or otherwise, during the day, and the desire to render them as numerous and perfect as possible; 3. The promise of performing or to have performed, should the petition be granted, some good work, spiritual or temporal, in thanksgiving—for instance, to have one or several Masses said for Father Charles's intentions, to give some one a copy of his Biography, to labor at the correction of a certain fault or the acquisition of a virtue, to be more faithful in fulfilling such or such a duty, etc. The most of these novenas have been made to obtain cures, conversions—favors, spiritual and temporal, of every sort. Frequently, to excite greater fervor, they have been so arranged in the order of time as to end on one of Father Charles's feast-days: the 29th of June, feast of SS. Peter and Paul, his two principal patrons; November 4th, feast of St. Charles, and December 25th, feast of Christmas, his two other patronal feasts; August 4th, anniversary of his death; on the anniversary of some one of the fortunate (as he

---

[1] Novenas and other prayers made in common, in families or even communities, provided they are not made in the chapel or in the choir, which would thus constitute them an act of public worship, are permitted to be offered the servants of God esteemed powerful in heaven.

styles them) days of his life, as mentioned in this Biography, or, again, on some one of the grand festivals of the Church.

To the prayers and novenas above mentioned is frequently added contact with Father Charles's picture or with something that had belonged to him, the latter being generally shreds or tiny portions of his linen, given the sick in their drink. Many cures have been obtained in this way.'

Many pious Christians, to touch Father Charles's heart and propitiate his favor, have given and continue to give him yet other marks of affection, devotion, and confidence, truly beautiful and inspired by the Holy Ghost. We regret that the limits of this simple Notice prevent our making known to our readers in detail a number of these testimonies of devotion so instructive and edifying. The two following, however, will give an idea of innumerable others that we might adduce, did space permit:

A very respectable citizen of Toulouse, who owed to Father Charles's mediation not only a notable portion of his fortune, which was considerable, but also repeated cures of the most of the members of his family, having made his will, dividing his possessions between his wife and children, ends the document thus: "I have now but one thing more to give them, and that the most precious devotion to Father Charles. Yes, this devotion I bequeath to each and all, earnestly desiring that it remain ever in the family as one of its treasures."

In the diocese of St. Flour, an illustrious family, having obtained many signal favors through Father Charles's intercession, among others two marriages most advantageous from every point of view, were inspired with the thought of testifying their gratitude by having an offering

---

' Thousands have asked for and obtained tiny fragments of these relics, which Father Charles's brothers give (of necessity) with a sparing hand.

made in his name of one or several tablets, costing three hundred francs, and a column, valued at a thousand francs, to the Church of the Sacred Heart of Mont Martre, Paris. This family itself was the first subscriber, by sending M. Vital a sum of money with that intention, enclosing therewith the surnames and Christian names of the first donors, which were to be sealed up in a vial and placed in the tablet itself, together with the names of such other clients of Father Charles as may help complete the needed three hundred or one thousand francs. The subscription for the tablet is ten centimes; for the column, one franc. This pious project, hailed with delight by the holy priest's devoted servants, is rapidly being realized; and ere long Father Charles will thus, even on earth, bear token of that ardent devotion to the Sacred Heart so consoling in his exile, and which now that he has reached his true country, his Father's house, must needs be more intense and holier still.

THE END.

PRINTED BY BENZIGER BROTHERS, NEW YORK.

www.ingramcontent.com/pod-product-compliance
Lightning Source LLC
Chambersburg PA
CBHW020346030726
47496CB00007B/2015

*9 7 8 3 7 4 4 6 5 3 7 2 5 *